WHEN the VIBE
is RIGHT

# WHEN the VIBE IS RIGHT

## SARAH DASS

BALZER + BRAY

*An Imprint of* HarperCollins*Publishers*

*For Gam.*
*For your support, wisdom, and love.*

**Bacchanal**. /bakənal/ *noun*

A Trinidadian term used to refer to an incident involving
  scandal, conflict, or disorder.

A large celebration.

Total confusion.

Much ado about a whole lot of nothing.

# ONE

"Why are you on the ground?"

It was a good question. The simple answer: there were no chairs available. The long answer: I'd been trying to find a peaceful spot to work when an impromptu dance party broke out around me. It hadn't been easy to focus on anything with a Machel Montano song blasting through Kate Melville's phone, the soca music tinny but loud in the empty community center hall. But the alternative to work was to join them. And that wasn't happening.

"Tess, get up." Sherlyn charged over to my hiding spot, behind the potted monstera bush. "You're going to dirty up the gown."

"Relax, I have my bookbag under me." I didn't bother looking up from my tablet. My stylus remained steady as I continued to sketch on the open design app. Normally, I'd never treat a piece of clothing this badly, but the gown in question was the same color as a potato sack, and just about as flattering. "Besides, even if I did dirty it up, I doubt anyone could tell."

"Ay, we do our best. The drama club budget is tight."

"Oh, I can tell."

She folded her arms. "Do you have any idea what I went through to borrow these?"

"Since you're the president of the drama club, I'm guessing not a lot." Then again, I wouldn't have put it past Sherlyn—the personification of a clenched fist—to take the process of borrowing a few stage costumes and props way too seriously.

For this year's Literatures in English project, we had to pick an adaptation of *Romeo and Juliet*, identify a change made to the original play, and examine how it impacted the story. Extra points if we took it a step further and highlighted this impact by making an adaptation of our own.

We'd been randomly assigned into groups, and I'd gotten dumped into the one with Sherlyn as a leader. Her pain-in-the-butt need to overachieve had us working on the assignment months before the deadline. Rather than a simple essay or quick presentation, she'd pushed us into filming a few scenes from the Baz Luhrmann movie. Whereas the film changed the setting and kept the dialogue, we kept the movie's settings and gave the dialogue a Trinidadian twist. Sherlyn even secured permission for us to shoot a few scenes in the community center not too far from school.

Unfortunately, Sister Thompson, our literature teacher, was running late. In her absence, Kate had pulled up a soca music playlist and turned the rehearsal into a small fete.

Sherlyn swatted the monstera leaves aside to glare at me. "For your information, it was not easy borrowing the costumes. I'd never abuse my power and take them just so. Our club had a vote." She leaned forward to see my tablet. "What are you doing over here anyway?"

I covered the screen. "Why are you harassing me? I don't even have any lines. Shouldn't you be rounding up your stars for rehearsal? Chris is somewhere outside. And Brandon and Kate have been doing nothing but wining and grinding on each other for the past thirty minutes—"

"What's that?" Brandon called out. "You talking about me?"

Damn it. How did he even hear that? Up until a minute earlier, he'd been dancing with Kate. The slinky gold Cleopatra costume she'd donned to play Lady Capulet was undeniably eye-catching, and Brandon had been effectively caught.

"What's your problem?" he asked me, stretching one arm across Kate's shoulders. "I'm only trying to get into character."

"You're trying to get into *something*," I muttered.

"What's that?" Brandon leaned forward, cupping his ear.

"I said you're trying to get into *something*." I raised my voice, enunciating each word to make sure he and the rest of the project group heard me. "By which, I meant her pants. In case that wasn't clear."

That earned me a couple of snickers and a few sighs. By this point, our classmates were more than used to our squabbles. I paid them no attention, holding Brandon's narrow-eyed gaze just as stubbornly as he held mine.

"Whatever," Sherlyn said, backing away. "Make sure you're ready for your scene when it comes up."

3

Ready for what? My brief appearance in the background, pretending to sing? Yeah. Okay. I'd get right on that.

I unlocked my tablet and returned to my other project—the one that actually mattered, not the farce unraveling around me.

While working, I didn't notice anyone approach. But I should've known he'd come over. No matter the place, the time, the circumstances—Brandon Richards never passed up an opportunity to annoy me. Whenever I least wanted him, there he was.

"Not bad," he said.

I hugged the tablet to my chest, blocking the screen. Brandon had slipped behind the plant pot, crouching next to me. I glared up at him. His smile, which was slightly crooked and unfairly pretty, betrayed his evil intent. The fact that he was currently dressed as the devil only reinforced it.

"No need to hide," he said. "I've already seen it. You're picking up the family business now?"

His tone sounded more amused than curious. I examined the situation from all angles, searching for any nefarious reasons he might have for asking the question. If he'd laid a trap, I couldn't see it.

"Yes," I said.

"Isn't it a bit early to be thinking about Carnival? It's only September."

I snorted. He had no idea.

Every year, in the two days preceding Ash Wednesday, tens of thousands of people filled the streets of Trinidad in a stunning array of costumes for the annual Carnival festival. There were traditional characters like dragons, devils, sailors, and Moko Jumbies, each with their own history and legends. Some costumes were elaborate and others simple. Some masqueraders played on their own, others in organized groups called mas bands. My family owned and ran one of these bands, called Grandeur.

For most people, those days of Carnival passed and then it was over. But for those of us who dedicated our lives to the festival, Monday and Tuesday were just the culmination of the rest of the year. Making Carnival costumes was an artform that took months of work, time, and commitment, and the process began days after the last festival ended.

I'd been fascinated with costumes for as long as I could remember. People thought they hid who a person was; I believed the opposite to be true. What you chose to wear, and what to project to the world—scary, sexy, cute, funny, not trying at all—said a lot about who you were under the flash and makeup.

Take Brandon, for example. When I'd heard he'd skipped on Romeo to play Tybalt, I'd been surprised he didn't leap at the chance for more attention as the lead. But now that I'd seen his devil outfit– black suit, red shirt, and horns—I understood. While others bought into his Prince Charming routine, I'd spotted the demon in him a long time ago.

Brandon slumped against the wall so he could be a little closer to my eye level. "You know what I think?"

"I'd never presume to know what you thought. That is assuming there's any thinking happening at all—which, from what I've seen, is doubtful."

"I think it's not fair that the rest of us are all contributing to the project," he said. "Meanwhile, you've chosen a role with no lines. Almost no camera time. And during rehearsals, you're working on something else."

"Or—and stay with me on this, because I know it's hard for you to focus on anything that's not the sound of your own voice—you could stay out of my business."

No power on earth could get me in front of a camera. Especially not Brandon Richards. Revealing my intense camera shyness would be like handing him ammunition to use against me.

"Clearly, you have an interest in costumes," Brandon went on like he hadn't heard a thing I'd said. He was good at that–brushing me off like nothing. "From what I've seen, you're not bad at designing them. So why didn't you offer to make some for this project?"

"I have an even better question," I said. "Why don't you go back to entertaining Kate? It looks like she misses her dance partner." I'd noticed her shooting me irritated looks from the corner, like I'd stolen him away from her.

"Don't be jealous, Boop," he said, using his ridiculous nickname for me. Through some ungodly means, he'd discovered my full first name was Beatrice. From there, he'd started calling me Betty, then Betty Boop. Then just Boop. If anything could illustrate how annoying he was, this would be it.

I glared up at him—into the face I'd grown to hate. To my regret, it wasn't a bad one. Brown skin, black hair, dark eyes. The angles of his jaw and cheeks were a little too sharp, his mouth a little too wide, and yet they came together to form a picture far too pleasing. As if I'd needed any more proof of the unfairness of the universe. I wanted to hate everything about him, so the fact that I found him attractive only made me angrier.

"Okay, first of all, what I make is a different kind of costume. The ones with feathers and beads and so on. I'm sure you're familiar."

Not that I couldn't make stage costumes too. My mother taught me to sew before I could write, but he didn't need to know that.

"Second, why would I bother going through the trouble of making something new, when we have such a beautiful wardrobe kindly provided by the school's drama club."

He tipped his head to the side, the way he did when he wanted to be extra condescending. "You know you're wearing a burlap sack, right? My jacket smells of mothballs. And Chris's metal suit has been leaving rust spots on everything."

"And? What about it?"

He threw his hands up, finally displaying some frustration. I felt a twinge of pleasure at making him break.

"You could contribute something," he said. "Anything."

"Look," I said, done with this conversation. "I didn't ask to be in this group. Believe me, if I had a choice, we wouldn't have ended up together. Hell, I'd prefer working alone."

"That sounds like a good idea to me," Sister Thompson said.

We both turned to our teacher and the rest of the literature group who'd all paused to watch our argument. At some point, the music had stopped. I hadn't noticed.

"I agree with Brandon," Sister Thompson said. "If you're not contributing to this project, you shouldn't be getting credit for it."

"I wasn't—" I started to protest, but she held up a finger to silence me.

"I put you into groups because I believe that for any project, collaboration is beneficial. Working with others is just a part of life that you need to learn. But I do not condone leeching." Her gaze slid to Brandon. "Can you still shoot your scenes today without her in it?"

"Yes," Brandon said, his lips tight.

"Good," Sister Thompson said. After one last disapproving look at me, she clapped her hands. "Okay, everyone. Let's get started." She led the rest of the group to the middle of the hall and I was left in the corner, alone. "Tess," she called back. "Feel free to leave whenever."

My skin burned with embarrassment.

I stood up and snatched my bag off the floor. After stuffing my tablet inside, I marched across the room, refusing to acknowledge any of them. I shoved open the door to the pool area. It slammed against the wall, the sound echoing throughout the building.

I searched for Hazel. Absolutely livid, I wanted nothing more than to vent about the crap that just went down. But my cousin wasn't alone. At some point, she'd acquired a knight in dull armor, and while I'd had mixed feelings on Chris's inclination toward nineties-esque sporty outfits, I could easily admit that this particular anachronistic look did suit him.

Sunlight poured through windows and ventilation blocks, casting patterns along the floor. Chris looked almost gallant kneeling beside Hazel, his floppy black hair falling across his forehead. Hazel sat on the edge of the pool, the legs of her jeans pulled up, her bare feet gently kicking in the icy-blue water.

They'd been classmates since preschool, but they only recently bonded over SAT classes. Both were applying to attend schools in New York the following year.

Something about the scene at the poolside felt private. Intimate.

Too bad I had to bust it up. "Time to go!"

Hazel turned to face me. "You're done already?"

"Can't be," Chris said. "They'd need me. And Sister T isn't here yet."

"She just got here."

"Oh!" He stood, the process slow and clunky because of his armor plates. A small rust stain remained on the tiled floor. "I should go then." He paused, smiling down at Hazel. "You'll come, right? The theater gave Brandon a bunch of tickets when he promoted their movie club cards. The only catch is that he has to use them tonight."

"Yeah, I don't know . . ." Her gaze darted toward me.

Chris noticed it. "Oh, Tess—you can come too, of course. It's just a movie lime with a few of us. We'll hang out. Free popcorn. But I'd need to check with Brandon first. Make sure he has enough tickets left."

Somehow, I suspected, if Brandon knew the ticket was for me, he'd find himself with none to spare. Not that I wanted to go anyway.

"I don't think so," I said. "And Hazel and I have a thing tonight, so she can't either."

Hazel blinked. "A thing?"

"Yes. *A thing.*" When she still didn't pick up my hint, I added, "You know, the thing with your father. The one that would cause problems if you went out tonight with Chris."

"Oh. That thing." Hazel's expression flattened with exasperation. "You know what? Since I refuse to acknowledge that thing—because it's silly—I think it'll be fine."

"Uh . . ." Chris shuffled his feet. "Was that a yes? No?"

"It's a maybe." Hazel smiled up at him. "I need to check with my parents first. Can I call you later?"

"Chris!" Brandon shoved open the side door and stuck his head through. "Come on, nah! We ready."

"I coming!" Chris backed away, his eyes still on Hazel. To her, he said, "You should know, *I* would really like it if you joined us tonight. If that makes a difference."

"Oh, for crying out loud," I said. "She said *maybe*, okay? Just take it and keep moving."

Chris's smile slipped a little. But he still threw Hazel a small wave before jogging off, his metal plates rattling.

Brandon glared at me, pushing the door wider to let his best friend through.

God, he was the worst. He'd probably known Sister Thompson

had been listening to us the whole time. Now, thanks to him, I had to think up a whole new project on my own.

After the door shut, Hazel continued to stare at it. She sighed dreamily.

I snapped my fingers in front of her face. "Pull it together. You're down so bad right now, it's embarrassing."

"I know." Hazel pressed her hands to her cheeks. "But he's so pretty, Tess. Has he always been so pretty?"

Chris? He was fine, I guess. If you liked the bland, generically handsome type—which, to be fair, a lot of people did. He played practically every sport, which gave him a muscular, broad build. And he had the perpetually cheerful attitude of a puppy, which I personally found annoying.

I held out a hand and helped her up. "I think Chris is exactly as he always has been." That seemed to be the most tactful answer I could give.

"I know!" She stood up and retrieved her sandals. "That's the strangest part. How can I like him so much now, when he's been there the whole time?"

"Well, to be fair to you, he does give off the impression of a . . ." I tried again. "He can sometimes . . . seem like . . ."

"You're trying really hard not to use the word himbo right now, aren't you?"

"I don't want to reduce him to his looks, but when he calls her Sister T, he makes it really hard."

She sighed, scooped her purse off the ground, and followed me across the room. "Chris has more interests than sports, okay?

Like music. He's taken up DJing."

As if I needed more reasons to object to this relationship. "Hazel . . ." I pushed the outer entrance door open and waited for her to pass through first. "Do you remember what I told you when you first expressed these feelings toward Chris?"

"Yes."

"And what did I say?"

"Don't."

"Exactly." I made a beeline for the car, more than ready to leave. The sooner I got away from my former groupmates—and out of this awful costume—the better. "Not only is Chris best friends with Brandon, but his mother has married into *that* family. By associating with him, you're effectively a traitor on multiple levels."

She unlocked the car door. "Don't you think you're being a little overdramatic? No one buys into that whole rivalry thing but you and Daddy."

"Because we're the only ones in our family that care about Grandeur."

"That's not fair," Hazel said. "I care about the mas band. I just, you know, don't want to design costumes. Or make them. Or have anything to do with the business."

"Exactly." I slipped into the car. "But you're wrong. The Kingstons are just as invested in this war as we are. Didn't you see the cheap shot they took at your father in the newspaper last week?"

The article had been a profile of the Kingston family and their mas band, Royalty. It had mostly focused on Mr. Kingston's son, Prince—the twenty-one-year-old who was all set to take over his father's company. They'd called Prince the face of the next generation of Carnival.

In the article, Prince had praised his father for being innovative and adapting to the changing times. It was because of this, he'd said, that his father remained relevant in the industry, unlike some of his father's contemporaries.

"We don't know he was talking about Daddy," Hazel said.

"Of course he meant Uncle Russell. Who else would he be talking about?"

The history between Mr. Kingston and Uncle Russell dated back to the 1990s. Mr. Kingston used to be Uncle Russell's apprentice, until they had an epic falling out. The details of that argument remained a mystery. However, after Mr. Kingston left to start his own company, rumors from his camp circulated that Uncle Russell was using Mr. Kingston's designs without giving credit.

Uncle Russell—being Uncle Russell—only addressed this rumor once. He denied the claim and argued that all anyone had to do was look at Mr. Kingston's work to know no one was going to bother stealing from him.

"When Chris's mother married into that family, he became the enemy," I said. "So, *don't*."

"Are you . . . *forbidding* me to date him?" She slid me a sly look as she started the car. "Because if there's one trope I love, it's forbidden romance. It makes everything so much hotter."

"Oh, God."

She laughed, maneuvering the car out of the parking lot.

Almost immediately we hit a line of traffic leading into Port of Spain. "He's like my very own Romeo. We're star-crossed lovers from rival families, kept apart by circumstances beyond our control."

"You do know how the play ends, right?" I had to ask. "And star-crossed lovers don't end up together. People have been misusing that term for ages. Think less Jane and Rochester and more Catherine and Heathcliff. If you're going to be a romance writer, you should know this."

"*Heathcliff*," she said, testing the name on her tongue. "Hang on." She reached across to pop open the glove compartment and grabbed a pen. After removing the cover with her teeth, she wrote *Heathcliff* on the back of the hand balanced on the steering wheel. Just below it had another scrawl, this one faded. It seemed to read something like *reverse fake date*, whatever that meant.

"Okay, seriously," I said. "Just use your phone to take notes like a normal person. Scribbling all over your hand is so weird."

"Hey," she said, her teeth clamped on the pen cap. "I believe the correct term for writers is eccentric. Oh shoot." The cars in front of us started to move. She tossed the pen and cover into my lap and returned her attention to the road. She hit the accelerator a little too hard.

"Hazel!" I shouted. The belt cut into my torso as we jerked forward. "Watch what you're doing. Please."

"Sorry," she said quickly. The car slowed as we slipped into more traffic. She glanced over at me. "Are you okay?"

"Yeah," I said, even as my heartbeat thundered in my ears. I focused on breathing slowly, deeply. Seconds passed as I willed the fear to ebb away. Hazel kept looking at me, checking on me. Rather than letting the silence grow awkward around us, I said, "My point is—where is your family loyalty?"

"Must've left it in my other purse."

"Along with your good sense?" I recapped the pen and returned it to the glove compartment. My heartbeat returned to a normal pace. "How do you know Chris isn't a spy? He might be using you to get information on our new designs. What if he's working for the enemy?"

"One word," she said. "*Hot.*"

"I'm not going to talk you out of this, am I?"

"No. But you can come with us to the movies tonight. Use it as a chance to get to know him better."

"No, thank you. If you want to go, fine. But I'm not about to subject myself to more time with my classmates than I already have to spend with them. And I'm sure they feel the same way about me."

"I wish you wouldn't say things like that," she said. "Maybe if you considered opening up a bit, and letting people see how great you are—"

"Dear, sweet cousin. I don't care what anyone thinks about me. Especially not my classmates."

She didn't look satisfied. "Okay. But for the record, I think you're great."

"Ugh. Don't get mushy on me. Please."

She sighed. "Fine. Forget it."

"Thank you," I said. "Just promise you'll let me be there when you tell Uncle Russell about you and Chris. Your father is going to be so pissed."

A sly smile stretched across her face. "Yes, I know."

Lord help us.

# TWO

Even before I'd come to live with my aunt and uncle, I'd been in love with their house.

The building and land had been passed down from Aunty Gloria's Indian grandparents, the massive two-story house still bearing some of the traditional architectural characteristics of their homeland, such as the square courtyard connecting the main house to the garage and Uncle Russell's workshop, and Jharokha-style balconies attached to a few of the second-floor rooms.

It sat on the edge of a hill, above an orchard, and offered a lush view of Maracas Valley to the north and the San Fernando Hill way to the south. Marble, brick, and concrete made up the structure—all earthy, neutral tones. The doors and windows were elaborately carved works of art, made of wood, steel, and stained glass. All that—coupled with a stunning garden, flush with palms, colorful crotons, and burning-red hibiscus—gave the place a dreamy, folkloric quality.

Even after seven years of living there, when we pulled up the driveway, I basked in awe as the house revealed itself.

And then I noticed the stacks of garbage bags on the front porch.

"Oh no." Hazel groaned as she parked the car. "She's still at it. How long is this vacation supposed to last again?"

"Too long," I said.

See, when a normal person took time off, they went on holiday. But not my aunt.

Gloria Messina was a household name in Trinidad and Tobago. After her win as Miss Trinidad & Tobago in the Miss Universe pageant, she traded her tiara for a microphone and became the face of Channel 8 news. She'd recently taken a few months off— her first in over twenty-five years of working—during which she'd spent approximately three minutes relaxing, then decided to embark on a multistage housewide cleaning project.

All the bags on the front porch were stuffed with family belongings to be trashed or donated. At the rate she'd been clearing things out, by Christmas, I doubted there'd be anything left in the house.

"Girls?" my aunt's voice came from somewhere inside the confusion. "Is that you?"

"Yes, Mummy. Wait—is that my sweatshirt?" Hazel reached out to yank a mass of faded blue fabric from one of the open bags. "You can't throw this out. I still wear this."

"Unfortunately," I muttered.

Aunty Gloria peered around one of the piles. She wore a

light sleeveless green dress, her long black hair tied up in a scarf. "Sweetheart, you already have so many sweatshirts and that one is in terrible condition."

"It's not that bad." Hazel pouted.

I took it from her, then shoved three fingers through a hole near the collar.

Hazel snatched it back, holding it to her chest. "It's comfortable."

"Hazel, drop it," Aunty Gloria said sternly, employing the same tone she'd once unleashed on a former government minister during an interview about alleged corruption.

"Fine." Hazel dropped the sweatshirt into the bag. The second Aunty Gloria looked away, she grabbed it and hurried inside. "It's not funny," she whispered when I laughed. "Just wait until she tries to Marie Kondo your dearest possessions too."

"Sure." I didn't really have dearest possessions. Perhaps it was a result of having my life suddenly upended when I was younger. I didn't see the point of getting attached when it could all be gone a second later.

"There you are." Uncle Russell came from the living room, his assistant, Melissa, a few steps behind, clearly struggling to keep his attention.

"Sir, please listen," Melissa was saying. "I can't send the invitations until I know where the venue for our launch party is going to be. And I can't decide on the venue until I have an idea of how many people are coming."

"Go ahead and book the same venue we had last year." Uncle

Russell's words curled into a slight English accent from his years living in London.

Uncle Russell's white cotton shirt hung loose on his tall, wiry body. Because he was a total workaholic, he sometimes skipped meals, too absorbed in his projects to remember trivialities like eating and sleeping. That being said, his Van Dyke facial hair was always immaculately maintained regardless. We all had our priorities, I supposed.

"Didn't Lauren already take care of all this before she left?" he asked. "I'm sure she did." He stopped in front of us. "Tess, where have you been? And why would you go there wearing that?"

It was a good question, from someone who actually knew what he was talking about.

While Russell Messina wasn't super famous internationally—a fact that I'd recommend never mentioning to him, even in his best mood—within Trinidad and Tobago, his name held a lot of weight.

He was a Carnival costume designer or—as we locals called people who did what he did—a mas maker. During the height of his career from the 1990s through the early 2010s, he'd built a reputation as a genius in his field. Since then, his star had been steadily fading, partly because of an influx of new designers, bigger bands, and several changes in the industry. But to those in the know, he was still *the* Russell Messina.

Basically, I wanted to be him when I grew up.

"Do you like it?" I held out the skirt so he could fully experience the awfulness of it. "I made it myself. It took so many long hours of blood, sweat, and tears."

He frowned. "Tell me you're joking."

"I'm joking. I only wore this for a school thing. But then they kicked me out of the school thing. So, bright side—I'll never have to wear it again."

"Love that positivity," Aunty Gloria said, passing through, an empty box tucked under her arm. "As we let out the old and welcome the new, only good vibes."

Uncle Russell watched her go with a small, soft smile. The second she was gone, his regular stony face returned. "They kicked you out?" He regarded me with narrowed eyes. "Knowing your penchant for backchat, I wouldn't be surprised if you deserved it."

Well, I mean, he wasn't wrong.

"Hi, Daddy," Hazel said peevishly. "I'm here too. Not sure if you noticed."

"Sir, please." Melissa interrupted. She flicked her long black ponytail over her shoulder, practically vibrating with nervous irritation. "I've been trying to tell you—the venue we used last year got damaged in the flooding last week. They won't reopen until at least November."

"Then find somewhere else," Uncle Russell said.

"Yes, but where?" Melissa asked him. She was only twenty-four, having worked with Grandeur for almost two years. Her predecessor and mentor, Miss Lauren, had been with the company for over a decade before abruptly retiring and moving to Maryland to live with her daughter. Poor Melissa had been blindsided by the sudden promotion.

Our upcoming Grandeur band launch would be her biggest challenge so far. During this event, the public would get their first look at our costumes that would be on sale for the upcoming festival.

"Melissa," Uncle Russell said, sounding a bit too unbothered by what—I had to agree with Melissa—did sound like a big problem. "My job is to create the costumes. Your job is to handle all the marketing and sales. So do that. If you really need help, call Miss Lauren. When she left, she said she'd be willing to give you advice if you needed it."

"I tried, but yesterday she asked me to cool it. She says I've been calling too much."

Uncle Russell wasn't listening, already heading out the front door. "Tess, join me in the workshop when you're done."

"Will do," I called back, excited to show him my new design. But before that, I turned my attention to Melissa—who'd fled. Sighing, I crossed the room and entered the kitchen. I yanked open the pantry, unsurprised to find Melissa standing in the dark, practicing her stress-relief breathing exercises.

She did this a lot.

Hazel stopped beside me. "Oh, Melissa."

"You okay?" I asked.

"The usual." Melissa inhaled. Exhaled. "In the middle of a breakdown, but otherwise pretty good. Met a guy at a fete last night. He seems nice."

"That's great," I said. "About the venue thing—why don't you try calling the community center? We just came from there, and the auditorium space would work. At most, we usually get about a hundred attendees, which should fit."

Since Grandeur was one of the smaller large bands, our numbers ranged between eight hundred to one thousand masquerade players a year. Most of them, particularly the foreigners, bought their costumes through the website, which meant we wouldn't expect them to show up in person.

Melissa inhaled, then exhaled, swaying slightly. "Yes. I think that might work. Thank you. Seriously, Tess. You're a lifesaver."

"No problem. I hope it works out."

The launch party wasn't only a tradition, it was a vital part of the band's promotions. The event catered to potential customers, journalists, and media influencers—all of whom were necessary to get the word out.

Melissa started to leave, then backed up. "I don't suppose you'd be willing to help me with the marketing, would you? I've tried to talk your uncle into hiring someone to handle it. But he won't listen."

"Me?" I laughed, waving my hands.

Like my uncle, I was good with costumes, not customers. I tended to rub people the wrong way—as evidenced by my ejection from the group project.

"Trust me, you don't want me promoting anything." I tried to inject as much confidence into my tone as possible, and added, "Besides, you've got this."

"Thanks," she said, looking a little more self-assured. "Nice dress, by the way."

I couldn't tell if she was being sarcastic.

After she left, I turned to Hazel. "Yeah . . . she's in way over her head."

A few hours later, Hazel hissed at me from the doorway of Uncle Russell's workshop. I looked up from the sewing machine. For the last few minutes, I'd been replacing a bent needle. She waved for me to come over.

I checked on Uncle Russell. For the moment, he seemed totally focused on reexamining one of the costumes. The recently finished design had been inspired by a blue heron, composed of a silvery-white two-piece, sapphire-colored jewels, and a dreamy blend of white, cerulean, and royal blue feathers.

He circled the mannequin, hunting for mistakes.

This type of costume was known as fantasy, or pretty mas. It was Uncle Russell's specialty. Over the years, this became the most popular type in the country. Best known for its bikinis and beads, these costumes were usually adorned with feathers, glitter, jewels, and sequins.

Each band had multiple sections with their own design, but they all fell within an overarching theme. This version of the Blue Heron costume would serve as the female backline of the section. There would also be a version for men, and a second version for women that was even more elaborate, called a frontline.

The look of pretty mas wasn't dissimilar to the costumes of the

Brazilian Carnival, but the festivals were different. Everyone could be a part of the festivities in Trinidad; everyone was welcome to take a break from their everyday cares and join the celebration, spectators and masqueraders alike.

Hazel hissed at me again, this time tapping an imaginary watch on her wrist.

I quietly rose from my seat and crossed over to the door, careful not to break Uncle Russell's concentration. He mostly worked in silence, the only exception the steelpan music that floated in through the window from the pan yard a few miles away. The sweet tinkling melodies played like background music and a timer of sorts. The closer to Carnival we got, the more frequent their practice sessions for the annual Panorama competition held around the same time.

"Last chance," Hazel whispered when I joined her in the doorway. "They have an extra ticket for you. Brandon said it was okay. You can come with us."

What an asshole. Of course he'd said that. This way he could look magnanimous by offering, well aware I'd rather chew my arm off than join him.

"Please tell him I appreciate his offer, but he can choke on it."

"I will definitely not be telling him that." Hazel tugged on the oversized sleeve of the ugly gray hoodie she was wearing. At least her straight-cut ripped jeans were cute, though it wasn't saving much of the overall look.

"Hold on," I said, retreating into the workshop. As I passed, Uncle Russell looked up. "What's this? You going out, Hazel?"

"Yeah. Going to the cinema with some friends from school. Mummy said it was okay."

"Fine, fine," he said, his attention already drifting back to work.

I reached into one of the clear containers that lined the shelves of the workshop—each filled with material and accessories of various shapes and sizes—and I pulled out a spool of glittery silver ribbon. Allegedly, Coco Chanel once said, before leaving the house, remove one accessory. My personal philosophy was the opposite. Especially when it came to my cousin, who seemed determined to drown in bland, oversized clothing.

I prayed for the day she'd agree to let me style her. She already had the advantage of stellar genes. With my help, I knew I could turn her into a stunner.

Hazel rolled her eyes but didn't object when I started to weave the ribbon into a braid in her hair. Then I scooped up and twisted her soft black locks into an artfully messy ponytail. Finished, I stepped back to admire my work. "There. Pretty as a painting. I see no reason you shouldn't land any guy you want. Even the ones that aren't related to Ian Kingston."

"What was that?" Uncle Russell asked, looking up.

"Nothing!" Hazel said. She mouthed the words *not yet* before she fled.

Uncle Russell squinted at me through a pair of rimless glasses. "Something I should know?"

"No."

I returned to the worktable. After I finished changing the

needle on the machine, I retrieved my tablet and resumed translating my uncle's sketches into cleaner designs that could be used for reference at the Grandeur mas camp. There, the costumes would be mass-produced by dozens of employees and volunteers and displayed in a special showroom for interested buyers to browse.

"Did Hazel say she was going to the cinema?" Uncle Russell belatedly asked, like he'd only just processed the information. He checked his watch. "Hell, it's almost dinnertime already. These hours slip by so quickly. I don't even know what day it is."

"Friday," I said.

"It's Friday night? And you didn't want to go lime with your friends too?"

"Not my friends," I corrected him. "Hazel's friends." I erased, then redrew part of a headpiece. I let out a small, dry laugh. "I only have one friend, and she's related to me." Well, maybe Melissa counted too. Though that relationship felt closer to a work friend more than anything else.

"Tess, that is not—" Uncle Russell hissed in pain.

I looked up.

My uncle stood next to the mannequin, a pair of thread scissors laying at his feet. His hands were balled into fists in front of him.

My heart dropped. I squashed my impulse to intervene immediately. Sometimes there was no need, his pain varying from day to day, hour to hour. So even though his arthritis had been getting worse over the past year, I'd learned it was best not to assume. He knew his limits better than I did.

"Tess, can you please . . . ?"

He did not have to say more. I retrieved the scissors from the floor.

Working with arthritis was frustrating for him. He was known for his hands-on approach; a bandleader who personally oversaw and helped construct every costume that went out. They were his art, his creations. He wanted to be the one to fine-tune the final project and be assured of the quality. But as his arthritis got worse, he couldn't do everything exactly as he used to. And if there was one thing my uncle didn't like, it was change.

"What was it?" I asked him.

He pointed out the tiny, errant thread almost obscured by a bejeweled applique. I snipped it off.

"Come on, Uncle. No one would've seen that." I turned to face him, smiling, hoping to lighten the mood.

My uncle stared at me, a deep groove working between his brows. Usually, when something similar happened, we'd immediately move on. Pretend it hadn't, and the air would clear.

This time, it felt different. This time, the awkwardness lingered long after we'd returned to our tasks. I had no idea why.

Later that night, the beep of the house alarm activating alerted me to Hazel's return. I paused *The Great Gatsby* and listened for her approach.

On a whim, I'd decided to check out more of the Luhrmann filmography and fallen in love with the aesthetics and over-the-top spectacle. While the movie played, I'd had to look up the costume designers for his films, tumbling down a rabbit hole of fascinating interviews with them.

I slid off my bed and opened my bedroom door. Hazel sailed past, a goofy smile on her face. Curious, I followed.

"So . . . how was it?" I asked, pausing in her doorway.

"Awful," she said, still smiling.

"What?"

"Very confusing." She unclipped her earrings. "Too much shaky-cam. And they fridged the only female character twenty minutes in—"

"Not the movie," I said, exasperated. Though, from her smile, I could see she knew what I meant. "Don't be a smartass."

She laughed, depositing her earrings on the vanity table.

"It was perfect. *Chris* is perfect." She giggled—like, actually giggled. "He was so clearly nervous and trying not to show it. It was adorable. We held hands at one point, and his palms were all sweaty."

"How . . . romantic?"

"It was!" She dropped onto the bed and clutched a pillow to her chest. "And we had so much fun. Brandon—you know how he is. He chatted up the girl behind the concession counter and we got free drinks too. And even though the movie was crap, he cracked jokes all the way through. It was hilarious. I wish you'd come with us."

Her phone chimed, and she pounced on her purse. She pulled it out and started grinning at the screen. "It's Chris. He's checking to see if I got home okay." She pressed the phone to her chest.

"Come on, Tess. Even you've got to admit that's sweet."

"I'm not admitting anything until he publicly renounces his stepfather, Royalty, and everything they stand for."

Hazel sighed, then lit up when her phone chimed again. She laughed at whatever popped up on screen and started tapping out a reply to him.

"Are you official then?" I asked.

She looked up. "What? Oh, no. Not yet. But maybe . . ." She got another message, and I lost her attention again.

"All right. I guess I'll go back to my movie. I'm watching *The Great Gatsby,* if you want to—"

"Okay, night." She turned away from me, curling onto her side.

Well, then. To be honest, her dismissal stung a little.

When I returned to my room, I finished up the movie, then went to bed. I flicked off the lights, burrowed under the sheets, listened to the hum of the air conditioner, and waited for the lure of sleep.

And yet, it did not come. Curiosity overpowered exhaustion.

I sat up, reached for my phone, and pulled up Instagram. Five minutes earlier, Hazel had posted a few photos of her, Chris, and some of my classmates.

Looking at them, I felt a twinge of something—not jealousy exactly, but an uncomfortable awareness that I would not fit into these pictures. My classmates seemed to communicate on a different frequency that I couldn't pick up. When it was just Hazel and me, it was fine. The disconnect came with adding more people.

The larger the group, the stronger my impulse to fade into the background.

Sometimes, I wondered why Hazel even put up with me. She could pick up their frequency—speak their language. And yet, she tried to be an interpreter, inviting me out and bringing me into conversations. Sometimes, I was grateful. Other times, I just wanted her to give up.

Using Hazel's list of followers to navigate, I bounced around a few other posts made by my classmates. I followed none of them, and none of them followed me. My account was set to private, visible to only Hazel and the rest of my family.

Finally, I got to Brandon. I'd left him for last because, unlike the others, I'd had to unblock him. After a couple of his posts went viral, his stuff ended up on my timeline way too often. To my shock, he'd gotten over eighty thousand followers—twice as much as the last time I'd checked.

When had that happened? How? I scrolled down to see what the hell he'd been posting for his number of followers to grow that quickly.

His profile, as I'd expected, was a colorful mosaic of selfies, food, his friends, lush Trinidadian landscapes, and clips from his YouTube channel where he played video games and reacted to movies. It all seemed so fake, so glossy and filtered to perfection. Even his photos from that night at the cinema had a staged quality to them.

"Shoot!" I'd accidentally clicked on his story. I'd wanted to avoid it since he'd be able to see everyone who'd watched. Before I could close it, though, the story played.

I sat up in shock.

In the very first photo, Brandon stood in front of a building, the logo of the enemy plastered on the wall behind him. The caption read: *Ready to launch. See you at the party #TTCarnival #Royaltyband #WeReady.*

# THREE

Here's the thing about Brandon—I didn't like him. In case that wasn't already clear.

Our ill-fated meeting occurred on my very first day at St. Mary's secondary school. I'd been eleven at the time, the wound from losing my parents still fresh. Naive enough to still care what people said about me.

It had been hate at first sight. Or rather, hate at first listen, to be more accurate. I'd heard him coming long before I'd laid eyes on him.

"Did you see it?"

"Of course I saw it. I'm pretty sure that shade of yellow is visible from space."

"You know who that is, don't you? That's Hazel's cousin."

I'd stopped at the top of the stairwell to the second floor, just about to turn the corner, when I'd realized they were talking about me.

Even if they hadn't mentioned Hazel's cousin, it wouldn't have been hard to work out. I was the only one wearing yellow, among the nuns and the other students dressed in the stark whites and moss greens of the school uniform. My transfer had been so abrupt—in the middle of the first term—I hadn't had a chance to get all my school supplies yet.

For my first day, I'd worn a yellow-and-red peplum top and a matching skirt that I'd made myself. I'd been so proud of the outfit until right then.

"Oh, she's a part of *that* family. That explains the Carnival costume."

"I was thinking less Carnival and more circus, if you get what I mean."

"That's a coincidence." I rounded the corner, no longer willing to listen to this. "'Cause now I've found myself a pair of clowns."

And there they were. Brandon and his good friend, David. Two people I wouldn't spit on if they caught fire.

At least when David saw me, he had the grace to look ashamed. Brandon, on the other hand, did not waiver. In fact, he seemed upset that I'd interrupted.

"I don't believe I was talking to you." He held my gaze, thoroughly unrepentant. "Anyone ever tell you not to eavesdrop on other people's conversations?"

"Anyone ever tell you, if you have nothing good to say, don't say it at all?" I asked in return.

"You're in Catholic school now, Big Bird. Here we learn thou shalt not lie. All I said was the truth."

"Oh, I remember that one. It's right next to thou shalt not be an asshole, right?"

And this was when our headmistress, Sister Rose, rounded the corner from the stairwell behind me. Needless to say, it had not been a great day for first impressions all around.

David would apologize shortly after. But for Brandon and me, the bonds of hatred between us would only multiply over the years, and it truly solidified when David and I started dating two years ago.

Believe me, no one was more surprised by my relationship with David than me. But the Martinique-born, bilingual, aspiring musician played a French song on his guitar once, and even though I didn't understand a word, it was the hottest thing I'd ever seen.

Brandon hadn't gotten onboard with the Tess and David ship. The second we engaged in anything couple-like, he'd leave the room. I didn't care what he thought. So long as he kept his objections to himself, it wasn't my problem. But of course, eventually he couldn't even do that much.

"What's the deal with you and Brandon anyway?" David had asked me one day after art class.

I remembered turning to him with clay-caked hands, my experiment in sculpture a bust—pun intended. "What do you mean?" I asked, thoroughly confused. "We don't like each other. You know this."

"Yeah. But some of that is for show, right?" he asked. "Like you play it up. Y'all are like frenemies or something?"

"No. It's very real."

He looked surprised and a little amused by my answer.

I wiped my hands on a rag and tried to make sense of his expression. "Why are you asking?"

"Just something he said to me."

Instantly, I was on alert. "What did he say to you?"

"He expressed some . . . opinions about us."

"Oh." I fought to keep my expression neutral, even as anger bubbled up inside me. "And what did you say in response to these opinions?"

"Let's put it this way—Brandon and I aren't speaking at the moment." He reached out to wipe off a smudge of clay on my cheek. The gesture had been so sweet that my heart bloomed with adoration.

I couldn't believe he'd picked me over his friendship with Brandon—the golden boy, the influencer, the guy that everyone and their mothers loved. It blew my mind and strengthened my resolve to be with him.

So, the next time I saw Brandon—chatting up one of the upper-form girls between classes—I couldn't let it slide. "Just so you know, he's an asshole," I told the girl as I passed them. "You might want to watch out for that."

The girl blinked, speechless, both of them slow to react. By the time Brandon recovered, I was already at the other end of the hall.

"What is your problem?" he demanded, catching up to me in the courtyard.

"Tell me, Brandon—are we dating?"

That brought him up short. "What?"

"Because I heard you have opinions about my love life, and since pigs aren't flying and my bar for a boyfriend remains higher than slightly above hell, I'm guessing the answer to that is no."

"What are you talking about?" he asked. But I spotted a flash of fear under his anger. Maybe he was afraid our confrontation would end his friendship with David for good.

The wind snatched my hair; I pinned it behind my ears. "David told me about your concerns about us."

"He did?" Brandon's posture turned rigid.

"Yeah, he did. And I don't care what you think. What's going on between David and me is between David and me. That makes your opinion about us worthless. Just like everything else you say."

Brandon's jaw flexed. "You have no idea what you're talking about right now. And the fact that you assume you do is the most arrogant—"

"Arrogant? *I'm* arrogant? As opposed to you, who posts his every random thought on the internet, because you believe everyone needs to know what you think."

"Twenty thousand followers and growing indicates to me that a significant number of people *do* care what I think."

"That's because they don't know you, Brandon," I said. "They see the carefully selected, filtered, edited version of you. But I see through all that, right to the ugly little faults that you try so hard to hide. So, even if everyone else in the world falls for your bullshit, I don't want to hear it."

"And that's it?" he'd asked me. "You've decided. You know exactly who I am."

"I think I've seen enough to make a decision."

"Fine." He'd lifted his hands up, backing away. "I got it. From now on, I'll keep my opinions to myself. Even when this relationship blows up in your face—which it will—I won't even bother saying I told you so."

And, to be fair to him, when my relationship with David did combust, he never did.

"Now that's embarrassing." Hazel laughed.

At first, I thought she'd meant me. I'd been checking Brandon's social media pages *again*. I'd been doing so at least once an hour, every hour, for days. I could not seem to stop.

Over the last week, he published seven Royalty-sponsored Instagram posts and two YouTube videos, the most recent one a behind-the-scenes look at how Royalty's mas camp operated. Brandon had his goofy charm dialed up to eleven while he interacted with the staff. Within a few hours, it had twelve thousand likes.

"That's not—" I started, defensive, then realized Hazel's comment hadn't been aimed at me. Her parents were dancing in the center of the plaza. A live band composed of guitars, a violin, bass, and steelpan were somehow pulling off a jazzy rendition of *Mr. Fete*.

"God, I hope I'm in love like that someday." Hazel rested her arms on the banister that separated the restaurant from the square.

Uncle Russell spun Aunty Gloria a little too enthusiastically, the couple beside them leaping out of their path.

"Okay, maybe not *exactly* like that," Hazel amended.

I finished off the last sip of my mocktail. "They really are doing too much."

"Please," Hazel said dryly. "You think holding hands in public is too much."

"Well, you are not wrong. Oh—" The waiter with the cute smile and the name I couldn't remember replaced my mocktail with a new one. "I didn't order this."

"It's on me." His eyes sparkled in the lights that hung overhead.

"Thanks," I said, then watched him retreat, intrigued by the way his shoulders filled out his white uniform shirt. My phone chimed, alerting me to a new video on Brandon's YouTube page. *Chatting with the next generation of Royalty*, the title read. The thumbnail featured none other than Prince Kingston.

"You should get his number," Hazel said.

"Who?" I asked, confused.

She sighed. "The waiter. He's into you. And he's really cute. He's giving me a young Hrithik Roshan vibe."

"He's fine." I stretched over to show her the YouTube page on my phone. "Look at what this asshole did now. He interviewed Prince. The both of them together. I'm pretty sure this video might be cursed."

She swatted my hand away. "Yes, Chris told me about it. Brandon filmed it at their house."

"And you didn't think to mention it?" I asked. "What am I saying? You failed to warn me about Brandon working for Royalty too. Why should I expect any better?"

Hazel rolled her eyes. "I didn't say anything because I knew you'd get like . . . *this*."

"Like what? Concerned? Because I am."

Even if I hated to admit it, Royalty was killing it with their advertising. Brandon wasn't even the only influencer involved. They'd collected all the local big names like Pokémon, each one of them polluting thousands of timelines with Royalty promotions. The hype for the band's launch party was like nothing I'd ever seen before.

"Tess, Royalty is a *huge* band," Hazel said. "Last year, they had over five thousand players. Grandeur can't compete with their numbers. If you insist on thinking of them as a rival—which is silly and pointless—then they're already crushing us. So, maybe, for your peace of mind, you should let this go."

"But they shouldn't be crushing us." It didn't make sense. "Our costumes are better. Why are we struggling to fill a community center for our launch, when they're renting out a whole stadium for a fete?"

Grandeur had a history. Awards. Industry recognition. It was the company my grandfather started. The one Uncle Russell and my parents helped build. The one, with any luck, I'd inherit one day. It deserved better than this.

Hazel resettled against the banister, returning her gaze to her parents. "Grandeur's a smaller band, Tess. We don't need a stadium. That's never been us."

But maybe it could be.

"Oh, no," Hazel muttered. In the square, Uncle Russell

dramatically dipped Aunty Gloria. "They need to stop. They're going to break something."

I pulled up Instagram and started going through the Royalty-sponsored posts again, trying to see what I could learn from them. Maybe if I studied what they did right, I could apply it to our band as well.

But studying the posts wouldn't be enough. I needed to see it all.

"I need to go to Royalty's launch party."

Hazel snorted. "Good luck with that. Tickets sold out. Plus, you've got to be eighteen, and you're a few months short."

"True . . . but lucky for us, we have a connection to the family in charge."

Hazel didn't get it at first. After a few beats, she slowly turned to face me. "You can't be serious."

I took a sip from my drink.

"You've been railing against Chris and me this entire time, and now you want to ask him for a favor?"

"Yes. And I need you to do the asking."

Hazel blinked. "I don't even know what to say."

"Okay." I set my glass down. "I promise, if Chris gets us into the party and helps us pull this off, I'll admit he may be trustworthy. And I'll support your relationship."

She narrowed her eyes. "Really?"

"What? You want it in writing?"

"Yes, please. I'll write it up when we get home."

• • •

"Sure," Chris said. "I'll do it."

"Really?" I could not hide my disbelief. The guy hadn't even hesitated. "You will?"

"Yeah, it's no problem," Chris agreed with confidence. "I can get you in."

"Great." I shared a look with Hazel, who seemed similarly shocked by how easy this turned out to be.

We probably didn't even need to meet in such a clandestine spot, under the blooming flamboyant tree at the very edge of the school campus. It was mostly used by the upper-formers to hang out, away from the eyes of the faculty.

"Wait." Hazel leaned forward. The light filtering through the leaves illuminated the natural chestnut streaks in her hair. "You realize what she's asking you to do, right?"

"Of course he does," I said, worried that Hazel's caution might change his mind. She was the one he wanted to impress after all. I certainly didn't think he was doing this for me. "He wants to help us. Right, Chris?"

"Oh, yeah." He squared his shoulders like a soldier ready for battle. "But what's the plan once you're inside? Do you want to start a scene? Rush the stage? Hack the sound system? Okay, I can't actually do that last one. But, if *you* can, just let me know what you'd need."

"Whoa, there." I held up my hands to stop him. "This is strictly a recon mission. I do appreciate the enthusiasm, though."

Perhaps I'd been wrong about him after all.

"Sorry." He laughed, ducking his head in embarrassment. "It's just that Prince has been driving me up a wall since he came home from university. He and his friends have taken over the whole house, including my room. Last week, they played with the football I'd gotten signed by Dwight Yorke and kicked it in the pool. And my dear stepfather didn't see any reason to punish his golden child for it."

"Yikes," I said.

"Exactly. So, when I say tell me if you need anything, Tess, I do mean *anything*."

"Oh," I said, touched by the sentiment. I could see it now, it seemed so obvious—the genuine loathing he had for the Kingstons. I couldn't deny it anymore. "Hazel, you were right. He is perfect."

"Tess!" Hazel hissed through her teeth.

Chris's eyes widened, his gaze sliding toward her. "You think I'm perfect?"

Hazel sputtered. "Well . . . it's just . . . she didn't mean . . . when I said . . ."

"And what's going on over here?" Brandon stood at the top of the hill, staring down at us. He wore his sports uniform, a football tucked under his arm.

It occurred to me that, while the spot under the flamboyant tree was secluded, it remained vulnerable to sneak attacks. Not the ideal location for a secret rendezvous then.

When none of us answered Brandon, he raised a brow. "Something *is* going on over here?"

"No," I said a beat too early, and the others echoed a beat too late.

43

"*Very* interesting." Brandon tapped the football. "Actually, no. I don't care. Chris, you forget we have practice or what?"

Chris shot to his feet, dusting off his pants. He started up the hill. "Sorry, lost track of time. We can go."

Brandon tilted his head, taking in the scene again. "Why do I feel like I'm missing something?"

"Like what?" I asked, unable to resist. "Self-respect? Humility? The ability to recognize when your presence is not wanted?"

"No, not that." He tipped his head to the side. "And I know it's definitely not bird shit. Which, from the look of it, you've already got that covered."

"What?" I asked, then caught sight of what he meant. "Ew!" I pulled at my sleeve, trying to put some distance between my face and the mess crusting on my shoulder. I was going to be sick.

"These days it's all about dressing to fit your personality, right?" Brandon called out as he retreated. "Well, I'll say you've really nailed it."

"Here." Hazel handed me a tissue.

"Oh, I hate him," I said, snatching it from her. "I hate him so much."

"Yes," Hazel said. "We know."

# FOUR

I hadn't expected that one of the hardest parts about getting to the launch party would be convincing my aunt and uncle that I wanted to go out. Apparently, after railing against social gatherings for years, my sudden interest in attending one raised some flags.

"Is someone forcing you to go?" Aunty Gloria asked me.

"Tess, blink twice for yes," Uncle Russell said wryly, swirling a tumbler of whiskey. Ice clinked against the glass.

Aunty Gloria turned a disapproving eye toward her daughter. "Hazel, are you blackmailing your cousin? You have to tell me. It's the law."

"They think they're comedians," Hazel muttered, then confirmed, "No, I am not blackmailing my cousin into going to the movies with me."

When we'd caught Aunty Gloria in the living room, she'd been in the middle of sorting through the random-item drawer of the cabinet under the TV. Every charger, cord, and plug we'd ever owned littered the carpet around her.

Our intention had been to ask just her for permission. But Uncle Russell had walked by about a minute into our appeal. Glass in hand, he paused to watch the show.

"There *is* some pressure being applied," I said, hoping to ease their suspicions. And technically, it wasn't even a lie. I just hadn't specified who was doing the pressuring.

"What sort of pressure?" Aunty Gloria asked.

"Bribery."

"Ah," Uncle Russell said. "That's fine then."

"Wait a minute," Aunty Gloria said. "What kind of—"

"Gloria, if Tess wants to go out, she should be encouraged. It's a rare occasion, so perhaps we should show more support."

"Thank you," I said. "And I'm sorry I won't be able to help you in the workshop tomorrow." We'd be deviating from our usual weekend ritual. But it was only one Saturday night.

"That's fine, child." Uncle Russell smiled wryly, his tone oddly somber.

"Don't worry," I told him. "It's not going to be a regular thing. Apart from this, I'll still report to the workshop as usual."

A groove appeared between Uncle Russell's brows. "You just focus on having fun tomorrow night." He started to swirl the glass of amber-colored liquid, then winced. He set it down and flexed his fingers.

"So, we can go?" Hazel asked, tugging on the long sleeve of her shirt. She seemed a little twitchy, likely nervous about the deception. Hopefully, it only came off as impatience to her parents.

"Yes," Aunty Gloria said after a pause. "I don't see why not. As long as you call me when you get there and when you're leaving." She shook her head. "I still feel like there's a hidden agenda here."

"They're teenage girls, Gloria," Uncle Russell said. "There's almost always a hidden agenda. We can let this one go."

Chris told us to meet him at the fence at the back of the field that adjoined the stadium. To my horror, when we found him, he wasn't alone.

I stopped dead in my tracks. "You told him?"

Chris blinked at me, utterly guileless, standing on the other side of the fence. "Why wouldn't I? He won't rat us out."

I glared at Brandon. "I don't know. If it looks like a rat and smells like a rat . . ."

"Look at you, Little Gray Riding Hood." Brandon took in my outfit—hoodie to trainers—an annoying little smirk playing about his lips. "Did you two switch clothes? If it weren't for the glare you're shooting at me right now, I might've suspected a full *Freaky Friday* situation."

Chris held open a little break in the chain-link fence. Hazel ducked and squeezed right through it.

"We are in disguise," I said.

"No, Hazel is in disguise. I wouldn't have recognized her." He nodded toward my cousin, who'd just stepped into the light.

In a rare but welcome treat, she'd let me dress her up tonight.

When she'd said yes, I'd almost started crying. Not one to waste what might be my only chance, I'd gone all out.

After some deliberation, and several vetoes on Hazel's part, we agreed she'd wear my white Calvin Klein bodycon dress, which hung slightly looser and longer on her smaller frame but remained flattering all the same. After some light makeup contouring, we added some product to her hair and let her natural curls hang loose.

I thought I'd done a pretty good job. If the way Chris couldn't look away from her was any indication, he agreed with me.

"You, on the other hand . . ." Brandon stepped back as I ducked through the fence to join them. "I'm not sure I'd call that a disguise, even if the gray is different from the usual neon festival you call outfits. Not saying it doesn't suit you."

"You know what color suits you? Puke green. Go on, ask me why."

"Because I look good in everything?"

He lifted his arms, drawing attention to his outfit—a pair of well-fitted dark jeans and a black short-sleeved shirt. An interesting gold detail adorned his shoulders and stretched across his back. It looked like a brush-on adhesive applied to the silk fabric. If so, it had been very well done.

"Can I help you?" Brandon asked.

I looked up and met his eyes. While examining the adhesive, I'd drawn startlingly close to him. My chest clenched, and I jerked backward. Glancing away, I muttered, "It's a nice shirt."

"Right." Brandon coughed into his fist. "Well. Chris, now that

I've seen you're going through with this nonsense, I'm going to go and pretend that I haven't."

"Thanks, man."

"I'm serious," Brandon said. "From this point on, I don't know anything." He held up a hand to stop me and quickly continued, "I've got a job to do, and the last thing I need is Prince catching me with them. He's made it no secret that he hates the Messinas. I'm not getting involved."

"See?" I elbowed Hazel. "I told you. Even Brandon knows the family vendetta is real."

"I never said it wasn't real." Hazel tried to lift the neckline of her dress, which inched up her skirt. "I just said it's silly." She pulled the skirt back down, which lowered her neckline. When she reached for her neckline again, I sighed.

So much for disguises.

"Here." I unzipped the hoodie, shrugged it off, and handed it to her. Cool night air settled against my exposed arms. Underneath the hoodie, I'd worn a fuchsia drawstring crop top with a layered silver necklace.

"Thanks." Hazel took it from me.

"And now you're back." Brandon sounded amused. "That lasted all of two minutes."

"Don't you have to be somewhere that is not here?" I asked him.

"Right." He stepped away from us. "I'm serious, all of you. Pretend you don't know me."

"I'd do that anyway," I said. "Though I do feel the need to

point out that you're the one still here talking to us."

"Good point," he said, and walked off.

"Unbelievable," I muttered, watching him filter into the crowd. "He's *got a job to do*. Please. He's just posting a few photos. That's it."

"He does more than that, actually." Chris readily accepted Hazel's purse while she pulled on her hoodie. "Brandon was hired as a social media consultant. He's more or less behind their whole social media campaign this year. He's the one who brought all the local influencers together and got them to agree to participate. I don't think the turnout tonight would've been anywhere near as big as it is without him."

"He. Did. What?" I'd thought Royalty only sponsored some of his content. I didn't realize he was the evil mastermind behind the whole campaign. That little snake.

"Uh . . ." Chris shrank back from whatever he saw in my expression. "You good, fam?"

"Why did you let him in on our plan?" I demanded. "It's clear he's picked a side and it's not ours."

Chris's shoulders slumped. "I can't say I'm happy about it, but this is a huge opportunity for Brandon. I couldn't take that away from him." He looked at Hazel, seeking support. "He's not going to snitch, I swear."

"It's okay," Hazel said.

I folded my arms. "Uh, no. It's not."

"Ease up, Tess," Chris said. "If anything, Brandon's been helpful. He's even the one who told me about the hole in the fence."

Chris shared a smile with Hazel. "You know how Brandon is—he knows everyone, including some of the workers who were setting up this morning. They knew fixing the gap would be more work for them, so they pretended not to see it."

"See," Hazel told me. "Brandon isn't so bad."

I eyed the hole in the fence with renewed suspicion. "Unless getting us in here is part of some setup."

When Hazel didn't comment, I looked back, only to realize she and Chris weren't listening to me. They were staring at each other, the pair locked in some silent conversation. He tried to return her purse, but she dodged it, laughing and backing away when he came closer.

As I watched them, something squeezed in my chest.

Well, I should've seen this coming. I'd been quietly and effectively slotted into the spot of the third wheel without even noticing.

# FIVE

I didn't hate parties, I hated *partying*. Not the noun. Not the clothes or the spectacle or the atmosphere of abandonment—all that was great. It was the verb, the action, the involvement. More often than not, I'd find myself drifting through, detached from the scene, simultaneously feeling invisible and sure that I stuck out like a sore thumb.

At some point, I'd given up on Chris and Hazel. The pair were too wrapped up in each other, more interested in having fun than helping me. I ditched them at one of the food tents, wormed my way through the crowd, and found a good spot near the stage. There, I listened and observed the partygoers around me.

Some seemed excited about seeing the costumes. Others clearly just came for the lime. Either way, the hype was real and maintained by the continuous pulse of the upbeat soca and dance hall music, and a DJ who regularly reminded us about the show starting soon. At one point, I almost bumped into a cameraman—just one of several members of the press who were present.

Finally, the stage lights flashed and it all went dark.

The music ebbed away, leaving a restless quiet. People started whispering excitedly, drawing closer to the stage. Goose bumps raised along my skin. The sound of drums thundered through the speakers, the beat getting faster, building to a woman's voice singing out. Lights illuminated the stage. Huge screens lit up with an explosion of color and a timer ticking down from ten seconds.

I watched it all in awe and horror. What had I been thinking? There was no way we could compete with this. Hazel was right. Royalty was operating on a totally different level. A wave of hopelessness washed over me.

And then I saw the costumes.

The models emerged from backstage, toned and long-limbed, and body-sprayed to perfection. But while they were hot, the costumes were not. Their theme for the year was *Galactic*, the different sections with names like *Solar Power, Stardust,* and *Andromeda*. But the designs were interchangeable—so generic, they could've slapped any name on them and it wouldn't make a difference.

"Having fun?" someone asked. The voice slithered over my shoulder, the source standing a little too close, even in the context of a gathered crowd. I suppressed a shiver and turned around.

Prince Kingston.

I hadn't seen him in person in years. The last time, he'd been in a disheveled school uniform, he and his friends harassing us younger students as we passed through the school gates.

Now, here he stood, dressed in a slick navy-blue suit, his shoes shined to perfection. He looked ready for a day at the office, rather than a fete.

"It is Tess, right?" he asked. "Russell's niece?"

Uh-oh.

"Who?" I stalled. I'd known there was a chance he might recognize me, but we hadn't exactly run in the same circles in school.

He shook his head. "I remember you."

On stage, the models lined up for the finale. They strutted forward, taking one last walk down the runway.

"Is your uncle here too?" Prince craned his neck, peering around me. "Has the great Russell Messina graced us with his presence tonight? It would be an honor."

"He would never." I snorted, dismissing the idea entirely. Belatedly, I realized by doing so, I'd confirmed my identity. Damn it.

The lights came up in full, illuminating his smug face. "But *you* would?"

I folded my arms. "What? Are you going to throw me out?"

"Oh, no. I'm taking it as a compliment that Russell would send a spy to our launch party."

"Why do you assume I'm a spy? Maybe I just wanted to fete."

"Maybe. Or maybe you're here to get a little inspiration from our showcase. Lord knows, Grandeur needs all the help it can get with someone like Russell at the helm."

"Excuse me? What's that supposed to mean?"

"I mean he's old," Prince said, enunciating the words. "Russell, his costumes, and the way he runs his band are dated. Your numbers have been declining for years. It's only a matter of time before it totally collapses."

"Okay, first of all"—I stepped closer to him—"Uncle Russell and your father are almost the same age, so cool it. And second, even if I was looking for inspiration, I definitely didn't find it here. Not with those overpriced generic pieces of fluff on stage that you charge people thousands of dollars for. They look as cheap as they probably cost you to make."

Prince's teeth clenched. "Our costumes are excellent quality. Made by a team of very talented designers."

"Wow. Really? Couldn't tell from looking at them."

"Who are you anyway?" he asked. "You're not a professional designer, you're just related to one."

"I'm not a professional *yet*," I said. "But I don't have to be to recognize a bad costume when I see it."

Prince's eyes flicked over my shoulder, then returned to me, ablaze with anger. His voice dropped to a sharp whisper. "You need to shut up."

"Why? I'm not saying anything anyone can't see for themselves."

"It's time for you to leave." He pulled out his phone. "I'm calling security. Are you even old enough to be in here?"

I froze.

"Maybe I should film this and post it online." He brought the phone to his ear. "Russell Messina's niece getting dragged out of a Royalty fete. Yeah . . ." He smiled with all teeth and no warmth. "I think I'd like to see that."

"Hold on a minute."

Somebody stepped between us. The back of a black shirt with gold detailing blocked my view.

"Things are getting a little too hot over here," Brandon said. "How about we all take a breath, grab some drinks, pick up something to eat. From what I'm hearing, everybody is really enjoying the beef rotis—"

"Go away, pretty boy," Prince said. "No one was talking to you."

"And that's the problem, isn't it?" Brandon said. "I love being the center of attention. But all yuh over here, hogging up the limelight. If I go too long without it, I start itching. Hives break out on my skin."

Prince glanced over my shoulder again. This time, I checked to see what he'd been looking at.

At some point, we'd captured a small audience, none of whom made any attempt to pretend they hadn't been listening.

"Fine." Prince hung up the phone. "You get her out of here. Now."

"Of course," Brandon said, sounding far more chipper than the situation warranted. He turned to face me. "After you, milady. You heard his highness. Let's get moving."

I had no intention of sticking around to see if Prince changed his mind about calling security, so I brushed passed Brandon and headed toward the main gate.

Brandon caught up to me. "Good job. You really managed to lay low. Excellent work."

"Why the hell are you following me?"

"I said I'd see you out, so . . ."

"And you have to do everything Prince says?"

"He is the boss."

"So, when he says jump—" My shoulder collided with a man heading in the opposite direction, knocking me to the ground.

Brandon reached for me. "Are you okay?" To the man who hadn't even stopped to say sorry, he called out, "Ay, nah! Watch where you going."

"I am fine." I dusted the dirt off my hands and ignored his attempt to help me up. The only thing truly hurt was my dignity.

Then, I rose to my feet and realized—*nope.*

Not just my dignity.

My ankle too.

Brandon caught me before I fell over again. "Something wrong with your foot?"

"No, obviously I'm just doing this to get closer to you."

"Well, you could have just asked."

I pushed him away, gingerly testing my weight on my ankle. The pain was sharp but not unbearable. Nothing seriously injured, but it would make walking to the gate a slow and difficult process.

"All yuh good over here, Brandon?" A passing guy stopped to ask.

"Yeah. We good." Brandon plastered on a smile and waved him off. "Thanks, man. And tell Mickie I didn't forget he owe me a drink."

The guy laughed, saluting Brandon before he walked off.

Brandon turned his attention back to me, all traces of his smile gone. "You want my help or not? I'm still going to walk you out, whether that means giving you a hand or watching you crawl the rest of the way."

"How kind of you." I extended my arm, and he let me hook it over his shoulder.

"Not at all." He slung his hand around my back, gripping my waist. His warm palm pressed against my bare skin. I jerked backward, surprised, and he quickly shifted his hand higher, holding me over the thin material of my top. My skin buzzed everywhere he touched.

"I'm not losing my job over you," he said, his voice a little gruff.

The scent of his cologne tickled my nose—spicy and not unpleasant. Even though I tried to keep as much distance as possible between our bodies, as we started hobbling toward the gate, we kept brushing against each other.

I swallowed, clearing my throat. "You know Prince is an awful human being, right?"

"I have noticed, yes," Brandon said. "But his company pays very well, so . . ."

"And it's all about the money for you?"

"Yeah, it is. Thanks."

"Unbelievable. Just when I thought I couldn't think any less of you."

"I'm sorry, are you judging me right now?" He stopped to look at me. "You were supposed to lay low. Do you have any idea how much trouble Chris would be in if his family found out he let you into the party?"

I had a fairly good idea. Regret washed over me, cooling my anger. "I hadn't thought of that."

"Well, you should have—hey!" He waved to a group of girls who called out to him. "Just helping this one to her car. She get on too bad. Wine too low and break something." He shrugged as if to say *what can you do?*

"I hate you," I muttered, as the group walked away laughing. "Do you know *everyone?*"

"Yes. Now come on, Boop. Hop to it. I've got better things to do than carry you around." We started moving again. When we almost reached the entrance, he asked, "Do you want to call Hazel?"

"Yes. Shoot." I made us stop, frustrated with myself. "I forgot."

"It's okay. I tend to have a kind of distracting effect on people."

"If you mean I've been distracted by irritation, then yes." I leaned against him. "Hold me."

"Of course, dear. And I'll never let go."

I ignored him, twisting my body to retrieve my phone from the pocket I'd sewed into the leg of my jeans. I expected some sarcastic remark, but Brandon said nothing. When I checked to see why, I noticed his eyes had dropped to my neckline.

He realized I'd caught him and looked away. "You calling them or not?"

"Yeah," I said, straightening up. "Hold on."

"Wait. On second thought, that might not be necessary."

I looked up from my phone. "Why not?"

He tipped his chin upward, directing me to turn around. I traced his gaze, stunned to find Hazel and Chris kissing in the shadowy corner of one of the merchandise booths.

Well, okay then.

"Good for them." Brandon stepped out of my hold. "Best of luck breaking that up."

"Are you serious?" I watched him retreat, precariously balancing my weight on one foot. "What about walking me out?"

He waved over his shoulder. "Close enough."

# SIX

A ROYAL FLOP?

"I don't have to be one [a professional designer] to recognize a bad costume when I see it."

While I wish I could take credit for this scalding takedown, I must attribute this very loud, very public assessment of Royalty's latest offerings to the young niece of Russell Messina, the celebrated Trinidadian mas maker and the leader of the band Grandeur. Having seen the costumes myself, I can confirm this spirited little lady knows what she's talking about.

Royalty's rapid growth over the past few years has not gone unnoticed. However, as they continue to focus on expanding their all-inclusive perks for players (free concerts, fetes, food, drinks, merch, etc.), they have seemingly abandoned any notions of making good costumes as well. While some bands, like Tribe and Ronnie & Caro, have figured out the formula for catering to players interested in both the costumes and the experience, Royalty is not them.

*That being said, I have no doubt that the general public will snap up their stock regardless, especially after the huge success of their recent viral social media campaign. Indeed, at the time of this article's publication, reports from company insiders confirm that several sections sold out within a matter of hours . . .*

"They sold out? How?" I couldn't believe it. "People saw those costumes and still bought them?"

Aunty Gloria rubbed her temples. "I don't think that's the most pressing factor at the moment, do you?"

"Sorry." I handed her the iPad with the article and molded my expression into something more contrite.

When Hazel and I arrived home from school that Monday afternoon, we were greeted by my aunt and uncle's stern faces. They marched us into the living room like we were sentenced to the gallows. Once we were seated, they presented us with the online article, written by one of Aunty Gloria's ex-colleagues for a Caribbean lifestyle digital publication called *The Write Vibez*.

Beside me, Hazel kept twitching and shifting in her seat, nervous and terrible at hiding it.

"Is it really so bad?" I asked. "Mr. Kingston takes jabs at you in the media all the time. This isn't any different."

"I don't care how many *jabs* he's taken at me," Uncle Russell said. "We do not stoop to his level. You and I—and Grandeur— we are supposed to be better than that. We let the quality of our costumes speak for itself."

"If I could just . . ." Melissa hesitantly inched into the room, through the kitchen doorway. She raised her hand like she was in class, then seemed to realize how ridiculous it was and dropped it. "To be fair to the girls, since the article came out last night, we've had a bump in ticket sales for our launch party this weekend. No press is bad press, I guess."

Uncle Russell said nothing. His glare said everything.

Melissa retreated into the kitchen.

"Uncle," I said. "Aren't you interested in what I learned from the party? I've been studying the Royalty model, and I've realized that their sales are entirely based on the experience they offer. Not the costumes. So, I've been looking into the different kinds of all-inclusive benefits we might consider adding—"

"Listen to me," Uncle Russell said. "We do not deal with all-inclusives. We do not need huge fetes and gimmicks. If the day comes when my name alone cannot sell a costume—when the Carnival landscape has changed so drastically that we do not have a place in it—Grandeur will close. It's that simple."

I couldn't believe it. How could he talk about ending the band so easily? "But everyone else—"

"It doesn't matter what everyone else is doing. We know who we are, and I'd rather be remembered for who we were than some knockoff we try to be." He sighed, scrubbing a hand over his face. "You shouldn't have gone to that party. What were you thinking?"

"In my defense," I said softly, "I didn't know people were listening to us. If I had, I wouldn't have been so loud."

"Again," Aunty Gloria said. "You're missing the point."

"You and Hazel lied to us," Uncle Russell said. "You told us you were going to the cinema. Instead, we find out this was all about the band again—" He closed his eyes and pinched the bridge of his nose. "I'm disappointed in both of you."

Ouch.

Aunty Gloria stepped forward. "For the next month, you're not allowed to go anywhere but school and home. That's it."

Hazel's jaw dropped. "Seriously?"

"Wait." I waved my hands, drawing their attention to me and away from my cousin. "Don't punish Hazel. This was my idea. She didn't want to go. I talked her into it."

"Oh, I don't doubt that," Uncle Russell said. "Which is why for the next month, you aren't allowed in the workshop. No mas camp either."

"Seriously?" I dropped my hands. This was so much worse than I'd thought. I searched his stern expression for some hesitance, some sign that he didn't mean it. But he seemed resolute.

"Yes, seriously," he said. "For a month. You should be focused on studying for your exams anyway. Your last set of results was less than stellar, to say the least."

I crossed my arms, trying to contain the hurt that sliced through my chest. "They weren't that bad." My grades had never been Hazel-level spectacular, but they were still pretty solid.

"Regardless," Uncle Russell said. "You could use this time to improve them."

For a few more minutes, I tried to reason with them, but they weren't having it. Once we were dismissed, Hazel and I retreated to my room where we could commiserate and plan accordingly.

"I can't believe this." Hazel dropped onto my bed, face down. "I finally got a boyfriend, and I can't go anywhere for a month."

"I'm sorry," I said, my chest tight with regret. My school skirt swished as I paced the length of my room, too wired to sit. "This wasn't your fault. You were only trying to help me. I'll talk to aunty and uncle again. Make them understand."

Hazel flipped over and sat up. "Hey, it's okay. Really. It sucks that they're mad, but it's not like I didn't know what I was getting into."

"No, it was a silly idea. I shouldn't have dragged you into it." Maybe I could've gone to the fete alone or kept up a disguise. I definitely shouldn't have given in to Prince's confrontation, or at the very least kept my voice down.

I'd never wanted to get my cousin in trouble. And I certainly didn't want to be banned from mas camp. The thought of not being there made me twitchy. There was so much work that needed to be done between now and Carnival, and I'd be missing it.

"Jeez." Hazel climbed off the bed. She caught me by the shoulders, and I stopped pacing. "You're actually freaking out about this."

No. Yes. Maybe?

Over Hazel's shoulder, my eyes settled on the one decoration I allowed on my walls: a blown-up photo of an overhead shot of masqueraders crossing the Queen's Park Savannah stage—thousands of people with different lives captured in a single moment of joy and celebration. All I'd ever wanted was to see my designs be a part of that day. A part of something so much bigger than myself.

Hazel's expression softened. "It's only a month. It'll pass so quickly you won't even notice."

Somehow, I doubted that. But I did take a little comfort in the fact that she didn't seem upset with me. "The thing is—I can't even say going to the launch party was worth it."

"Well . . ." She let go of my shoulders, a sly smile on her face. "I can't say I agree with you on that one."

It took me a second to grasp her meaning, and when I did, my guilt melted into exasperation. "Yeah, whatever. Congrats on you and Chris finally giving into the urge to eat each other's faces. Well done."

She smiled. "Thanks."

"Does that mean you're official now? Everything all sunshine and roses?"

"Yeah. We are. It's just . . ." She bit her lip.

"What?" I asked. Something was clearly off. "You just got together. How can there be a problem already?"

"It's nothing. Really." She sighed, dropping onto the bed again. "It's just . . . well . . . do you know who his ex-girlfriend is?"

"Am I supposed to?"

Hazel reached over the edge of the bed to retrieve her bag. "Her name's Nora."

"Nora what?"

"Just Nora. One name."

"What? Like Rihanna?"

"Basically." Hazel pulled out her phone, found what she needed, and showed it to me. "She performs cover songs on YouTube." On screen, a girl with dip-dyed black-blue hair and perfectly applied winged eyeliner leaned closer to a microphone. The opening notes of "Love on the Brain" started to play.

"Chris used to date her?" I asked.

"They met through Brandon," Hazel said miserably. "Look at her. She's pretty, older, taller, way more interesting than me. And she's smart too, studying to be a lawyer. She posted a photo of her bookshelf and it's all textbooks and Man Booker and Pulitzer Prize–winning doorstops."

"Hazel, *you're* pretty and smart. And you read doorstops as well." I wasn't seeing the problem here.

"Not like her," Hazel muttered, swiping the app off the screen. "She probably laughs at romance novels too."

"Too?" Suspicion snuck up on me. "Did Chris say something about you writing romance?" He wouldn't dare, would he?

"No," Hazel said. "Because he doesn't know that I do."

"How is that possible?" I asked. Hazel wrote all the time. On everything.

Actually, no. Now that I thought about it, she hadn't been writing on her arms for a while.

Did she stop because of Chris?

Hazel picked at the quilting of the duvet. "A few weeks back, he asked me what I was reading. When I told him it was a romance book, his immediate reaction was—oh, like *Fifty Shades of Grey*? Then he laughed." She pulled the duvet over her face, embarrassed. "How could I tell him I wrote romance too after that?"

"This happened a few weeks ago? And you still wanted to date him?"

"It seemed like a small flaw in an otherwise perfect person."

"Maybe you should stop calling him perfect. No one is perfect. And if you're serious about him, you're going to have to tell him about your writing eventually."

"Not if I use a pseudonym when I publish," she said. "I could keep it secret. Like a second life."

"That sounds like borrowing trouble," I said, standing up. My attention turned to the photo of the masqueraders on my wall again, and I felt a sharp tug of shame. "The article wasn't that bad, right? Like, I really didn't know a reporter was listening. I don't want to cause problems for Uncle."

"I'm sure he knows that you were just trying to help." Hazel waved a dismissive hand. "It's just an article. No one will care. I'm sure it'll be fine."

Except it wasn't.

It turned out someone had cared. We'd find out how much a few days later.

Aunty Gloria was the reason we'd gone to the community center that morning. She'd insisted that Friday was the day to send Hazel's car for detailing and offered to drop us to school herself. On the way there, she'd answered the distressed call from my uncle. Without a second thought, she adjusted our route to meet him at the community center.

Uncle Russell hadn't been happy she'd brought us along. But

his objections faded into faint background noise as I took in the ruined costumes on the floor. The hall had been thoroughly trashed—graffiti on the walls, decorations torn, potted plants overturned.

This was all my fault.

"What do you want to do now?" Melissa asked, her anxious tone slipping through my haze.

I walked past one of the custodians tasked with sweeping and scooping and scrubbing the walls. A familiar shock of blue and silver caught my attention. I bent to pick it up. It was the tattered and twisted remains of the blue heron headpiece. The room could be fixed, but these costumes could not.

"Don't you have backups?" Aunty Gloria asked.

"For some," Uncle Russell said. "Not all."

"Some of the materials needed to be imported in bulk," Melissa said. "They haven't come in yet." She let out a groan. "It's going to be hell calling all the guests. And the vendors. We're not getting a refund for canceling this late."

"We can't cancel," I insisted, surprising even myself. The launch was an important promotional event. Even more than that—it was tradition. We couldn't not do it.

"We can work on replacements—"

Even before I'd finished talking my uncle was shaking his head. "No. We don't have time."

"We can set out the costumes that we do have and use the concept art in place of the others."

"No—"

"It can work," I insisted. "I'll help. I can skip school today."

"No!" Uncle Russell said. "Beatrice, enough. I am not setting out rushed costumes and concept art. It's not professional. The best we can do is cancel and apologize and pray that that's enough to save face."

I snapped my mouth shut.

*Beatrice*? No one called me that. The formality of it cut right through me.

Uncle Russell's chest fell with a heavy sigh. His tone softened, but his stony expression remained. "You and Hazel should be at school." He threw Aunty Gloria a pointed look. "Melissa, come on. We've got a lot of calls to make."

"You know this was the Kingstons, right?" I blurted as he started to leave. "It's Prince. This is him getting back at me."

"You don't know that," Uncle Russell said.

"I do. This is his retaliation for the article. He feels like I messed up his launch so he's doing the same to us."

If I hadn't gone to the party—if I hadn't insulted their costumes and publicly embarrassed their band, then none of this would've happened.

"Come on, Tess." Aunty Gloria wrapped an arm around my shoulders. "Russell is right. I shouldn't have brought you here."

She led me out of the hall, Hazel trailing behind.

I couldn't say what happened in school that day. Most of the time, all I could do was sit and pretend to listen, breathing through the heavy block of ice lodged in my chest.

We had a mock exam in French, and I'd handed in the paper with most of the sections empty. Not because I didn't know the answers, but because I'd zoned out midway through. By the time I returned to the moment, time was up. Class dismissed.

Prince had to be behind this. I knew it in my bones. He shouldn't be allowed to get away with it.

"*Hello?*" Brandon stood on the other side of my desk, waving a hand in front of my face. "Anyone home?"

"What?" I glanced around, confused by the new faces filtering into the classroom.

"It's seventh period," he said. "Last I checked, you're not in Accounting."

Shoot. I reached for my bag. My class had ended and another was starting.

"No need to rush," Brandon said. "Mr. Brathwaite is always late anyway. And it looked like you were doing some deep thinking there."

"Not today, Brandon." I shoved my books into my backpack and zipped it shut. "I'm not in the mood."

His brows raised. "Did you have a bad night? Conscience bothering you over that article? What did they call you—a *spirited little lady*? When I read that, I couldn't help but think, well, that's one way to put it."

"*My* conscience?" I asked, fuming at his choice of words. "You want to talk about *my* conscience. You're the one working for a snake." I shoved my chair back and stood. "The article was an accident. I didn't plan that. What he did was malicious with intent."

Brandon folded his arms. "What are you talking about?"

"I'm talking about your boss and how he wrecked our venue the night before our band launch. He trashed the whole place and destroyed—" I stopped, breathing through a wave of emotion. "Destroyed all our costumes."

"Prince did what?" Brandon dropped his arms. "Are you sure it was him?"

"Who else would it be?" I slid out from behind the desk. "And the worst part is, my silly article won't affect Royalty's sales at all. Not even a blip. But Grandeur . . ." I bit my lip and shook my head. "What he did might've ruined our whole year."

"How do you know it was him?" Brandon asked, following me out of the classroom. "Prince is an asshole, no question. But what you're talking about is criminal."

"Yeah, it is. And you work for someone like that, so what does that say about you? How's *your* conscience?" I asked, then backed away without waiting for an answer.

# SEVEN

The sales numbers for the first week came in. They weren't good.

We got quite a bit of backlash for canceling the party at the last moment. Responses ranged from irritated understanding to straight vitriol. A few guests, who didn't get the update, even showed up at the venue expecting a party, only to be turned away.

It didn't help that Uncle Russell wouldn't explain what happened. He said he didn't see the point. If it were me, I'd have been pointing fingers at the culprit, solid proof or not.

The atmosphere in the house was thick with tension, Uncle Russell perpetually moody, Melissa in the pantry up to three times a day. And yet, the full extent of the damage didn't quite hit me until I overheard Uncle Russell and Aunty Gloria talking about it.

It was a late night. I'd been up working on my literature project, and I'd come downstairs to the kitchen for some water.

"—call some people?" Aunty Gloria was saying. "See if I can drum up some interest?"

"No," Uncle Russell said. "Besides, who would want to tie themselves to a sinking ship. Grandeur hasn't made a profit in three years. We can't go on like this."

I froze behind the doorway, numb and listening.

"If we don't at least break even this year," he said, "we can't afford a next one."

"You mean shutting it down?" Aunty Gloria asked him. "Are you ready for that?"

"I don't know. But a man can only swim against the current for so long before he's tired. And I am."

He couldn't mean that, right?

This wasn't the end. It couldn't be.

After that, I returned to my room and settled in for a night of fitful sleep. I dreamed of long-necked birds, great big waves, and vicious currents dragging me underwater.

Help came the next morning from the most unexpected source.

"Uh . . ." I stopped on the threshold of the living room. No matter how many times I blinked, the scene in front of me remained: Aunty Gloria on one end of the couch, Brandon sitting on the other. Both of them drinking from the "good" teacups that Aunty Gloria brought out only for special occasions.

"I see what you mean," Brandon said, after taking a sip. "It's the ginger. It's like a punch in the face. Really wakes you up."

"Exactly," Aunty Gloria said. "I swapped out coffee for this and never looked back. One of the members of my meditation group recommended it." She set her cup down. "I've been trying to get my family to join our group for ages. But every time I bring it up, they zone out, which is ironic—"

"Aunty Gloria." I found my voice. "What are you doing? You're not supposed to invite them inside." I approached the couch, pointing to Brandon. "We'll need holy water to get him out now."

"What's that, sweetheart?" Aunty Gloria asked.

"She's insinuating I'm a vampire, Aunty," Brandon explained. "It's a joke. Just something we do." He smiled at me. "Not her best, though. She must still be sleepy."

Hazel entered from the kitchen. "Oh, good. You're awake. Brandon's here."

"Yes. I noticed. Thank you, Hazel." I returned my attention to the interloper. "Why *are* you here?"

He took one last long sip, set the empty cup down, and stood. "I actually came to talk to you."

"Me?"

Aunty Gloria laughed. "You two can talk in here." She stood and gathered the cups. "Brandon, let me know if you change your mind about joining our meditation group. You'd be surprised who's involved. We've even got young people like yourself."

"I'll think about it, Aunty," he said. "Thank you for the tea and for answering my questions. And let me say, we miss seeing you on TV every night. The man they've got filling in has nothing on you."

Aunty Gloria laughed, waving off his flattery. "Hazel, come. Grab that plate for me."

Hazel did as she was told, and the pair left the living room.

Brandon and I stared at each other. For the life of me, I couldn't think of a single reason he should be here, much less why he'd want to talk to me.

"Surprised to see me?" he asked.

"Surprise is definitely one of the emotions involved."

A small smile tugged at his lips. He stuck his hands into his pockets and strolled over to the shelves. To my irritation, he started inspecting the various framed photos that adorned them. If I didn't know better, I'd say he looked nervous.

He pointed at one of the photos. "Is that you and Hazel?"

"Yes." I didn't have to look to know which one he meant. Hazel and I had been about four when it was taken. My arm slung around her shoulder, the both of us in matching floral dresses, our hair adorned with multi-colored baubles.

He moved on to the photo of Uncle Russell and Aunty Gloria's wedding, the both of them in profile as they grinned at each other. "Your uncle with hair. That's so . . ."

"Wrong?" I supplied, having thought something similar myself. Uncle Russell was bald. Had been since I could remember. Anything else didn't compute.

"*Yes*. Exactly." He did a double-take and backed up. "And who's this?" He picked up the frame to get a better look. "Is this your parents? Wow."

I crossed the room to join him. Somehow, I knew he'd notice that one. To be fair, it did stand out. My parents, in their early twenties, glittering in fiery-red and gold Grandeur costumes. The camera focused on them, amid a sea of other masquerade players, their youth and beauty and joy forever captured in that moment, exactly the way I wanted to remember them.

"Talk about couple goals," he said.

I snorted. Not really. But they did work really hard to make people think they were. I snatched the frame from him and returned it to the shelf. "Why are you here, Brandon?"

He let out a small laugh and retreated to the couch. "This is very hard for me to say. So give me a second." He perched on the armrest, drew a deep breath, then exhaled slowly. "You were right."

"I'm sorry—what?" I leaned forward, cupping my ear. "I think I misheard you. Can you say that again?"

"No," he said.

I rolled my eyes. "Can you at least tell me why I was right?"

"Do you remember a recent conversation we had? The one where you implied that I was a soulless, greedy bastard."

"*Implied*? I mean, I may not have used those exact words, but—"

"Yes, yes." He folded his arms. "Well, that same afternoon, I had to stop by the Royalty offices to pick something up. While there, I started chatting with some of the admin staff. They mentioned how nice it was that Prince didn't stick around for their weekly after-work lime. Usually, he and his friends turn up, make a mess, and harass everyone."

"Somehow that doesn't surprise me," I said.

"Right? But this part will. That office lime was the same night your venue got trashed. And for the first time since Prince started working at Royalty, he didn't turn up."

"I knew it," I said. My mind whirled with anger and vindication.

"Wait, wait. Don't jump ahead. All that proves is that he wasn't at the lime. He and his lackeys could've been wreaking havoc somewhere else. But it is suspicious."

I dropped onto the loveseat. "It can't be a coincidence."

"It might be. Which is why I asked around some more. I tried to find out where he was that night." He grimaced. "I guess I wasn't being as subtle as I thought."

"What happened?"

"Nothing at first. Then Prince started asking *me* questions. About you. About us. About how you got into the party."

"And you said . . . ?"

He gave me a dry look. "I didn't rat out Chris, if that's what you're asking."

"I didn't say that you did." I might've thought it. But I didn't say it.

"Sure," he said. "Anyway, later that same day, my latest video for them got mysteriously flagged. They used that to claim I'd breached our contract, and they ended our sponsorship agreement."

Well, damn. "Can they do that?"

"Apparently," he said. "It's clearly bullshit, but what can I do? And the worst part is they don't have to pay me what I'm owed because of it."

"Well, that sucks, but I'm not sure why you're here telling me about it."

"It's because—" He broke off, his lips pressed into a thin line. He watched me for a moment, his brow furrowed under the weight of some decision. Then, with a sharp exhale, he seemed to give in. "I want you to convince your uncle to hire me."

"Oh, really?" I folded my arms. After he'd basically handed our rivals their best year ever, he wanted to switch sides? "What makes you think we'd want you?"

"Do you know what people's first reaction is to hearing about Grandeur?"

"Awe? Respect? Admiration?"

"More like—*oh, they're still around?*"

"That's not true."

"It is and you know it. Almost all promotions are done online these days, and your band's social media game is weak. I can help with that."

"Why? Out of the kindness of your heart?"

"Yes. And for a fee."

I rolled my eyes. "Yes. Of course."

"And for revenge," he added. "Prince can't be allowed to get away with this."

"I see. Not that I'm against what you're suggesting, but how would you do that? You can't turn Grandeur into a big band like Royalty."

"Give me some credit. I'm well aware of the limitations. But in my experience, you don't have to surpass your enemies to annoy them. Just thriving is often enough."

"In your experience?" I slid him a side-eye, trying to work out if that was some veiled reference to our relationship.

He shrugged, smiling.

"You're forgetting something," I said. "A big problem."

"What?"

"I don't trust you. For all I know, Prince put you up to this. Maybe he's paid you to sabotage or spy on us."

His smile fell. "You'd believe something that farfetched before believing me? You really do think I'm a complete asshole, don't you?"

I shrugged.

Brandon stood. "I thought, seeing as we had a common enemy, we could work together for once. But if you want to continue acting like a know-it-all—"

"*I'm* a know-it-all? *Me*? You're the one who strutted in here, so arrogant, so sure you could help us."

"I do not strut."

"Oh, you do and you know it."

We glared at each other. Not for the first time I noticed we happened to be almost the same height. Even when arguing, we stood eye to eye.

"I know I can help." He stubbornly held my gaze. "It's not arrogance if it's true. Just look at what I did for Royalty."

He was right, and I knew it.

"Fine," I said, through gritted teeth. "I'll talk to my uncle. But

I wouldn't hold my breath, if I were you." Uncle Russell would never agree to this.

His smug smile was instant and irritating.

"On second thought, maybe you should hold your breath."

"Aw, Boop," he said, following me out the front door. "Your confidence in me warms my heart. Truly."


"We're not hiring at the moment," Uncle Russell said. He looked tired, hunched behind the desk of his workshop. In the last few days, he'd been quieter. More distant than usual. Almost impossible to reach.

But I had to try.

"Brandon isn't looking for something permanent. He'd only be consulting for a few months. Just until Carnival."

My uncle sat back in his chair, apparently unimpressed.

I'd told Brandon to wait outside the workshop, sure that my uncle would see through his charm as clearly as I did. Rather than risk it, I came in here alone. Not that it seemed to be helping. My uncle had his mind made up.

"Melissa is handling marketing and promotions," Uncle Russell said.

"No, Melissa is bumbling through marketing and promotions. Don't get me wrong, she's doing the best she can, but—" I had to grit my teeth to force the words out. "Brandon would be better. He is actually good at what he does."

"I really am," Brandon said from the doorway behind me.

I turned to glare at him. *Get out*, I mouthed. Why did I ever think he'd listen to me? No doubt he'd say something annoying and ruin any chance we might've had.

Brandon strolled right in. "Mr. Messina," he said, approaching the desk with far more confidence than most strangers had when facing my uncle. "Thank you for hearing us out. I know your time is valuable."

Uncle Russell said nothing.

"I hope Tess has mentioned how much I admire your work. Honestly, it's inspiring what you and your family have accomplished with Grandeur."

I closed my eyes, unable to watch the unfolding trainwreck. This was why I'd told him to wait outside.

"Is that so?" my uncle said finally. "Tell me, then, Brandon— do you play mas?"

The question seemed to throw Brandon off. His smile dimmed. His answer took so long to come that I'd almost expected him to lie.

"No," he said eventually. His tone sounded so resigned it had to be true. "Not your kind of mas."

My uncle folded his arms. "My kind?"

"I've played J'ouvert and my parents join the mud mas sometimes. But your kind—with the beads and feathers—no. My parents don't like it. They feel that the large Carnival bands have overcommercialized and diluted the traditional aspects of the festival."

Oh God. Just when I thought this couldn't get any worse. The complicated conversation around the commercialization of

Carnival came with no easy answer. Definitely not the topic to bring up when trying to convince my uncle—who owned a mas band—to hire him.

Why couldn't he talk about the number of Instagram followers he had instead?

"And what do you think?" Uncle Russell rested his elbows on his desk and leaned forward. "You agree with them?"

"I'm clearly not an expert on this," he said carefully. "But I think it has in some ways, yes."

Mentally, I kissed this silly plan of ours goodbye. Maybe it would've worked. Maybe it wouldn't. Now, we'd never know.

"But," Brandon said, "I also think there are a lot of massively talented artists in this country. Many who genuinely love Carnival and its traditions, and dismissing their work because they design for a particular type of mas isn't fair. They help keep the festival fresh and exciting. And I think you're one of those people."

Uncle Russell blinked. "I am?"

"Well, at least when it comes to costume design." Brandon let out a small, nervous laugh. "Your marketing strategies are dated. You have almost no online presence. I think if you keep operating exactly the way you have, Grandeur will fade away. And I think that's sad because, over the years, you've inspired a lot of people."

Uncle Russell said nothing. I was similarly speechless, stunned by his response.

Where had that come from?

He'd sounded so confident, so genuine. I believed he meant it. That he could help us. Though, to be fair, I'd already been on his side when he'd walked in. My uncle would be much harder to sway.

"But that's just my opinion," Brandon continued. "Like I said, I don't know anything about—"

"All right, son." Uncle Russell held up a hand. "Stop while you're ahead."

Brandon snapped his mouth shut. Then he lit up. "Have I got the job?"

"Yes, fine," Uncle Russell said impatiently. "If all your sales pitches are anywhere near as eloquent as that one, I don't see why not."

"Oh. Okay." Brandon let out a laugh, breathy and relieved.

He'd done it. He'd convinced my uncle.

I couldn't tell who was more surprised by the outcome—Brandon, Uncle Russell, or me.

# EIGHT

"I hate him." I dropped onto the spot on the steps next to Hazel.

We sat in front of the empty music room, facing the football field. Around us, students lunched or limed in clusters. A handful of first formers kicked around an empty Chubby soda bottle with all the enthusiasm of a FIFA World Cup Final.

"What did Brandon do now?" Hazel didn't bother to look up, steadily scribbling in one of her notebooks.

"He wouldn't look at my binder," I said bitterly.

"What?" She lifted her head.

I pulled the yellow ring binder out of my bag and showed it to her.

My ban from the mas camp hadn't been lifted yet, so I'd had some time. For the last two days, I'd been collecting all the material about Grandeur I could find—photos, article clippings, and magazine cutouts. Everything about the mas band's background, the awards, the designs. How my grandfather started it, and

Mummy and Uncle Russell inherited it.

"This is . . ." Hazel seemed to be at a loss for words.

"Yeah, I know it's a bit much." And as someone who deeply cared about aesthetics, I could admit the final product was a bit of a bulky mess. "Still, Brandon could've at least looked at it. I just want to help."

Hazel narrowed her eyes. "Tess, be honest. How did you approach Brandon with this? Did you offer your help or demand he take it?"

"Well . . ." I picked at the edge of the plastic cover. "I suppose my timing could've been better." Perhaps I hadn't needed to interrupt his study session. And I could've waited until he was free instead of glaring at his friends until they left us.

"You have such a way with others," Brandon had said dryly once we were alone.

"Thanks," I'd said and sat across from him. "So, what's your plan?"

"My . . . plan?"

"For social media?"

"What about it? I'm already running everything through Melissa."

"Yes, but if you're looking for more content, I think I can help." I flipped the binder around and flicked it open. "I've put it all in here. The whole history of Grandeur. Everything you'd ever need to know."

"And . . . what am I supposed to do with this?"

"Use it." Obviously.

He pushed the binder toward me. "That won't be necessary."

I nudged the binder toward him. "Why don't you have a look first, before you decide."

"You're forgetting that I've worked with the entire marketing department at Royalty for weeks. I've learned how they operate. Not to mention I've been managing my own platforms for years." He pushed the binder back again. "I think I know what I'm doing."

"I didn't forget. But while you might know social media, you don't know Grandeur." Not the way I did.

He sighed, pulled the binder closer, and flipped to a random page. "You really think that people are going to care about a pheasant feather shortage? Or that the mas camp changed location in 2002?" He slapped the cover shut. "And why a hard copy? How many trees had to die for this?"

"Brandon, this"—I tapped the cover—"this is Grandeur. It's not just about the costumes. It's about the history. The people who make it what it is."

"And that's great and all," he said, checking his phone. "But people won't care. Trust me, they want to see the costumes. That's it."

"Because you always know what people want?"

He raised a brow. "Do you?"

The school bell rang.

He stood, grabbed his backpack off the chair, and headed for the door. "Trust me. I know what I'm doing."

Trust him? *Him?*

Two periods later, I was still fuming.

"Why did you make it a hard copy?" Hazel asked, inspecting the binder.

"Because I like working with my hands. It makes the progress feel tangible, like something's getting done—you know what? It doesn't matter." I snatched it back from her. "My point is Brandon's an asshole."

"An asshole with ninety-two thousand followers on Instagram."

"Ninety-two?" When did it go up? I pulled out my phone to check.

"And wasn't the whole reason you wanted Daddy to hire him because he knows what he's doing?"

"Well, yes. But—"

"So maybe you should give him a chance to show you what he can do before you decide he's messing up?"

I glared at her. "For future reference, when I'm venting, your only job is supposed to be unconditionally agreeing with me."

"I am agreeing with you." Hazel scribbled something on her arm, then immediately rubbed it off, leaving a black splotch. She flipped her notebook open and started writing in that instead. "I'm only suggesting that you might want to change your approach and compromise a little. Like, for example, you could've digitized the files for Brandon, but you didn't. Even though it would've made the information more convenient to him, you still did things the way you wanted to."

"That doesn't sound like unconditional agreement to me."

"I do agree with you. Brandon didn't have to be so dismissive. He could've heard you out." She shrugged. "Then again, if you were coming at him with a closed mind-set, isn't it understandable that he'd respond the same way?"

Damn it. She made a good point, and I hated it. "So, what do you suggest I do?"

"I think you should try being nicer to him."

"Ew."

"Nothing too dramatic. All you'd need is a slightly softer approach." She laughed at my expression of total revulsion. "Would it help if you knew Chris said Brandon is actually taking this job very seriously? He even skipped one of their football matches to work."

"How generous of him," I said dryly. "Though, speaking of Chris . . ."

Hazel's boyfriend sat down next to her.

"Speaking of me?" he asked, delighted.

Hazel flinched, her pen dropping and bouncing off the step. It landed somewhere in the patchy grass below.

"I got it." Chris leaped off the side of the steps and landed in a crouched pose.

Hazel shoved the notebook into my hands. "Here."

"*Okay* . . ." I took the book from her—not that I seemed to have a choice in the matter.

"This is for you." Chris handed her the pen, which she promptly passed on to me.

"Oh, no. This is for Tess."

Chris retook the spot beside her. "So. You were speaking of me? Were you saying good things?"

While Hazel sputtered, trying to cover her small deception, I examined the notebook. Sure enough, she'd been writing a scene for her novel. I didn't see why she still felt the need to hide this from him. Eventually, he would find out.

I skimmed the page. Normally, I wouldn't read Hazel's early drafts. Not because she didn't want me to, but because most of her first drafts were done longhand, and her handwriting was head-ache-inducingly atrocious. This time, however, my eyes caught on the name *Heathcliff*, and I couldn't resist.

> *Of all the people to find sitting in her grandmother's parlor, she'd never envisioned him.*
>
> *Heathcliff.*
>
> *Her enemy. The bane of her existence.*
>
> *"What's he doing here?" she demanded.*
>
> *"Drinking tea, obviously," he returned. His eyes danced with mischief, and his dark-brown skin glowed in the golden light spilling through the open window. The air smelled of the nearby sea and the chamomile steeping. The delicate teacup appeared tiny in his large hands.*
>
> *"Would you like some, sweetheart?" her grandmother asked. The sweet, gentle, naive woman seemed thoroughly oblivious to the trouble she'd let into their home.*
>
> *"No!" she exclaimed, then felt compelled to add a polite, "Thank you, Gran. But are you aware of who this is? Who his family is?"*
>
> *Gran lifted a shoulder dismissively. "You know I've never*

*subscribed to petty rivalries."*

*"Gran, nothing about this is petty." She thrust an
accusatory finger toward the man on the couch. "He's
threatening our business. Our livelihood."*

*"Please excuse my granddaughter's impoliteness," Gran
told Heathcliff. "She can be very dramatic. Her father and I
agree that she must get it from her mother's side of the family."*

*Heathcliff smirked. "Yes, I'm well aware of how . . .
spirited she can be."*

*Julie burned with embarrassment. "Why are you here?"
she asked him. "Really? Is it just to have tea with Gran?"*

*He set the teacup on the coffee table. "I'm here to talk to
you."*

*Julie froze. "Me?" That was an even stranger reason than
tea with her grandmother.*

"What the hell?"

Chris and Hazel turned to me. My cousin must've realized
what I'd read, because she widened her eyes in a silent plea.

"Sorry," I said. "Sometimes, I get so excited about my writing,
I just can't hold it in." I let out a forced laugh, pointedly holding Hazel's gaze. "Sometimes, it's like *wow*. I can't even believe I
would write something like this."

"What did you write?" Chris asked, shifting closer.

"It's nothing," I said, then paused. Wait---why was I hiding it?
"A romance novel."

Hazel seemed to choke on nothing.

Chris laughed, and I resisted the urge to smack him with the binder. "You're writing a romance novel? For real? I never saw you as the romantic type."

"Most don't," I said. "But I have layers. Besides, I love how fictional guys always know the right thing to say, no matter the situation. So different from real guys."

"*Oh.*" He still sounded amused. "I think I know what this is about."

I highly doubted it.

"This is about Brandon."

"No."

"Sure. What did he do now?"

"He wouldn't take her binder," Hazel supplied, probably happy for the change of topic.

Chris frowned. "Is that a euphemism?"

"What? No. Don't be gross." I lifted the binder so he could see. "This is what she's talking about. It's something I put together for Brandon. I thought it might be useful for his new job with us. But he didn't want it, so whatever."

Chris stared at the binder for a moment, before reaching for it. "Can I have that?"

"Uh, okay." It wasn't like I had any use for it now.

"Thanks." He took it, pressed a kiss to Hazel's cheek, and stood. "I've got to go. But meet me at the gate after school?" he asked her.

"Yeah . . ." She watched him retreat up the steps. The second he was out of earshot, she snatched the notebook from me and smacked my shoulder. "What the hell, Tess?"

"Not *me* what the hell. *You* what the hell? I didn't realize you were writing nonfiction now."

"Oh." Hazel grimaced and lowered the book. "Do you want me to take out the scene?"

I considered it for a moment, then decided, "No, do whatever you want. But you're definitely using a pseudonym."

# NINE

The next day, I decided to take Hazel's advice. Brandon's number wasn't hard to find thanks to the group chat Sherlyn made for the literature project. Even though I'd been booted out within seconds of leaving the community center, I could still access all the messages that came before.

With the latest DJ Bacchanal album set to repeat, I laid back on my bed. Focused on the hypnotic rhythm of the music, I breathed through my reluctance and opened a new chat.

Hi! This is Tess

There. Short and sweet. Good start.

Or was it too curt? Too peppy? Did the exclamation mark make it look like I was trying too hard?

I quickly added a bit more.

I just want to make sure you have my number in case you had any questions

About the band obviously

Dots popped up to indicate typing on his end. His reply appeared a few seconds later.

Sorry I don't accept messages from strange people

I frowned. Did he not see the part where I said it was me?

This is Tess

He replied:

Yes, I know

Unbelievable.

My thumbs flew across the keyboard, typing out a few choice words of my own. Couldn't he see I was making an effort here?

The memory of Hazel's advice hit like a bucket of ice water. I smashed the delete button and watched my anger vanish, letter by letter.

There were three facts I needed to consider:

1. Brandon could be the solution to the band's bad sales problem.
2. I still didn't totally believe that Brandon wouldn't mess this up because of ego or some misunderstanding of how the band worked.
3. If I wanted him to keep me in the loop, I'd have to soften my approach. In other words, I'd have to be nicer.

So much easier said than done.

I wrote out a new message.

I see what you did there lol

Pressing the send button caused me physical pain.

The dots appeared and then vanished. Appeared. Then vanished. Appeared, then . . .

Ok. Who IS this?

Ugh. I dropped my phone onto the bed, recoiling in a full-body cringe. That *lol* had made me feel dirty.

My phone chimed with another message. Before I could read it, someone knocked on my door. "Come in!" I called out.

Aunty Gloria entered, a cardboard box cradled in her hands. "Do you have a second?"

I pushed the phone aside. "Yeah?"

She set the box on the floor. "When I was going through Hazel's closet for donations, I found a few things that she said were yours. They must've gotten mixed in there somehow."

I sat up, eyeing the box. So far, I'd avoided getting swept up in the great cleaning project. Last week, things had gotten tense when Aunty Gloria went after Hazel's library. In the end, Hazel had given away two boxes full of novels. Aunty Gloria had wanted more and Hazel tried for less. Neither party was satisfied with the outcome.

I peeked at the box, reluctant to investigate further. "If I didn't notice these things were missing, I don't need them. You can give them away."

"I'd still prefer if you had a look first. Then sort everything into what can be donated or thrown out."

"Okay," I said, sighing. It seemed like a total waste of time.

When Aunty Gloria lingered, I started to wonder if she meant to watch me sort it out. "Actually," she said finally. "There's something else I want to talk to you about as well." She wiped her palms on the side of her house dress.

Her tone held a cautious note, which caused my chest to constrict. Perhaps it was an overreaction, but after the memorable experience of an adult needing to *talk to me about something*, only to have them break the news about my parents' accident, there was no controlling it.

My shoulders tensed, bracing for the worst.

"Do you remember the Nelsons?" she asked. "The ones currently renting your house?"

*My house.* It felt strange to think of it that way. But technically it was.

"Yes, I remember them."

Instead of selling the house where I'd grown up, we'd rented out the first floor to the young couple. The upper rooms, which still contained some of my parent's belongings, had been sealed off. Money hadn't been the motivator for renting, though all funds were set aside for my attendance at the University of the West Indies next year. Instead, my uncle and aunt thought it would be better to not leave the place empty. It seemed like a good solution until I was old enough to decide what to do with it.

"They made an offer to buy it," she said.

I guess now I was old enough to decide. A heavy feeling settled on my chest.

"They made a very good offer," she said. "And since they've been living there for so many years now, I thought we should at least consider it."

Despite my best efforts, Aunty Gloria must've seen the reluctance on my face. "If you don't want to, that's fine," she hurried to assure me. "The Nelsons will move out, though, if we refuse—which, again, is fine. But I thought you should know what's going on."

"Can I think about it?"

"Of course, sweetheart. But the Nelsons would need to know before the end of January. And we would have to clear out the upstairs before that."

With a smile, she left me, and I remained anchored to the bed, unmoving. My mind flashed over the memory of our house in San Fernando, with the fishtail palm trees and the backrooms overlooking the Atlantic Ocean.

I didn't want to think about it.

Instead, I focused on the box that sat in the middle of the room. I considered throwing it out right away, without opening it at all.

Sighing, I slipped off the bed and knelt on the cool carpet. I pried the flaps open.

Aunty Gloria had been right. It was mostly my belongings. Not sure how they got mixed in with Hazel's things, though my cousin did have a tendency to borrow and forget to return. At first glance, the box seemed stuffed with only clothes and accessories and a couple of battered Stephen King novels nestled at the bottom. I'd recommended the books to Hazel for her dip into the horror genre. After she finished *Pet Sematary*, she wouldn't speak to me for a whole day.

Within a few minutes, I'd almost cleared the box. Everything, as expected, fell into the piles for donation or trash. Then, I spotted a familiar yellow-and-red peplum top—the same one that captured Brandon and David's attention on my first day at school. I thought I'd gotten rid of it.

How different would my life have been if I'd never worn it? Would David and Brandon not have insulted me, or would they have found some other reason to do so anyway? But I do know David wouldn't have apologized. And maybe he wouldn't have spent the next few years trying to win me over.

Even at the time, I'd wondered if it had all been a challenge to David—to see if he could charm the girl who'd hated him.

But he'd been persistent and sweet, and I'd become infatuated—utterly taken in, not only by his perfect smile or hazel eyes, but because of the way he seemed just as infatuated with me. His kisses felt like little miracles, every second together a small pearl to be treasured.

Around his friends, he could be annoying. Sometimes a little mean as he gave into unnecessary posturing and competition. But around me, he was different. When it was just us, we could be ourselves.

We talked a lot. He'd told me about his dream of becoming a pilot, like both his parents. That he'd taken a small stone from every country he visited, hoping to collect a little piece of the whole world. That he loved but didn't particularly like his father. That he suspected his father felt the same about him.

I'd told him that for weeks after my parents' accident, I couldn't get into a car without throwing up. That even now, I still felt uneasy when riding in one. That even though I loved Hazel, I resented the way everything came so easy to her. That my biggest fear was my uncle and aunt regretted taking me in.

Maybe it would've been okay if I'd stopped there. If I'd only handed him my secrets to hold. But my family was such a big part of my life, of who I was, it seemed natural to share theirs with him as well.

So I told him about the *Twilight* fanfiction Hazel posted anonymously online. That Aunty Gloria had a fear of elevators after getting trapped in one as a child.

That my father, when he was nineteen, made the biggest mistake of his life. Drunk and angry, he'd jumped into a bar fight, picked up a bottle, and slammed it over another man's head. The glass had shattered, blinding the man in one eye. My father served two years in prison and spent the rest of his life trying to make amends. All his charity work, the donations, the community development projects—he worked himself to the bone, not to erase what he'd done, but so it wouldn't be all that people remembered of him.

I told David all of this.

And then David told his friends.

Soon talk of my father's conviction started kicking around the school. It passed from one mouth to another, twisting in the relay so my father became a murderer, and my parents' crash maybe wasn't an accident after all.

The second I found out, I confronted him.

It was a bad idea. I should've waited until we were alone. But better sense folded in the face of fury. I could not contain it.

100

He'd been in the music room with his friends, before fourth period. Hazel and Brandon were there too, along with a good chunk of our entire class. I hadn't meant to make a scene, but when I'd tried to pull him aside, vibrating with hurt and urgency, he shrugged me off and something inside me snapped.

"What is wrong with you?" I demanded. "How could you . . . ?" I couldn't say it, emotion clogging my throat.

His brows raised. "How could I . . . what?"

For a second, I lost my nerve. Maybe I'd been mistaken. Maybe he hadn't been the one who told everybody. My father's record wasn't exactly a secret. In fact, Daddy had talked about the experience openly and frequently, in an attempt to deter people from landing themselves in a similar situation.

But no. The timing couldn't be a coincidence.

"Tell people . . ." I said, dropping my voice. "You know what."

"Oh. You mean how your father went to jail for almost killing a man?"

Stunned, I couldn't speak. He'd said it. Just like that. Like it was nothing.

"What's your problem?" he asked. "It's not like no one knows."

Our classmates hadn't. And he knew what they were like. How hard it had been for me to fit in, and he'd told them anyway.

"No need to overreact." He glanced over his shoulder, sharing a smile with his friends. "At least now we know where her short temper comes from."

The rushing in my ears intensified, the classroom closing in. I'd been stunned—blindsided by his casual cruelty. It came out of nowhere, so different from the boy I thought I knew. As I grew conscious of the attention of my classmates, my skin burned with embarrassment.

Looking back, I wished I'd spoken up. Told him off. Said something. Anything. But even more intense than the anger coursing through my body, more potent than the embarrassment, was the feeling of heartbreak and the subsequent need to get away from him.

I did not run or cry. I just walked out, a strange numbness spreading from my chest to the tips of my fingers and my toes. The school nurse offered me refuge. Menstrual cramps, I'd told her. I didn't think she believed me.

My first heartbreak hadn't felt like breaking. More like shrinking. Like I was becoming smaller, collapsing inward.

I didn't know who called Uncle Russell to pick me up early. Probably Hazel. I think she'd tried to talk to me at some point, but it was all a blur. He took me to the mas camp. There, I could pretend like this was any other visit. Like this was any other day. And I sat among the seamstresses and decorators and lost myself in the creative haze of a beloved routine.

Slowly, feeling started seeping back in—a warmth laced with a reassuring certainty that this was something I loved. Something I was good at. Doing this for the rest of my life could be all I needed. And that would be enough.

For the rest of the school year, I barely talked to anyone. Like a broken reflection of who I once was, I'd been reassembled with all my jagged edges facing outward.

David tried to talk to me a few times, but I refused to listen.

In a beautiful coincidence, while this was going on, David's parents accepted a new job in Martinique. They moved before the start of the following year. His absence made it easier to pretend that none of it ever happened.

Now, I dumped the yellow top into the trash pile and stared at the empty box. As I'd suspected—nothing here worth saving.

My phone chimed again. I picked it up without thinking.

Seriously who is this?

What did you do with Boop?

I rolled my eyes and replied:

Forget it

Then I muted the chat.

# TEN

I'd completely forgotten about Career Day. Not that it was a standout event on the school calendar. It was mostly parents giving presentations about their jobs, their kids running behind them to make sure they weren't too embarrassing. At least we got a break from our regularly scheduled classes.

The only big difference this year was that, for once, one of Hazel's parents was available.

"If we don't look at her, maybe we can pretend it's not happening," Hazel told me.

We stood in front of the board with the posted list of speakers, their scheduled times, and their assigned rooms. Behind us, a swarm had converged on Aunty Gloria, mostly students and a handful of other parents.

"This is the worst," she said, then violated her own advice, glancing back. "Oh God. Now there's more of them."

"Hey, look." I tried to distract her. "They've got a newspaper journalist. It's not the same type of writing you're interested in, but it's close."

"Sure, if it's all they've got. Hey—" she pointed at one of the items. "Let's go to the marine biologist's talk. I heard she bought actual specimens."

"What? Like fish? Ew."

"Okay. If that's your reaction, then I guess not." Her finger slid down the list. "Not much else going on."

As was expected. The options for Career Day talks were usually limited.

Her finger stopped. "What the . . ."

"What?" I asked, leaning closer to read it.

She flattened her hand, covering the words. "Nothing."

"Ay, do you mind?" said one of the lower-form girls, who stood next to us. She shot us a bad-eye. "We're reading too."

"Sorry." Hazel lifted her hand so we could all see it.

*The Business of Carnival by Ian Kingston, 10 a.m., Main Auditorium.*

"Interesting," I said.

Hazel tugged me away from the board, the other students filling in the gap. "Promise me you won't go to that talk."

"Who? Me? Why would I want to go to that?"

"Because I know you," she said. "You'll go and you'll make a scene. Need I remind you how much trouble we got into because of the last one?"

"Yes, I remember," I said, still bitter. With a week of our punishment left, my aunt and uncle seemed no more inclined to lift our sentence than they'd been at the start, even though Hazel and I had been on our best behavior.

"Why don't you check out the architect's talk?" she suggested. "That's a type of design, right? It could be interesting."

It was also, I noticed, the same time as Mr. Kingston's presentation.

"Sounds like fun," I said.

While Hazel was off playing with tuna or whatever, I fought the urge to doze through the architect's presentation. It didn't help that she spoke with a soft, droning voice that made the already-dry content even drier. Next to me, Sherlyn took copious notes, hanging on every word. Good for her, I supposed.

I unzipped my backpack, found my phone, and subtly checked the time. We had about half the presentation left. Very quietly, I slipped out of the room.

Mr. Kingston's presentation had been assigned to the main auditorium, the biggest room in the school. It made sense. As the organizers must've expected, he'd drawn a large crowd. Because all the seats were taken, some of the attendees had to stand at the back. I joined them.

The man himself occupied center stage. Mr. Ian Kingston. The bandleader of Royalty. The man who had tried—and failed—several times to bring down my uncle's career.

"Do you know how many tourists come for Carnival every year on average?" he asked, surveying the room. He crossed the stage, commanding the space and our attention. "Go on. I want you to guess. Closest number wins."

With movie-star white teeth and a head of full jet-black hair, he looked ten years younger than he was. He wore a suit as sharp as his smile, strutting across the stage, engaging the audience. Every word that fell from his lips was infused with a laid-back charisma.

When a fourth-form student guessed thirty-five thousand, she got tossed a Royalty-branded T-shirt and pen for the answer. When she didn't catch it, he laughed, and I noticed the resemblance to his son.

Someone shifted into the space next to me, their arm brushing against mine. I glanced over, put off by the proximity.

"Surprised to see you here," Prince said.

Uh-oh.

I side-stepped away from him. No matter what he said, I could not engage.

"Did you come to try and learn something?" he asked. "That's good."

*Don't engage. Do not engage.*

"Because last I heard, Grandeur's sales were tanking. Surprised you're not taking notes. Pen?" He offered, holding one out to me. It was blue and Royalty-branded.

"Yes," I said, taking it from him. Never turned down a free pen before, and I wasn't about to start now. "So far, I've learned that the Royalty stationery comes in both blue and red. It's been very educational."

Damn it. So much for not engaging.

He laughed without a trace of humor. "Might've helped your sales if you'd gone ahead with your launch party. Sorry to hear about what happened to your venue. Such a shame."

Anger, hot and ugly, burned through my body. How dare he?

I faced him, ready to let him have it, when the impossibility of what he'd said registered.

Wait a minute.

"How did you know our sales are tanking?" I demanded.

"Heard a rumor somewhere." Prince smiled. "Thanks for confirming it."

On stage, Mr. Kingston threw his head back, laughing way too hard at a comment from one of the first formers. He tossed a T-shirt at the student. The tagline printed under the logo read: *We're not just the best. We're Royalty.*

I snorted. "The best? Yeah, okay."

"You have something you want to say?" Prince asked with a flat stare, daring me to go on.

"I'm just curious," I said. "The best meaning the biggest? Because that's not true. You're not the most popular. Not even top five. We all know it's not a question of costume quality and design, and you've never won a single award. So, what is Royalty *the best* at exactly? Because I'm drawing a blank."

Someone behind us laughed.

Oh no. Not again. How did I keep getting myself into these situations? Time to strategically relocate.

"Thanks for the pen," I said, then bolted.

Thankfully, he didn't seem inclined to follow me out of the auditorium. Just to be safe though, I didn't slow down. While checking over my shoulder, I collided with someone.

"Tess?" Chris reached out to steady me, holding my arm. "You good?"

"Sorry." I backed up.

"No worries." He laughed. "In a rush?"

"Yes, I had another run-in with your stepbrother. You know, I'm starting to think that repeatedly antagonizing him isn't my best move."

His smile faltered. "Yeah, I learned that the hard way." He rubbed the back of his neck. "Just so you know, I didn't invite them today. Mom heard about it at the parent-teacher meeting. She signed them up."

"Good to know," I said. "Otherwise, I definitely would've held it against you. No offense."

"None taken."

After a few steps, it became clear that we were heading in the same direction. We walked on together.

"Brandon told me what happened to your launch party." He let out a sigh, his body seeming to deflate. "I wouldn't be surprised if Prince did do it. Ever since he came back from school, living at home has been hell."

"I'm sorry." Any lingering suspicions I'd had about him harboring a secret loyalty to his family's company evaporated. I could see the truth in his face, hear it in his words.

"No worries." He waved a hand to dispel the sad topic. "What keeps me going is knowing that I'll be in New York next year, far away from him."

"With Hazel," I prompted.

A smile softened his face. "With Hazel."

I elbowed his arm. "I'd say I'm happy for you two if you weren't, you know, stealing my cousin from me. No offense."

"You say no offense a lot. I'm starting to wonder if I should be offended."

"I don't see how that would be productive. But you do you."

He laughed and stopped to sit on the bench that faced the main gate of the school. Only a handful of students milled about, the quad mostly empty. "I didn't steal your cousin, though."

I took a seat beside him. "Just her heart?"

He ducked his head, bashful. "I honestly don't know what she sees in me. She's so smart. And not just in the bookish way. Like she'll say these things—these things that I've never thought of before. It's like she's a wise old woman. Except, you know, she's only eighteen."

"That's . . . good." I shifted to face him. "Can I ask you a question? I'm curious. You and Hazel have known each other forever. Why get together now? Did something change?"

"I know, it's strange, right?" His forehead wrinkled. "I can't give you the exact moment. We started spending a lot of time together, studying for the SATs. And after a while, after getting to know her, it felt like I was actually seeing her for the first time. Do you know what I mean?"

"Sure," I said. At least, in theory. I still didn't get how feelings for a person you'd known forever could shift so drastically in a short time. Even with David, some part of me always knew who he was, even if I'd tried to overlook it.

# ELEVEN

"And have you learned your lesson?" Aunty Gloria asked Hazel and me, on our first morning of freedom. It amazed me how one month could feel like an eternity. But the time had finally come.

"Yes," I said. "Next time I bad talk a competitor, I'll make sure there aren't any reporters within hearing distance."

Hazel, who stood at my side, solemnly nodded in agreement.

For some reason, Aunty Gloria did not find this as funny as we did.

After school, Hazel dropped me off at the mas camp, but she didn't stick around. She and Chris were going to spend the afternoon organizing their university and US visa applications. As thrilling as that had sounded, I found myself turning down their invitation to join.

As I watched Hazel's car drive off, the truth hit me: I'd effectively lost my partner-in-crime. It would've happened anyway, when she moved to New York. But I hadn't been prepared for the hollow feeling that opened in my chest.

I turned away from the road and headed inside.

The mas camp stood on the outskirts of the busy capital city. On the outside, it appeared no different from any of the bland boxy office buildings beside it. That was, until you went inside. There, the difference was stark—the bright color almost startling.

The walls were all sunny yellows, turquoise blues, and hibiscus reds, many plastered with posters and framed photos of masqueraders in glittering costumes. The decor had been designed to straddle the line between stylish and comfortable, the chairs plush and available for the visiting customers who came in for fittings or to browse the showroom.

I exited the elevator and bid good evening to the part-time receptionist. She waved back, busy on the phone, the receiver for the landline tucked under her ear. I breathed deeply, inhaling the familiar jasmine-scented air freshener.

A short hall led to two doors. The first to the offices; the second to the heart of the building, where the magic happened.

I chose the magic. Excitement bubbled in my chest.

The first thing anyone notices when entering the mas camp's workshop is the size. It was huge. Several tables and chairs were laid out in individual workstations, equipment and materials littering every surface. Mountains of unused supplies were packed into boxes and clear plastic containers and stored on shelves or stacked in every available corner.

Eighteen mannequins stood out front, each sporting one of the different costumes being made in this very room. Overhead thin ropes had been hung from one wall to another, completed head-pieces clipped onto them. They were stored that way to save space as well as ensure each one maintained its voluminous shape.

Rhythmic beats of calypso music blunted the gentle chatter of the dozen or so decorators present. I entered slowly, eyes lifted to the number of finished headpieces, marveling at how much had been done, and a bit sour that I'd missed it.

And then I ran into Brandon.

I recoiled, horrified that he'd dared to invade my favorite place. Then I remembered—oh, right. He was supposed to be here.

Brandon raised a brow, apparently noticing my confusion. He still wore his uniform, his tie askew, the top button of his shirt open. "All good?"

*Well, it had been a few seconds earlier . . .*

. . . is what I would have said, if I weren't trying to be nicer.

"Great, thank you for asking." I plastered on a fake smile. My cheeks hurt.

Brandon backed away, like I'd sprouted an extra head in front of him.

"You're back." Morris's deep voice rumbled from the corner. "About time."

"Agreed," I said. Delighted to see him, I pushed thoughts of Brandon aside.

Morris, our grizzle-haired production manager, oversaw the making of the costumes. He and my uncle had met many years earlier—two young Trinidadians working in the West End in London. Even though Morris and his husband still primarily lived in England, they split their time between there and here.

"Welcome back," Morris said, never looking up. While he spoke, he did not stop working, his hands and attention occupied with threading a sewing machine. "When your uncle said that you'd gotten yourself banned, I couldn't believe it. Not Tess. Could never be. Then I saw the article."

"What?" I asked. "It wasn't that bad. Everything I said was true."

"Unrepentant to the end."

"If you'd seen the costumes, you'd agree."

"I have and I do. I just have the good sense not to broadcast it." He tipped his head toward the people working on the other side of the room. "See if you can help me with the newbies. They're design students from the institute. I swear, if I have to remind one more person not to touch the glue from the hot glue gun, I will scream."

I couldn't imagine Morris ever screaming. Even though his personality was just as prickly as my uncle's—which was saying something—he remained a rock in all situations. Steady and imposing. Quiet but never silent.

"What they need is a chance to grow thicker skin." I held up my fingers and wiggled them. "I touch the hot glue all the time and don't feel a thing. Lost sensitivity in them years ago."

"You weird child, that is not something to brag about."

I laughed, glancing away only to catch Brandon's eye for a moment. He was watching me with a small frown of confusion.

"Fair enough," I said, returning my attention to Morris. "I'll help the newbies out. But I've got to work on my school assignment for a bit first. I need to borrow some of the equipment."

"That's fine. You do what you need to do. Let me know if you need any help."

I smiled at him in parting, found a free workstation, unzipped my backpack, and pulled out the material I needed. I'd only just started when a shadow fell across my table. Assuming it was Morris being curious about my project, I lifted my head, excited to show off a bit.

It was just Brandon.

"Oh." My smile started to fall, but I caught it at the last second. In a voice a little too high-pitched, I asked, "Can I help you?"

"What are you doing?" he asked.

My eyes dropped to the contents on the table. "I'm working on—"

"No. Not that. I mean, why are you acting all polite and agreeable. It's weird."

"I'm not—"

"Don't try that. I know you're faking. Every time you smile at me you look like you're in pain."

Busted.

I sagged against the table, defeated. "Okay, fine. I really want to help with the band's promotions. Hazel thought if I was nicer to you, you'd be more likely to consider it."

"Ah," he said. "I see. That must've been very hard for you."

"It really was."

And I knew it wouldn't work. Why did I even bother?

"All because you want to help me?" he asked.

"To help the band. Obviously."

Brandon tilted his head, considering. I shifted in my seat, unnerved by his focused attention. My gaze slipped down to his open button and the glimpse of his collarbone. Did he do this on purpose? Was he aware of how good he looked, ever so slightly undone?

He sat on the open chair beside me, jostling the table.

"I did have a look at your binder," he said.

"How?" I asked, then realized, "Chris gave it to you?"

"Yes, along with some advice that I pull my head out of my ass."

Not for the first time, I noticed he gestured a lot when he talked. It was a little distracting.

"Most of it was boring," he said. "As expected. But some of it could be useful. I shouldn't have dismissed your help like that. I'm sorry."

Amazing.

I laughed. "Are you seriously apologizing to me?"

"Yes, that's what *I'm sorry* usually—" He bit off the rest of his words and closed his eyes. "I'm not trying to start a fight with you right now."

"But we do it so well."

"Yes, I'm aware."

I stared at him for a moment, then admitted, "I'm sorry too. For getting you fired from your job with Royalty."

He sat back in the seat, his long legs outstretched. "Don't

flatter yourself too much, Boop. I'm the one who decided to play Sherlock Holmes."

"I know, but Chris told me they also blamed you for sneaking me into the launch party. If that influenced their decision at all, I am sorry."

"Okay . . . Apology accepted." A smile tugged at his lips. "Now, tell me, how much did that hurt you to say?"

"So much," I said. But it hadn't really. It felt more like a relief than anything else.

He let out a soft laugh, his fingers tapping out a staccato beat on the table. He tipped his chin toward the pieces of my project. "What's that? It doesn't look like any of the costumes I've seen so far."

"That's because this is mine. It's my version of Juliet's costume from the Baz Luhrmann movie. As you may remember, you got me kicked out of the group project, so I have to do my own."

Brandon winced. "You know I didn't know Sister was there, right? I'm not saying I didn't enjoy watching you get kicked out at the time, but I didn't set you up on purpose."

I wasn't sure that I believed him, but I let it slide for now. "It's fine. Focusing on the costumes in the adaptation was a better fit for me anyway."

Brandon lifted a brow. "If only someone had suggested something like that."

"Don't be smug. You had no idea what you were talking about. But some of the wardrobe choices in that movie are actually fascinating."

"Okay . . ." He sounded unimpressed.

"Seriously. Like the designer dressed Juliet as an angel to represent her innocence and naivety, but also because it's a direct reference to Romeo's line—*O speak again, bright angel*. By doing that, when you watch the film, the line now has a double meaning. Not just a metaphor or endearment, but she is literally dressed as an angel. Just that simple choice gives a whole new layer to text that was written over four hundred years ago." I threw up my hands. "How is that not amazing?"

"Wow." His tone was dry, but his smile betrayed amusement. "You really got into it."

"Because costumes are fascinating," I said, on a roll now. "Just look at where we are." I waved my hand around, referring to the mas camp and everything in it. "Think about Carnival. It's a festival born out of rebellion, resilience, and resourcefulness. Think of all the creativity that has gone into it—the characters, the traditions. The costumes reflect our history and where we are now—"

I stopped and snapped my mouth shut, embarrassed about my rambling. "Sorry." I dropped my eyes. "I never get to talk about this stuff. It must have been building up."

Brandon said nothing for a moment. He'd stopped tapping on the table, the tips of his long, elegant fingers resting against the surface. When he finally did speak, his tone was surprisingly soft. "You really love this, don't you?"

"That's what I've been trying to tell you. Grandeur means everything to me. That's why I want to help."

"Well . . ." he said, squinting at me. "Would you be okay with talking about this on camera?"

"Excuse me?"

"For the band?"

Me? In front of a camera? "No."

"You did say you wanted to help."

"Yeah, like coming up with ideas and pointing out when you're wrong. You're the influencer. Some of us don't feel comfortable plastering our face all over the internet, or require a certain number of likes for self-validation."

"It's not . . ." He huffed out a breath of frustration. "Look, Grandeur needs a face online. Someone for people to connect with. Mr. Russell, unsurprisingly, turned me down. But you're the young protégé. The next generation. We can work with that."

"Aren't you the online face? Isn't that what we hired you for?"

Even as I said the words, realization sank in. So far, Brandon had posted behind-the-scenes photos, pictures of the costumes, and clips from recent festivals. But he hadn't posted himself.

He grimaced. "I can't. I'm not allowed to."

"What are you talking about?"

"According to the terms of the contract I signed with Royalty, I'm not allowed to publicly endorse another Carnival mas band for at least twelve months."

"But the Kingstons ended the contract. Screw their terms."

"Believe me, I'd love to. But I can't. Even if they were being shady about it, they were within their right to terminate our collaboration. But if I violate it, they've got the money and power to come after me. I can't afford that."

I gaped at him. "And . . . you didn't think this was something you should have mentioned before my uncle hired you?"

"I know it sounds concerning, but even if I could post about Grandeur, I wouldn't. I was just posting about another band not even a month ago. In addition to confusing the hell out of my followers, they'd think I was being disingenuous."

"Brandon," I said. "That doesn't just sound concerning. It's a concern."

He waved his hand in a dismissive gesture. "It's okay. I can still consult. And I've got a plan."

"Which involves putting me online?" I asked, my worries mounting. "Because if that's the best you've got, we're in serious trouble."

"Relax, Boop. Obviously, you don't have to if you don't want to. It was just an idea."

"Please, *please* tell me you have a better one."

"I do." He smiled, all confidence. "Since I can't be the face, I just have to find someone else who can."

"And who would that be?" I asked, still doubtful. "Didn't you already enlist every local influencer to work for Royalty?" If he'd had a contract with Royalty that barred him from endorsing another band, wouldn't all his friends have signed similar ones as well?

"Don't worry about it. I already have somebody in mind." He stood and started to leave. But then he turned back. "Okay, wait," he said, as if he wasn't the one walking away. "I know you don't want to be on camera, but would you be okay with talking to someone in person?"

"The way I'm talking to you now?" I asked.

He huffed out a laugh. "No, I think you could help me convince Jenni Baptiste to collaborate with us. Nothing I've tried has worked on her so far."

"Jenni Baptiste? The lifestyle influencer?"

"You've heard of her?"

"Yeah. A couple of her posts came up on my timeline."

Jenni fell into that category of online personality who promoted personal growth through healthy living, a multitude of self-help books, and inspiring—though often misattributed—celebrity quotes. Not really my thing, but one hundred thousand followers wasn't something to dismiss easily.

"Your timeline?" Brandon's eyes widened. "So you *do* have an Instagram. Interesting. How have I not found it?"

Whoops. "Why Jenni Baptiste?" I asked, hoping he'd let go of my little slip.

"Because she's the only big influencer left who's not currently on Kingston's payroll. She didn't want to work with Prince. In her words, he gave her bad vibes."

Understandable. "You think you can convince her to work with us?"

"No, I think you can," Brandon said, then frowned. "Your account can't be set to private because I'd still see it. Does that mean I've been blocked? Boop, have you blocked me?"

"Brandon, focus." I snapped my fingers. "How am I supposed to convince her?"

"Say what you just said to me. I think half her problem with Prince was that he came off as insincere. Anyone who listens to you talk about costumes will know you're . . . not."

"Thanks?"

"Trust me. It'll be great. Just remember to put out good vibes while we're there."

"There where?"

"At her house, of course. Where else would you meet her?" He started walking away, like that was the end of our conversation. Like I'd agreed.

"I never said I'd talk to her!"

The chatter around us halted. All the decorators turned to look. Even Morris lifted his head to see what was going on.

"I'll pick you up Saturday," Brandon called back. "At seven!"

# TWELVE

"I can't believe you're actually going to Jenni Baptiste's house," Hazel said. She sat at my desk, writing. All my sewing equipment had been pushed aside for her laptop.

"Me neither." I really didn't want to go. But I'd do anything to help Grandeur, and Brandon knew it.

On the bright side, going out did give me the chance to dress up. Between the ugly vestiges of colonialism that were our school uniforms and my nonexistent social life, opportunities to turn up were rare.

Even though a part of me wanted to crawl back into bed and spend the rest of the evening watching *Scream* for the millionth time, I got dressed, more than a little excited to test out my new Anastasia eyeshadow palette.

When I finished, I stepped back to get a full look at myself in the long mirror. The vivid gold and russet-brown pigments of my makeup matched the drama of my black-on-black outfit. The cut of the top reminded me of Katniss's style in the chariot scene in *Catching Fire*. It would be a lie to say I wasn't trying to channel some of that kick-ass energy tonight.

"What do you think?" I asked Hazel.

She didn't answer, furiously typing. Caught in some wave of inspiration, she wasn't listening to me.

I crossed the room, about to tap her shoulder, when I glanced at the screen. The words *Heathcliff* and *Julie* popped out from the text. Curious, I leaned forward to see what they were up to now. If Hazel had taken inspiration from another one of my conversations, I'd have to demand royalties if it ever got published.

> "I don't know what you want me to say." *Heathcliff's eyes glimmered in the low light; the dark-brown orbs fixed on her, as fathomless and hostile as the stormy sea.* "I told you this would happen."
>
> *Julie's fists curled at her sides.* "I might've listened if you'd explained the entire situation."
>
> *The nerve of this man. At a moment like this, he dared to utter an I told you so. Then again, she shouldn't be surprised. It appeared no amount of money in the world could polish his rough edges. He was as tactless and rude as ever.*
>
> "Would it have made a difference?" *he asked.* "When have you ever listened to a single thing I've said? Every piece of advice I've ever given, every offer of help I've ever extended, you've immediately disregarded or else criticized to death."
>
> "I wouldn't criticize you so much if you didn't say so much

*that's worthy of criticism." Julie lifted her chin, meeting his gaze.*

*When did he get so close?*

*Was he moving closer?*

*Was she?*

*"Or perhaps you shouldn't always expect the worst of me," he said, definitely moving closer.*

*She could see the delicate fan of his eyelashes. The flecks of gold in his eyes. Her chest rose and fell with rapid breaths, her heart thundering with unchecked abandon.*

*They seemed to be sharing the same air. The same tension. The same thought.*

*Julie could not say who moved first. Only that, when they finally collided in a hungry, devouring kiss, it felt long overdue.*

"Hazel!"

My cousin nearly fell out of the chair, startled. "What are you doing?"

I pointed at the screen. "Julie and Heathcliff are kissing?"

"Yes?" She sounded confused. "It's a romance book, Tess. What did you think would happen?"

"Julie and Heathcliff are the couple? I thought Heathcliff was the villain or something. Not a love interest!"

After reading her earlier interpretation of our fight, I'd drawn parallels between Brandon and me, casting us in the respective roles of Heathcliff and Julie. Naturally, I'd assumed they were enemies. Instead, they were kissing on-page, and in my head, and the whole thing weirded me out.

"In the last scene, they were arguing," I said.

"That wasn't arguing." Hazel wrinkled her nose. "Did it come off as arguing? It was supposed to be romantic banter."

Romantic *what*?

"But—that's—how—why would you?—Brandon and I would never—" I couldn't get the words out. The thread of thought that ran from my brain to my mouth hit a snag.

"You know it's just fiction, right?" Hazel asked. "This isn't actually you and Brandon I'm writing about?"

"Of course I know that." Except, when they'd kissed, in my head, I'd been picturing them as us.

The image would haunt me until the day I died.

Hazel's confusion melted into a sly smile. "You seem . . . weirdly affected by this. I don't think I've ever seen you lose your cool like this before."

"It's the idea of me and Brandon. It's . . ." I released a full-body shiver. There were no words to encapsulate the full scale of horror that would entail.

Hazel sat back. Her gaze turned narrow and searching. "The lady doth protest too much, methinks."

I gaped, thoroughly offended. "That is so . . . *wrong*."

She, of all people, knew how I felt about Brandon. I'd told her about the incident on the first day of school, and the many offenses, arguments, and competitions that came after. She'd even witnessed tons of it herself. And yet, knowing all that, Hazel's eyes continued to sparkle with unrestrained mischief.

"Or have I accidentally tapped into something right?" she asked. "You didn't interpret your arguments as romantic banter, but for some reason my writing muses did. Why is that?"

"Okay. Cool it, Shakespeare." Forget the royalties. I wanted no part of this book. "All I wanted was to show off my new eyeshadow. Not to have the foundations of my character thoroughly tainted with your unseemly assertion—"

"Do you notice your vocabulary gets more convoluted when you're flustered?"

"That's preposterous," I said, fleeing the room.

To my irritation, she followed me downstairs.

"Evening, girls," Aunty Gloria called out as we entered the living room. She sat on the floor, using fishing line to restring the old bamboo chime that usually hung outside. "You look nice for your meeting, Tess."

"Thank you." I flopped onto the couch.

"She does, doesn't she?" Hazel sat beside me. "It's almost like she wants to look especially good for some reason." In a whisper, she added, "Or someone."

I glared at her. She smiled back.

"I'm happy to hear that you and Brandon are working together." Aunty Gloria unspooled more line, wrapping the excess around her finger. "He's such a sweetheart. I've always liked him."

"You may not be the only one," Hazel mumbled under her breath.

*Stop it,* I mouthed.

She widened her eyes. *What?*

"Oh!" Aunty Gloria lifted her head. "Tess, have you had a chance to think about the Nelsons' offer yet? They've been asking for an answer."

Right. The house.

I'd been putting it off, a swell of dread rising whenever I thought about it. "Yeah—no. I haven't yet."

Aunty Gloria's expression softened with a slight frown. "You know you don't have to accept their offer if you don't want to."

"I know." I wiped my damp palms on the side of my jeans. Logically, I knew I should sell it. Like everything else I owned, there was no reason to get overly attached. "Can I have a little more time to think about it? If that's okay?"

"Of course," Aunty Gloria said easily. She shifted so her back rested against the leg of the winged-back chair. "Don't worry about that now anyway. We've got time. Tonight, just focus on your meeting with the Instagram person."

Yeah, that didn't make me feel any better.

A tinkling chime rang through the house. The bell indicated someone at the gate. I leaped to my feet and hurried for the door. Without bothering to check who it was, I hit the button to let them in. I grabbed my sandals, then bent over to put them on. The shoes had an intricate tie around the ankle. I loved the style, but at the moment, it was taking way too long to do up.

Hazel met me at the door. "Eager, are we?"

I leaned my back against the wall for balance. "To get away from you and your ridiculousness? Yes." I was already nervous enough about tonight, the last thing I needed was for her to get into my head with this foolishness.

"And what about Brandon?" Hazel opened the front door and stalled on the threshold. "Do you think he'd find it ridiculous too?"

"I think that attempting to understand Brandon's mind would be an exercise in futility."

"There you go again with those big words."

I said nothing, refusing to feed the troll any longer.

I finally twisted the last tie in place, pushed the door wider, and sprinted right past her. Brandon had been mere feet from the front steps when I caught him. Grabbing onto his T-shirt, I tugged him backward.

"Move," I said, though he wasn't resisting.

"Hello to you too." He sounded amused. "I didn't realize you'd be so excited to see me. Hi, Hazel!"

"Hi, Brandon!" Hazel called out, all sweetness and light. No trace of the menace from seconds earlier.

I opened the driver's side and shoved him in. After I made sure all of his limbs were inside, I shut the door and got in on the passenger side. After buckling my seat belt, I folded my arms and waited to get going.

Seconds passed in silence, the car not moving. I looked over to find him watching me. "What?"

"Why are you dressed like you're revolting against a futuristic dystopian government?"

I tried not to take too much pleasure in having my inspiration recognized. "Because not only is *Catching Fire* one of the best movies ever made, it has incredible costume design, which goes thoroughly underappreciated."

Not to mention, in a way, I was going into battle, these clothes and my makeup a form of armor.

"You have a problem with it?" I asked him.

"No way." He snapped his seat belt into place and started the engine. "Last time I criticized your outfit, you started a seven-year-long vendetta against me."

At least he was learning.

"I'd like to avoid a repeat," he said and smiled, drawing my attention to his mouth and his jawline. He looked good tonight, his broad shoulders snug in a wine-red shirt. My eyes strayed to the sleeve that clung to his bicep. When I realized what I was doing, I immediately looked away.

This was all Hazel's fault. She'd gotten into my head.

When I was mad at Brandon, it was so much easier to ignore how hot he was. Ignore the way his rich, brown skin seemed to glow with a golden undertone. Or the way his long lashes framed his dark-brown eyes, giving them a smudged, sexy quality.

In the privacy of my head, I could admit all this, but even that was dangerous.

I pulled my eyes back to the road ahead, and the tiny droplets of rain that sprinkled the windshield. The radio had been turned down low, I could only just make out the melody to Beres Hammond's "Rockaway," the familiar melody easing my nerves a little.

"I'll admit," I said. "I'm surprised you knew exactly which

movie inspired this outfit."

"Only because I remember your very loud debate with Hazel over the book versus the movie. You mentioned the costuming as a point in your favor."

"You heard that?" And even more surprising, he remembered it?

"The whole class heard it." He flicked on an indicator, slowing to a stop at an intersection. "I agree with her, for the record."

"Of course you do. And as usual, you're wrong."

"I'm surprised you read the book at all, given that you only read horror," he said.

I did a double take. "How the hell do you know that?"

"Because the best way to defeat your enemies is to know them as well as your dearest friends." He sounded like he was quoting someone. "We've known each other for almost a decade. If anything, I'm disappointed you don't know me better."

"You think you know me that well?"

"I do," he said with far too much confidence.

"Okay. Prove it then."

"How?" he asked, glancing at me. "You want me to guess your favorite color?"

"Only guess? You sounded so sure a second ago."

He wouldn't get it. Even though it was the most basic of basic questions, I had no right answer. My favorite color changed from day to day, mood to mood. Did that make the question unfair? Yes. But if he knew me as well as he claimed, he should've seen this coming.

Brandon snorted. "First of all, from the way you dress, I'd be surprised if there was a color in existence that you didn't like." Then, he quickly added, "That wasn't an insult—just a fact."

"Hey, if you have to clarify it isn't an insult . . ."

"My point is," he said, "I don't think you have a favorite color, exactly. I think you have favorite color combinations. Like blue and gold, green and silver, and white and red."

My jaw dropped.

He glanced over at me. His laughter filled the closed car.

"How—?"

"I told you," he said. "We've known each other for seven years. You've gotten a little predictable."

I snapped my mouth shut. Okay, so what? He'd noticed I liked to mix certain color combinations. "That's just basic observations. It doesn't mean that you know me. Know who I am."

"Okay. I know you're a pessimist."

"I prefer to think of it as healthy skepticism."

"Or just plain old bitter cynicism. I mean, you're the type of person who'd see a pothole in front of them, and rather than swerve to avoid it, you'd fumble right through, then relish in complaining about government spending for the rest of the drive."

"Amazing," I said. If he really knew me as well as he thought he did, then he'd know I'd never drive. Period. "And you think you're the type who would swerve to avoid it?"

"Of course."

"I don't. I think you'd be the type to say screw it. Speed up and have someone film the fallout for content."

Brandon paused at a red light. "Yeah, you're right. That does sound like something I'd do." His lips tightened. For some reason, he didn't sound happy about it. "I guess you know me after all."

Did I, though? Because, from the look on his face, it seemed like I'd said the wrong thing.

For the life of me, I didn't know what.

# THIRTEEN

Jenni lived in Cascade, just north of Port of Spain. The gravel-lined road to her gated community cut around a hill, hidden unless you knew where to look for it. I couldn't help but think that was on purpose.

"Oh, definitely," Brandon said, when I mentioned it to him. "The people up here have *money*-money. The last thing they'd want is bandits finding them easily."

"I didn't realize Jenni's Instagram was doing that well."

"It's not. Jenni's father is Larry Persaud, the cricketer." When I blinked at him, silent and utterly nonplussed, he added, "For the West Indies team? The sport with the bat and ball? Pitch? Wicket? None of this ringing a bell?"

"I know what cricket is. I'm just baffled that you'd think I'd know anyone who played it."

"Well, he's considered a national icon for breaking a world record back in his day. For that, I thought anyone living in this country would know him. My mistake." He slowed the car, rolling up to a security booth. He stopped before the barrier.

"Didn't realize you were so sensitive about cricket players," I said.

"*National icon.*"

"Sure." My focus shifted to the stern-faced security guard glaring at us from the window of the booth. "Looks like he wants to talk to you." Actually, he looked more likely to growl at us than talk.

Brandon lowered his window. "Night, Mr. Lewis. How's it going?"

Oh. Of course Brandon knew him.

"Good, good," Mr. Lewis answered, though his angry expression did not change. With each word he spoke, I became more convinced it was just the set of his face. "I enjoyed your recent video on *Midsommar.* A very disgusting movie. I regret watching it, but your reactions to it were too funny."

"I'm glad my suffering amused you," Brandon said, smiling.

Mr. Lewis laughed. "You still haven't taken my advice and watched *Kuch Kuch Hota Hai.* Now that is a great movie. Very wholesome. No heads going *splat.*"

"I'll consider it." Brandon smiled. "Uh, but right now we really have to . . ." He tipped his head in the direction of the road ahead.

"Oh. Yes, yes." Mr. Lewis reached for something, and the barrier in front of us started to lift. "But don't forget my recommendation. It's a great, great movie. It's actually—"

"Will do," Brandon said and drove off.

"That was a bit rude," I said.

He closed the window. "If I didn't cut him off, he'd never stop talking. Trust me, he can chat for hours. We'd be stuck out there all night."

"He is right about *Kuch Kuch Hota Hai*, by the way. It's pretty cute if you're into romances." I wasn't as big a fan of Bollywood movies as Hazel, but she'd made sure I'd seen all the Shah Rukh Khan essential films, including that one.

He smiled. "Well, I don't mind a romance. But those don't bring in the big views. The people only want to see two things from a reaction video—tears and fear. The series I did for *The Haunting of Hill House* has my highest views to date."

"Never seen it."

"You have to. It's a masterpiece." Brandon pulled into an open space, guiding the car into a parallel park. "Well, if you ever want to watch it, and you've changed your mind about being filmed—"

"Ha. No, thank you. I told you, I'm not putting my face out there."

"See, I don't get that." He cut the engine. "Anyone who wears as many colors at once as you do cannot be shy or self-conscious. It does not add up."

I got out of the car. "Like I told you, not everyone needs to plaster every part of their life online for the approval of other people."

"Is it the approval you don't need? Or the idea of being rejected that you subconsciously fear?"

"Okay, cool it with the psychoanalysis, Freud, and fill me in on the plan for tonight."

"Well, first of all, Freud's work has been largely discredited by modern psychologists." He met me at the front of the car. "And second, there's no big plan. We chat with Jenni for a bit. You bring up the band. Talk about why you love it, and what it means to you, et cetera, et cetera."

"And what's your part in all this?"

"You mean apart from facilitating this entire meeting?"

"Yes, that. And being your usual asinine self."

"Just think of me as your backup."

A small, dry laugh burst from my lips. "Yeah, I feel very supported. Thanks."

"Wait," he said, sounding exasperated. "Before we get inside, we need to talk." He stepped in front of me so I had to stop. "Jenni isn't just a friend, okay? For lack of a better word, she's also a colleague."

"Colleague?" Who did he think he was? "Calm down. You film yourself playing *Five Nights at Freddy's*, not competing for tenure at some prestigious university."

"That is what I'm talking about," he said. "I'm begging you not to walk in there, ready to dump on us and what we do online. Not only will you put Jenni off, but you'll embarrass me because I brought you here."

His words stung. "Give me some credit. I don't want to dump on all influencers. Just you."

"Well, it doesn't come off that way. And I'm not going to be able to focus on what needs to be done if I spend the whole time worrying about who you might offend."

I held up my hands in a gesture of surrender. Clearly, this was something he'd been stewing over for a while. "Okay, okay. I'll be good."

He didn't look like he believed me. "We need to call a truce."

"A what? Why?"

"Because we need to work together," he said, without a trace of amusement or sarcasm. He searched my face, his gaze so intense I could almost feel the touch of it like a caress against my skin. It made me nervous in a way I couldn't explain, sure that I did not want to examine it. "Are you in this with me or not?"

I glanced away. "Yeah, sure. No need to be so dramatic about it."

Brandon closed his eyes for a moment, breaking off the tension far more effectively than my attempt at flippancy.

A few seconds later, we entered Jenni's villa, greeted by a wall of chatter and music. A dozen or so university students wandered about. A few nursed paper cups or chilled bottles of Stag beer. Others stood in one corner, apparently learning choreography from a video they were watching on a phone.

"Brandon." I leaned closer to him to be heard over the Nailah Blackman song pulsing through the air. A girl with shoulder-length braids and a croaky voice enthusiastically sang along with the music. "This is a party."

Brandon's gaze made a circuit of our surroundings. "I wouldn't call it a party. It's only a small lime with . . . thirty people. Give or take."

I clutched his sleeve. "You said this was a meeting."

"I never said anything about a meeting. I did say we were *meeting* her."

Oh my God. "How am I supposed to get Jenni's attention with all this going on?"

As if answering my query, Jenni appeared. A few people in front of us quickly stepped aside to let her through. I supposed when you had the stature and the strut of a supermodel, people tended to notice you coming faster than usual. She wore a floral maxi dress, her long curly hair held back with a matching hairband. Both of her ears glittered with multiple piercings.

"Brandon!" She smiled, revealing perfectly whitened teeth. "I didn't know you were coming tonight." She hugged him, holding him for a few beats too long.

Brandon pulled back first. I watched his expression, checking to see if I'd correctly interpreted a second layer to that very warm greeting. But Brandon's smile was no different from usual.

Well, that didn't make sense.

Brandon pointed to me. "Jenni, this is—"

"Hold on," Jenni cut him off, her attention straying toward the living room. "Jo's got his crusty old Timbs up on the couch again. I swear, some people have no home training." She squeezed Brandon's arm, reestablished eye contact, and held it. "Give me one second. I'll be right back. Promise."

After she glided away, I tapped Brandon on his shoulder. "Exactly why did you need me here? She's clearly very into you. Just bat your eyelashes at her, ask her to do the sponsorship, and our problems are solved."

Brandon shook his head. "Jenni doesn't like me like that. She's just one of those people who feel comfortable being slightly more affectionate than usual."

So, basically the opposite of me. Noted.

"If you say so," I said, still skeptical. But what did I know? These were his people after all. He'd understand them better than I did.

"*And*," Brandon said, "if nothing else, she's had a serious boyfriend for the last three years. So, that's that."

"Back again," Jenni said, sliding up to us. She wrapped one arm around Brandon's, locking him to her. "What were we talking about? Was I telling you about how Xavier and I broke up? It feels like that's all I talk about lately."

"I'm sorry to hear that." Brandon's smile stiffened.

"Not too sad, I hope." Jenni knocked her side against his. She glanced away, the smile sliding from her face. "Seriously, Jo?" She untangled herself from Brandon. "That's it. I'm throwing them shoes outside!"

The second she stalked out of earshot, Brandon whispered, "Okay, she's definitely into me."

"Amazing. Who could've seen this coming?"

"This might be a problem."

"Why? You don't even need me now. If you two get together, she'll help us out."

"Flawless plan. Except for one little problem. I'm not into Jenni like that."

"Really? But she's, like, perfect. If you two got together, you'd be like the Trini Instagram power couple."

He tipped his head and gave me a narrow-eyed look. "I know you think I'll do anything for followers, but I do draw a line at leading a friend on." He winced. "Rejecting her is going to make things so awkward. She's probably not going to want to be around me for a while, much less work with us."

Shoot. That hadn't even occurred to me. "Well, think of something fast. Because she's really into you. Like I don't think she even noticed me standing right here. Which—now that I'm saying it aloud—is kind of rude. Like, we came in together. Hell, we could've been on a date."

Brandon snorted.

"What? I'm not good enough to be your girlfriend?"

"Anyone who knows about us wouldn't believe that for a second."

"Yeah, but she doesn't really know about us, does she? For all she knows, I *am* your girlfriend."

The music cut off just in time for the tail end of my words to slice through the sudden silence. Brandon and I froze as several people turned toward us. Jenni, who'd been reapproaching, slowed her steps.

The music started again, but the damage had been done.

The tall boy who'd been accompanying Jenni, a pair of sneakers in his hand, started laughing. "Brandon, you have a girlfriend?" The guy—Jo, I guessed—shoved Brandon's shoulder. "You? Mr. I'm-not-looking-for-anything-serious?"

"Why haven't I heard about this?" Jenni said, recovering from her initial shock. Her smile was weak but present. For the first time that night, she looked at me. "I don't think we've met."

"Did I miss the official announcement?" Jo dropped his shoes on the floor and pulled a phone out of his back pocket. "I don't remember seeing anything."

I shook my head. "Actually, we're not—"

"Putting anything online for now." Brandon shifted closer, until our shoulders touched. "We're still feeling each other out. Our relationship's new."

"Yeah . . ." I said, catching on. "Very new. In fact, I'm still processing it." For the moment, I'd play along, even if I thought it was a terrible idea.

"Cute," Jenni said, making it sound like anything but. "Have we met before . . . ? Sorry, what was your name again?"

"Tess," I said. "And, no, we haven't met before. But I've seen your Instagram. It's very inspiring." I smiled and hoped it didn't come off as insincere as it felt.

"Thank you." Her eyes flicked from my head to my feet and back up again. I held myself still, trying not to fold under the weight of her assessment. What did she see when she looked at us—Brandon and I, together? Did we look like a couple?

The memory of Hazel's story flashed in my head, and I flinched.

"*Brandon has a girlfriend.*" Jo stretched the words so they flowed in a slippery rhythm. "I see, I see. You've got to meet the whole crew then." Abandoning his shoes right there in the middle of the floor, he retreated to the living room in socked feet, waving for us to follow.

"Yes," Jenni said. "Let's."

As we followed them toward the seating area, in front of a massive TV, I caught Brandon's eye and tried to telepathically transmit my objections to the current trajectory of the evening. He widened his eyes in return. I could only assume he was telling me to shut up and go with it.

At least I didn't recognize anyone at the party. All we needed was one classmate—or anyone who'd witnessed Brandon and I interacting at any point in the last seven years—to expose our sham.

Brandon may not have wanted to offend Jenni with a rejection, but if Jenni found out that we were faking it just to avoid that rejection—it would be so much worse.

Resigned, I tapped the back of Brandon's hand with mine. When he shot me a look of confusion, I held his hand. The gesture was meant to show him I was all in. That, if this was the only way to keep Jenni from outright rejecting our proposal, then I'd do it. For Grandeur.

Brandon ducked his head in a move that might've been mistaken for bashfulness, except his shoulders started shaking. He was laughing.

*What?* I mouthed.

He leaned in close to whisper in my ear, the scent of mint on his breath. "I'm thinking about how much you must hate this."

"Shut up."

In the living room, we took a seat beside Jenni on the expensive-looking leather couch. Across from us, a girl and a guy cozied up on a tipped-back recliner. The TV played music videos on mute. The second we settled, Jenni shifted, closing the gap between her and Brandon.

I watched her smile at him, a heavy, sinking feeling in my gut. Was Jenni the type of person who wouldn't care if Brandon had a girlfriend? He and I had taken it for granted that she'd see my presence as an indicator to back off. But if she dismissed our relationship, this could get awkward.

"And who is this?" The boy sitting on the recliner asked. He leaned around the girl with dip-dyed blue-black hair who sat on his lap. His high fade haircut reminded me of something out of the early nineties. His smile wasn't exactly glowing with warmth, but it wasn't unkind either.

I studied their faces, trying to figure out if they were also influencers. The girl did look a little familiar. But, then again, Trinidad wasn't that big. I could be recognizing her from the supermarket.

"This is Brandon's girlfriend, Tess," Jenni said with a tight smile. "Tess, this is Rondell and Nora."

Wait—so this was Nora? As in Chris's ex-girlfriend? As in the person who'd cheated on him? No wonder she looked familiar.

"Since when do you have a girlfriend?" Rondell sat up, causing Nora to slide sideways onto the cushion.

"Watch it, nah." Nora held onto the back of the recliner for balance, squeezing into the small space between Rondell and the armrest.

"Sorry," Rondell said. "But this is big news."

"Big?" Jo flopped onto the couch beside me. "More like mind-blowing. Earth-shattering. Potentially a sign of the apocalypse."

"Way to understate it," Brandon said mildly.

Rondell clasped his hands under his chin. "What happened to all your talk about being too busy for anything serious? That girlfriends are too much trouble and you don't have time to focus on one?"

"That's what I asked him." Jo slid closer, pushing me against Brandon. "My boy changed his tune real quick."

"I did say all that," Brandon conceded, and I tipped my head back to look at him, curious about his answer. "But then I met Tess. And I decided she was worth the effort." Amusement tugged at his lips. "So, *so* much effort."

I narrowed my eyes, irritated. He seemed to be having too much fun with this.

Well, two could play this game.

"Should I be worried that your friends are so surprised by this, honey?" I asked in a teasing tone. "That seems like a big red flag to me."

"I don't see why you should put much thought into anything they say, dear. I know I don't."

"Rude." Jo reached over me to smack Brandon's shoulder. "Just wait until you're in UWI next year. When you need someone to help you move into the dorm—don't call me."

"I wouldn't have expected you to show up anyway," Brandon said.

"You're applying to UWI?" I asked, surprised.

"You didn't know?" Jenni said.

"Of course she does." Brandon squeezed my hand. "It's an inside joke between us. She's teasing me about turning down the football scholarship to Florida."

*Scholarship?* I almost blurted out, but I caught myself this time.

"We're both applying to UWI next year," he said.

"Right," I said. "We are." Apparently.

I didn't know why, but I'd assumed Brandon would be going away for university, and from the sound of it, that had been an option.

Until that moment, I thought this year would be our last in the same school. Now that I knew it wasn't, I didn't know how to feel about it.

"Tess?" Jo reached out and waved a hand in front of my face.

I flinched backward, alarmed to see they were all staring at me. I realized they must've been trying to talk to me for a while, during which I'd been basically gawking at Brandon.

"Sorry, what was that?" I asked.

"Your Instagram handle?" Rondell asked.

Right. "I don't have one. I'm not on social media."

From the way their jaws dropped, one would think I'd just told them I used mayonnaise to shave my legs.

"What—are you like a spy or serial killer?" Jo asked. "Those are literally the only reasons not to."

"Uh . . . no?" I laughed nervously. "Honestly, I don't really have anything interesting to post. I mean, who really cares about the food I eat? Or what I'm wearing today? Plus, there are so many cringey bathroom selfies already out there, I don't need to add to them."

A silence filled the space. With slow, dawning horror, I remembered who I was talking to.

"Present company excepted, of course." I laughed and no one laughed with me. Damn it.

"Tess has some . . . interesting opinions about social media." Brandon shifted, putting a little space between us. My chest clenched.

"Which makes her interest in you that much more puzzling." Jenni raised a manicured brow.

I scrambled to think of a reply, an excuse, but nothing came. I'd done exactly what Brandon asked me not to do. Not only had I insulted them, but I'd also made them doubt him and our fake relationship.

"Actually," Brandon said. "It's not really that much of a puzzle. Tess doesn't care about followers and views. And I like that. She keeps my ego in check. If not, I might spend the whole day taking cringey bathroom selfies or something."

The others laughed. Brandon smiled, soft and self-deprecating. But it seemed off. He wouldn't look at me.

"Besides," Brandon said. "Tess's life isn't half as boring as she claims. You know the mas band, Grandeur?"

"Of course we know them," Jo said.

"Russell Messina's band, right?" Nora sat up. For the first time, she seemed interested in what was going on.

"That's her uncle," Brandon said.

"Really?" Nora not-too-subtly looked me over. "That's cool. My parents used to play with them. I didn't know they were still around."

"They are," Brandon said. "And they're better than ever, now that I'm consulting for them."

"Hold up," Jo said. "You hooked Nora into representing Royalty and now you're Team Grandeur?"

"I was," Brandon said, his attention sliding to Jenni. "But you were right about Prince. I shouldn't have taken the job with him. He messed me up. Bad."

"I knew it!" Jenni's face brightened with the joy of vindication. "Didn't I tell you something was off about him? I told you he gave me bad vibes. No amount of money in the world is worth inviting that kind of energy into my life."

"I didn't think he was that bad," Nora said.

Brandon didn't seem to hear Nora, nodding along with Jenni's words. "You did tell me. I can see it now, especially since I've started working with Grandeur. They're much more professional, and the costumes are amazing." He squeezed my hand. "Right, Tess?"

It took me a second to recognize my cue. "Uh, yeah. This year's theme is *The Wonderous and Wicked Seas*. It's based on—"

"Didn't Harts band have a sea theme last year?" Jo interjected. "Is it similar?"

"Uh . . ." I fumbled, thrown off course by the question. "I don't think so."

"Nah, that was Bliss," Jenni said. "My older sister played with them. She was—oh my God! Did I tell you what happened to her on Carnival Monday last year? She got lost on the streets, even with the band tracking app. The girl cannot read a map . . ."

Jo leaned closer to hear her story, and I pressed into the couch, trying to make room. The plush cushions seemed to swallow me whole.

Their conversation meandered from Carnival to movies to music. They talked over me about people I did not know and places I'd never been. As the discussion strayed further and further away from Grandeur, I grew more and more dejected. Not to mention I was very conscious of the fact that the length of my side was currently pressed against the length of Brandon's. And we were still holding hands.

What had started as a ploy was beginning to feel too intimate. I was too aware of his every move, and all the places where his skin and warmth pressed against mine. My body hummed with an inexplicable thrum of energy. A barely restrained need to do *something*. All that, mixed with the burning shame that usually accompanied my failure in these types of social situations, pushed me to my feet.

"What?" Brandon asked.

"Bathroom," I said.

He started to get up. "I can show you."

"No, stay. I think I saw it when we came in. Next to the stairs, right?"

"Yes—"

"Got it," I said, then left before he could say more. I needed to get away from him. From them.

Why had I come here tonight? I knew I couldn't pull this off.

As I left the living room, I glanced back at the group. Brandon was watching me, his brow knitted with concern. A silent question passed between us, and my steps slowed. But not even a second later, Jenni tugged on his sleeve, leaning closer to whisper in his ear. When Brandon turned to talk to her, cutting that connection between us, I left the room.

As I neared the bathroom, I noticed the line, for it extended to the bottom of the stairs. The wait deterred me from actually going in. I didn't really have to. Instead, I wasted time, wandering through the rest of the lower floor, well aware that I wouldn't be missed in the living room.

In the hall, some of Jenni's father's trophies and sports memorabilia sat on display shelves. I paused to inspect them, pretending that I knew what I was looking at. In the kitchen, an open cooler had been packed with drinks and ice. Used and unused cups, bottles, and cans littered the counters. Two guys were picking through the contents of the fridge, while a third plated their findings.

Everyone seemed to be having fun. I didn't understand how they made it look so easy. When I tried, I usually messed up. And on the rare occasions I didn't, I'd feel so drained afterward.

When I finally returned to the living room, everyone had

squeezed onto the couch. Jenni perched on the armrest, her leg hooked over Brandon's knee. If we really were dating, the sight would've destroyed me. As it was, I felt a heavy, sinking disappointment.

In that moment, I decided I was done.

They hadn't noticed me yet, so I retreated. I spotted a side door across from the stairs. It seemed to lead to a balcony. When I pushed it open, the cool air slapped me in the face.

Brandon could do whatever he wanted. I had no intention of rejoining them.

Instead, I checked out the length of the narrow balcony, which ran around the side of the house. I followed it, a little curious at first, then more so when I noticed the cool blue glimmer of a pool in the backyard. To get to it, I skirted around a handful of people sitting on the stairs.

"Tess?" someone called out.

I stopped and turned around. One of the people I'd passed on the stairs stood and stepped away from the rest. Belatedly, the familiarity of his voice registered. As he approached, his face illuminated in the light from the house, all I could do was stand there and catalog all the ways he hadn't changed.

David looked the same. Same slim physique. Same smile. Same black curly hair.

The sight of him took me back to the girl I was two years ago. The girl who'd been naive in love. The girl who'd gotten her heart broken.

"Is that you, Tess?" A little laugh fell from his lips.

Yes, his laugh was the same too.

The closer he drew, the tighter my skin felt. Slowly surfacing from my stupor, I said, "Hi."

Chris had warned me he was back. I wasn't as careful as I should have been.

"How are you?" He stopped in front of me, looking me over.

"Fine."

He paused as if he'd expected me to ask the same. I did not.

A silence dragged out between us.

"How do you know Jenni?" he asked eventually.

"I don't really. I came with . . . someone." With a sting of annoyance, I realized that if Brandon and David were friends, it stood to reason that David would be Jenni's friend too.

Did Brandon know that David might be here tonight? Did he know and not tell me?

"Someone?" he asked.

"It's . . ." Why was I even talking to him? "I should go back inside. Someone will be looking for me." It wasn't true, of course. But he didn't need to know that.

"Wait." He stepped in front of me. "I'm actually glad we ran into each other. Now that I'm back in Trinidad, I wanted to talk to you."

Uh-oh. "I don't think that's a good idea."

"Tess!" Brandon appeared around the same corner I'd come from earlier. I watched him approach, very aware of the exact moment he noticed David in front of me. A range of emotions flashed across his face, none of which seemed particularly friendly.

"Hey." David raised a hand in greeting.

"David," he said, his jaw tight. He nodded once before transferring his attention to me. "Where have you been? I've been looking all over for you. Did you forget why we came here?"

"You two came here together?" David's eyes darted between us.

I couldn't fault his skepticism. A month ago, I wouldn't have believed it either.

"Yeah, we did," Brandon said. "You have a problem with that?"

I froze, confused. What was going on here? Why had the atmosphere tensed all of a sudden? Weren't they friends?

Then, just when I thought it couldn't get more awkward, Brandon took my hand and held it.

David's gaze dropped to our laced fingers. "I didn't expect that."

No kidding. He wasn't the only one. My brain also had trouble wrapping itself around our current predicament.

I couldn't understand Brandon's reasoning. It was one thing to hold my hand in front of Jenni, who didn't know us. But this was David. We couldn't fool him.

David squinted at Brandon for a moment, assessing. "Actually, now that I think about it, it's not that much of a surprise at all."

Brandon's grip on my hand tightened. "If you're done talking, Tess, I'm ready to go."

"Yeah." I'd been ready since the moment we got here.

# FOURTEEN

"What happened back there?" Brandon's profile lit up in the flashes of orange streetlights. The roads, buildings, and cars of Port of Spain slipped by in snatches of light and sound.

"It was nothing," I said, not wanting to get into it. Seeing David again, after all this time, shook me more than I'd wanted to admit. "Did you get a chance to talk to Jenni about the band?" Maybe she'd turned us down. That would explain his mood.

"Funny you should ask," he said. "Funny in the sense that you'd know if you hadn't disappeared. You know, you were the one who wanted to help me."

"And I tried," I said. He'd been there. He'd heard me. "They cut me off. And Jenni clearly didn't care about what I had to say."

"So you gave up? Just like that?" His grip on the steering wheel tightened. "I know you think we're all shallow, vain assholes. But those people back there—*my friends*—are actually really nice, if you tried to get to know them."

"But I did try!"

"By insulting them two minutes in?"

I winced. Okay. That hadn't been my finest moment.

"You went in there ready to hate them," he said. "It's what you do to me. And to our classmates. And everyone at school."

"Excuse me? The only one who was ready to hate was Jenni. She didn't even acknowledge me at first, then totally dismissed me after you introduced us."

"She would've opened up if you'd stuck around. She's a really sweet person. All that stuff she posts about personal growth, creativity, and self-love—that's all her. It's real. That's why I brought you there tonight. I truly believe if you'd been honest with her about what the band means to you, she would've listened."

"Please. She can't be all that sweet if she still hit on you after she found out you had a girlfriend. While I was right there. And can you slow down, please." I noticed the car accelerating, the number on the speedometer climbing.

"She was not hitting on me."

"Brandon, even you're not that dense." I tried to breathe through my rising anxiety, my attention on the speedometer.

"You don't know what you're talking about."

"I know what I saw. By the end there, she was two seconds away from climbing into your lap."

"I told you—we've known each other for years. We're just that comfortable together."

"Brandon, please slow down." My voice dropped to a whisper. I could barely talk now, my throat tight. My breath coming too fast and too shallow. I started to feel lightheaded.

"What?" Brandon said.

I didn't answer, closing my eyes as they started to water. My heart beat so hard I thought it would burst through my chest. I recognized the feeling of a panic attack. It had been ages since the last one.

Brandon let out a string of curses, slowing the car. "What's happening? Are you okay? What do you want me to do?"

I tried to tell him to wait. There was nothing he could do until it passed. And it would pass, even if it didn't feel like it would just then. In the moment, it felt like I was free-falling, grasping for some piece of reality to cling to and finding nothing.

"I stopped the car, okay?" He turned the music off. "We're not moving. I'm sorry, I didn't realize something was wrong."

I leaned against the car door and focused on breathing, counting in my head. After a while, the tight bands around my chest started to ease. The rush of air felt like surfacing from the sea.

"It's fine," I said, voice raspy. All the energy had drained out of me. "It's nothing," I insisted. "I don't know why it affects me like this. I wasn't even in the car when it happened." But I'd seen the photo of the wreck published in the newspapers the following day. I'd spent countless nights picturing what they must've gone through.

Brandon inhaled sharply, like he'd been punched in the gut. "Your parents. I forgot. I'm so sorry."

"You didn't know. I thought I was over this."

"Tess, I've never lost anyone close to me," Brandon said. "So I don't know what you're going through. But I don't think there's a time limit for this kind of thing."

I knew he was right. But I wished there was some sort of limit. A time when the hurt would just stop. When grief wouldn't hit with this powerful, uncontrolled feeling of unraveling. I hated it. And even more than that—I hated showing it to him. Or anyone.

I wiped the tears from my cheeks, hands shaking. "Okay. I'm okay now. We can go."

"Or we can wait for a bit," Brandon said with forced casualness. "It's only eight. There's no rush."

"We can't stay here. On the shoulder of the highway."

He nodded, his eyes on the road ahead. "Then we should stop off at this gyro place that's nearby. Their lamb is next-level amazing. We can pick up something to eat."

I knew the place he was talking about. And while I agreed that it was excellent, my stomach churned at the thought of food. All I wanted to do was lie down and forget this night ever happened. "I'm not hungry."

"I am." He restarted the car, then slowly pulled back onto the road. "I'll only be a few minutes. You can watch me eat."

"Lucky me." I knew what he was trying to do. He wanted to give me more time to recover. I didn't need it. But I was too exhausted, too hollowed out to argue.

A few minutes later, he parked in the lot of a small shopping center. I got out with him, surprised when he started walking in the wrong direction.

"Where are you going?" I asked, pointing to the restaurant behind us. "It's over there."

"No." He pointed to the place ahead of us. "It's over here."

Surely, he had to be joking. "No. *This* place is better. It has the best gyros on the island."

"Well, that's a strong statement." He folded his arms. "Have you ever tried the food at my place, much less every gyro on the island?"

"No." I mirrored his pose, crossing my own arms. "Have you?"

"Oh, I see how it is," he said, nodding slowly. "I think there's only one way to solve this."

Later, we returned to the car with two gyros from our respective restaurants of choice. We left the doors open and the night air chilled my skin. He handed me one of his, and I gave him one of mine.

"You remembered no tomatoes for me, right?" I asked.

"Yep." He set the bag with one of the gyros on the dashboard and started unwrapping the one I'd bought him. "Honestly, I don't like them that much either. Especially when they're raw." He screwed up his face in disgust.

"Aunty Gloria says only babies pick vegetables off their food."

"Since tomatoes are fruits, I think you're good."

I laughed, something easing inside me. I was still shaky from earlier, but as the scent of the spiced lamb filled the air, I felt the stirrings of hunger. As much as I didn't want to admit it, stopping here hadn't been a bad idea.

He was being so nice to me—which was weird, but not

160

unwelcome. Obviously, I'd scared him. It only made me feel guiltier for ditching him tonight.

"Did I really mess things up with Jenni?" I asked.

Brandon paused in the act of unwrapping his gyro and looked up, his face illuminated in the pink-neon lighting of the nearby storefront. "Honestly? I don't know. She said she'd think about it. We'll have to wait and see."

"I'm sorry." I picked at a paper napkin. "I didn't mean to abandon you. I'm not . . . good at parties. Or with people. I never know what to say." Brandon—who always seemed to know exactly what to say in every situation—wouldn't understand.

"You've never had a problem talking to me," he said.

"Yeah, but I don't really care what you think."

"Clearly."

"You know what I mean."

"Yeah, I do, actually," he said. "Sometimes, it feels like I have no filter when it comes to you. I say things, even though I know I shouldn't." He lifted his eyes to meet mine. "I am really sorry about earlier. For driving too fast. And I didn't realize you felt that uncomfortable at Jenni's. I thought you were just being contrary to annoy me, or something like that."

"It's okay," I said, surprised by his apology. "You didn't know."

"Yeah, but it feels like I'm always saying the wrong things to you. Even when I'm trying not to."

I didn't know about that. "You seem to be doing okay at the moment."

The smile he gave me sent a rush of warmth through my chest.

It was as sudden as it was unexpected. Struck by a wave of inexplicable nervousness, I dropped my eyes, focusing on the food in my hands. I took a bite of the gyro and my mouth flooded with the taste of the most perfectly spiced meat I'd ever eaten.

"Damn it." I covered my mouth with the napkin.

The sound of his laughter filled the car.

When we neared the house, I didn't even notice. We'd been talking nonstop the whole time. After Brandon failed to get more information on my secret Instagram account, he tried to convince me to make a public one instead.

"Okay, I understand you don't want to put your face out there, fine. But you could still post your designs. Your costumes. Maybe make how-to sewing tutorials."

"And why would I do that?" I asked.

"I don't know. Maybe you'll meet people interested in the same things? Join a community."

"Brandon, my uncle is Russell Messina. I already have access to the Carnival costume-making industry, and the community around it."

"Carnival, yes. But what about movie costuming?"

"What about it? That's just for fun."

"Then do it for fun." Brandon sounded frustrated. "You might end up enjoying it. Can you open this or do we have to ring the bell?"

I glanced ahead, surprised to find we'd arrived at the gate to the house. After we'd finished eating, the drive back felt absurdly short.

"Oh, right. No, I've got it." I retrieved the tiny key fob from my pocket and pressed it. The metal of the gate creaked and rattled as it slid aside. As we rolled up the driveway, I refused to examine the disappointment I felt, knowing the night had ended.

When the car stopped, I unbuckled my seat belt. I reached for the door handle, then hesitated. There was something I'd wanted to ask since we'd left the party, but I'd held back at the risk of making things awkward.

Since the night was over, I figured I might as well do it now.

"Brandon. About David . . ." My words trailed off as my courage slipped. I struggled to find the best way to phrase what I wanted to say, certain that something needed to be said.

He grimaced. "I swear, I didn't know he'd be there."

"Okay." Good to know. But while that seemed to answer some questions, it sparked a few more. "I'm confused. Aren't you two friends?"

Brandon jerked backward, looking horrified. "Of course not. You know that."

I shook my head. "I think I'm missing something."

"Why would I stay friends with him after what he did to you?"

My breath caught in my throat. "To me?"

"What he said about your father," Brandon clarified. He searched my face, as if checking my reaction, before he continued, "We all heard him that day. What he said was messed up."

Yeah, I'd thought so. But I was surprised he had too.

"After you left the classroom, we confronted him about it. He was an ass and tried to play it off as a joke, but our friendship was already on shaky ground before. After that, I was done."

I sat there, at a loss for words.

"You really didn't know?"

I shook my head. "Wait—you said *we* confronted him?"

"Yeah. Me and a couple of people in our class. Hazel, though . . ." He pursed his lips in a silent whistle. "She did not hold back."

"What?"

"Yeah. Hazel completely ripped him apart. Didn't she tell you any of this?"

"No. Maybe she tried to, but . . ." At the time, all I'd wanted to do was be alone. I'd shut everyone, including Hazel, out. Then, after David transferred, I did everything I could to make sure I never spoke about him.

"What did Hazel say to him?" I had to know, finding it impossible to imagine my sweet, mild-tempered cousin going off on anyone.

"It's been a while, so I don't remember exactly. But she basically tore him apart in front of the whole class. It was beautiful. David was so lucky that transfer came, because no one in school was letting him live that down."

"Hazel did that?" For me? I still had trouble believing it.

"Yes." His smile slipped. Something like hurt flashed across his face, but in the shadows of the car, I couldn't quite catch it before it melted into the darkness. "Did you really think, all this time, we were just okay with what David said to you?"

Well, yeah. But from his tone, I could tell he thought it was ridiculous that I had. "I thought, since everyone sort of hated me, and liked him, they'd take his side." Everyone, but especially Brandon. He'd been my enemy and David's friend. At the time, it made sense.

But now, he was saying that hadn't happened at all. And I didn't know what to do. Didn't know what to think. It felt like my world had been shattered and then rearranged into something strange.

The gate behind us started to close, on a timer.

I opened the car door. "Yeah, I should go in." It had been a long night, and I needed to think. "Thanks for . . ." I wasn't sure what I'd wanted to say exactly, but he seemed to understand.

"Sure," he said.

I shut the door and stepped back. While I reopened the gate for him, he turned the car around. As he passed next to me, he stopped and lowered his window. "For the record, Tess," he said. "Everyone doesn't hate you."

My skin warmed. He called me Tess. Which was my name, so I didn't understand why that felt so important that he'd used it.

"Everyone? Not even you?" I tossed back, hoping to lighten the moment with a joke.

"Especially not me," he said before driving off.

I watched him leave, then closed the gate. As I entered the house, I thought over his words, confused by the fluttery feeling they provoked.

In the living room, I found Hazel on the couch, her feet propped on the coffee table. She balanced her laptop on her knees. When she spotted me, she frowned. "Back already? Did the date go that badly?"

"It wasn't a date," I said automatically.

Overwhelmed by a wave of fondness, I leaned over the back of the couch and gave her a hug. The angle was awkward but serviceable.

"What—?" Hazel held on to her laptop before it tipped over. She went very still. "What's happening right now? Are you voluntarily showing affection? Did something happen? Did someone die? Did you actually kill Brandon?"

"Thank you," I said. "For being . . . you. And for always looking out for me."

"Okay. Random," she said. "You don't have to thank me for that. We're family. It's what we do."

"I know." My eyes burned. "I'm going to miss you next year."

Her shoulders slackened, and she reached up to squeeze my arm. "Me too."

We stayed like that for a moment, and I tried to blink away my tears and my worries about a future without Hazel here, watching my back.

I didn't want to need or miss people, but it happened anyway. And as I hugged my cousin, and thought of what she'd done for me, and what that meant to me, I started to wonder if perhaps letting someone in wasn't the worst thing after all.

She patted my shoulder. "Sorry to break the moment, but you didn't answer my question about Brandon, and I'm getting a little concerned. I just need to know if there's a body that needs to be moved or . . ."

"Brandon is not dead."

"Thank you for confirming," she said.

# FIFTEEN

*"Why?" I asked.*

*His hands trailed down the length of my spine. His touch, soft but firm, pulled me closer. "Because . . ." he said, and his mouth slanted over mine, answering my question with action and stealing the breath from my lungs.*

*The miracle of his kiss almost brought me to my knees, right in a way that I didn't know existed, like the secrets of a forbidden fruit that couldn't be experienced until consumed.*

*I pulled away panting, breathless, as he proceeded to press fervent kisses along my neck. Impatient, I reached out, pushing the gold half-mask off his face. I already knew who it was, but I needed to see him.*

*Brandon stared back at me.*

I sat up in bed, startled from the dream. The warm sheets had fallen to my waist, exposing my sweat-damp skin to the biting chill of the air conditioner. My heart hammered in my chest, out of control.

"Oh no," I muttered into the inky darkness of the room.

For the rest of the night, I did not sleep.

Aunty Gloria hummed an upbeat tune as she set a plate of coconut bake slices in the center of the table. That Monday morning, the kitchen was full of light and the scent of breakfast. Steam curled from the warm, doughy surfaces of the bake. Despite the pretty picture they presented, I was not hungry.

"I think something's wrong with me," I said.

Aunty Gloria's song stopped. She wiped her hands on a kitchen towel. "You think you're catching something, sweetheart?"

"I don't know. But I don't think I should go to school today."

"Then stay away from me." Hazel reached across the table for a slice of bake and slathered it in butter. "I've got my SATs coming up. I can't get sick now."

I glared at her. "This is all your fault."

She'd done this to me. Her novel planted the insidious romantic idea in my head. If she'd never written it, I wouldn't be having disturbing dreams. And if I hadn't had any disturbing dreams, I would've gotten more than two hours of sleep the night before.

Hazel wrinkled her nose. "What are you talking about? I didn't give you anything. I feel great." She pulled the plate of baigan choka closer to her. "Maybe you caught something from Brandon and his friends."

At the mention of his name, flashes of my dream appeared in

169

my head. I recoiled in a full-body shiver.

"Are you feeling cold?" Aunty Gloria frowned. She pressed the back of her hand against my forehead. "You don't have a fever."

That wasn't surprising, since I strongly suspected my problems were more emotional than biological.

Melissa and Uncle Russell entered the kitchen. Uncle Russell wore his usual expression of bland indifference, but Melissa practically skipped into the room, smiling.

"Good morning, all," she said.

"Breakfast, Melissa?" Aunty Gloria asked. "We've got more than enough."

"No, thank you, Aunty," she said. "I just came over to finalize some details with Mr. Russell, then I'll head back to the camp. I'm actually hoping to finish up early today."

*New boyfriend*, Hazel mouthed at me.

On any other day, this would be interesting information. But today, I wasn't in the mood. All the joy and love floating around made me uneasy. Even Uncle Russell's perfunctory kiss on Aunty Gloria's cheek made me want to pull my hair out.

"You still okay with me borrowing your car again?" Melissa asked Hazel. "Mine is still at the mechanic."

"Sure," Hazel said. "As long as Mummy can still pick us up this afternoon. Or, I guess, just me, if Tess isn't going to school today."

"What's going on?" Uncle Russell said, pouring out a cup of coffee.

"Tess isn't feeling well," Aunty Gloria said.

Uncle Russell examined my face. I tried to look sufficiently diseased.

"In my day," Uncle Russell started ominously, "we were only sick enough to stay home when we were sick enough to need a hospital. Should we take you to the doctor?"

I shook my head. "Not that sick. But I still think I should stay home." An idea popped into my head. "Or I could go to work with you?"

A few hours at the mas camp might clear my head. I'd pretty much do anything to avoid school and avoid facing . . . a certain person I didn't want to think about.

Uncle Russell's eyebrows rose. "You want to skip school . . . for the mas camp?"

"Please." I gave him my most pitiful expression. "Just for today. The only thing I have is a practice exam."

"Those practice exams are important."

"It's only French," I said. "It's not even one of the important subjects. I don't really need it, since I'm going to end up working for Grandeur anyway."

Rather than agree, as I expected him to, my uncle swelled with anger. "You seem to be under a misapprehension. You are a student. Your first priority is school and exams."

Surprised, I sat up, looking over to Hazel for assistance. Why was he so mad? "I know that, but the band—"

"Enough about the band! With the way things are going there won't even be a band next year."

*What?* I tried to ask, but the words wouldn't come out, my

throat too tight with alarm. Had he decided then? Was it over? It couldn't be. Brandon and I were still working on it.

"Russell." Aunty Gloria approached him. They shared a moment of tense, silent communication, and Uncle Russell's shoulders eased.

He scrubbed a hand over his face. "I'm sorry, Tess." The line of his gaze fell somewhere left of my face. "I shouldn't have said that."

"Is it true?" I had to know.

"There's a possibility," he said, still not looking at me.

Why wouldn't he look at me?

"That is why your attention should be on school—hell, that's where it should've been from the start. You've been spending far too much time involved with the band. I realize that is my fault."

"How have I been spending too much time?" I asked, my own temper rising. "I was banned for a whole month."

"And it wasn't enough." His tone hardened again. "In fact, I'm reinstating it. You're not allowed to come to the camp until your exams are done."

"My last exams are in July," I reminded him. "Way after Carnival."

He shrugged. "Then I guess you're not coming back until next year."

My heart plummeted. "You just said that this might be Grandeur's last Carnival. If that's true, you can't ban me again."

"Last I checked, this is my band, and I'm your guardian. So, yes, I can." He waved to Melissa. "Come on. We have a lot to do this morning, if you want to leave early."

He left without his coffee, and Melissa rushed to keep up with him.

"Excuse me, girls." Aunty Gloria dropped the kitchen towel on the counter before following them as well.

I didn't know how long I sat there before Hazel reached over to squeeze my wrist. "Don't worry," she said. "He's probably stressed about the sales. He'll let up eventually."

"That's what you said last time he banned me." My tone was way harsher than it should have been, but my emotions stretched beyond good sense, dangling wildly between anger and sadness with no place for purchase.

I hadn't even done anything wrong. At least, I didn't think that I had. Honestly, I was so sleep-deprived and confused, it was too much for me.

I stood up. "I'm going to get ready for school."

"You okay?" she asked.

Not really. Uncle Russell had never been that angry at me before. Never like that. I didn't even understand what I'd done. Or, more important, how I could fix it.


My plan for school that day came down to one objective: Avoid Brandon.

Pretty simple. And it turned out to be a lot easier than I'd expected. The only class we had in common was Literatures in English, which we didn't have that day, so all I had to do was eat lunch in the art room and slip out of French immediately after dismissal, before he arrived for Accounting.

What I hadn't taken into consideration was football. The team had a big match coming up, which meant a rearrangement of certain practice times. Which meant, as I'd entered the east stairwell, about to go up, I heard him and his friends coming down. I quickly retreated, ducking into the girls' bathroom nearby.

I leaned my ear toward the closed door, listening and waiting for the voices to fade.

"What are you doing?"

I flinched, dropping my backpack. It hit the tiled floor with a worryingly loud smack. "Oh, crap." I quickly retrieved and unzipped it, praying that the tiara I'd been working on in the art room hadn't been ruined.

"Uh, hello?" Sherlyn tapped her foot. "What are you—actually you know what? I don't care. Can you move from the door? Some of us have places to be."

I ignored her, unable to relax until I was sure that the tiara hadn't been damaged. The deadline for the adaptation project was fast approaching. I pulled it out of the bag and looked it over, relieved to see every jewel in place, the plaster and paint smooth and unblemished.

Sherlyn moved closer. "You made this?"

"Yeah," I said, irritated by the shock in her tone. I placed it back into my bag, resting it on top of my books, then carefully closed the zip. "It's for the Literatures in English project. I'm re-creating Juliet's costume with a twist."

For some reason, she looked pissed. "So, you mean we had to settle for fourth-hand musty old props and costumes for our project when you could do this all along? You never said anything."

I was tempted to point out that she'd insisted we use her drama club's costumes right from the start, but it felt like a waste of energy. "You never asked."

Sherlyn sucked her teeth. "You're determined to be the worst, aren't you?" She started to move past me, then backtracked. "Is the full costume as good as this headpiece?"

Confused, I searched her face for a hint of the hidden motive behind her question. "Why do you want to know?"

"Because even though I suspect working with you would drive my blood pressure through the roof, the drama club's putting on another play next term, and I'd prefer not to repurpose the same costumes for the fifty-millionth time."

"You want me to make costumes for your play?"

She crossed her arms. "It'll be my last show before I leave for university. I want it to be special."

Oh. That did sound like a good reason.

"Sorry," I said, and found that I actually meant it. "I'll be too busy with exams and my uncle's mas band to help." At least, I would be, once my uncle realized he was being unreasonable.

"Okay." Sherlyn shrugged, "If you change your mind, let me know. We start rehearsals in January." She stepped around me, opened the door, and peered out. "The coast is clear, by the way."

It took me a second to realize she was referring to my shady behavior from a minute earlier. "Thanks," I said.

"Weirdo," she muttered and left.

• • •

Finally, the last bell of the day rang. I took the long way off campus, through the side gate, cutting across the school garden, and then following the line of the fence to the parking lot. I hesitated, spotting Hazel waiting for me under the tamarind tree. I surveyed the area, then proceeded when she seemed to be alone.

Halfway across the lot, I heard it. "Boop!"

Dammit.

What if I just kept walking? Pretended I hadn't heard him?

I picked up my pace. But Hazel, always helpful, caught my eye, and despite the intense glower on my face, she called out as I approached. "Hey, Tess. Behind you!"

A handful of passing students glanced at us, curious. Rapid footsteps crunched over gravel, then Brandon skidded to a stop beside me.

"Wait! Just . . ." He hunched over breathing hard. The sweat-soaked material of his football shirt clung to his chest as it rose and fell. "Just give me a . . ." He held up a finger.

I looked everywhere but at him, the memory of the dream too vivid in my head.

Brandon dragged in a great lungful of air. "Look . . . I know what you're . . . going to say."

Well, that made one of us.

"You're mad at me," he said. "But I swear . . . it's not the end of the world."

"Brandon, are you okay?" Hazel asked, joining us. "Did you run out on practice? Chris told me y'all were going until five today."

"It's fine." Brandon waved off her concern. "I mean Coach is going to skin me alive when he realizes I'm gone. But it's fine."

"What are you talking about?" I asked him. "What's not the end of the world?"

Brandon straightened up. "You didn't hear about Jenni yet?"

"What about her?"

"She agreed to a sponsorship," he said. "With Royalty."

I didn't know what I'd expected, but that wasn't it. "You're joking." I pulled out my phone to check.

"I wish. She posted about it this morning. I thought maybe you'd seen it, which is why you were blanking me."

"I wasn't blanking you," I said, perhaps a little too quickly. So he had noticed me avoiding him. Thankfully, he hadn't landed on the right reason.

Hazel had her own phone out. "How did that happen? It can't be a coincidence. Did Royalty know that you were trying to get her?"

I opened the app and searched for Jenni's profile, my hands trembling with fury. "What's her handle?"

"It doesn't matter," Brandon said.

He couldn't be serious. "Of course it matters! Prince has to be behind this. He knew what we were up to, somehow, and he hired Jenni to mess with us."

"Sounds like him." Chris jogged up to us. Like Brandon, he was similarly winded. "Like he really hates you. A lot."

"Well, the feeling is mutual," I said.

"Coach sent me to find you," Chris explained to Brandon. "He is not happy."

"Great."

While they talked, I finally found Jenni's Instagram page. I pulled up the photo of her standing in front of the Royalty mas camp. "She really did it. Unbelievable."

Brandon sighed. "Look, I'm not saying that Prince wouldn't do something like this. What I'm saying is—it doesn't matter if he did, we don't need her."

"But you said we did. You said she was your last Instagram friend not corrupted by Royalty."

"I'm fairly certain I've never used the term *Instagram friend* in my life."

"I don't understand. Why did she agree to work with them now, when she turned them down before? What changed?"

"Well, it's not because Prince's vibes have improved, I can tell you that." Brandon's laugher trailed off weakly, his gaze sliding away from mine. His feet shifted. "Look, I'm sure Jenni has her reasons. But we don't need her because we're going to get someone else. Someone bigger. Someone more famous."

"How? You've literally hit up everyone you know."

"That's why we've got to step outside the local influencer bubble. We've got to go mainstream. I'm working on a plan."

"What are you talking about? What's mainstream? And can you please stop fidgeting? You're making me nervous." I held onto his shoulders and he stilled. "What plan?"

"I'm working on it," he said.

"Brandon . . ." He had no plan. I could tell. And despite his assurances, I doubted he'd have one later.

"I know what you're thinking," Brandon said, his gaze level with mine. And as we stood, eye to eye, I believed that he did know what I was thinking. That he could see, not just my skepticism, but the bone-deep disappointment that left me wary.

Maybe it was time to accept this wasn't going to happen.

"Don't give up yet," he said. "Jenni may have been a bust, but I think I can still fix this, Tess. Let me try?"

He used my name again and something inside me softened.

"Okay. Fine." What did it hurt to give him this chance? Maybe his plan would work and the sales would improve. Then my uncle wouldn't be so stressed, and he'd let me help with the costume-making again. "I mean, I'm not going to stop you . . ."

"Great." He smiled.

My breath caught in my throat. With my hands on his shoulders, his face so close to mine, I caught a glimpse of déjà vu. A memory from the dream. It had me rooted to the spot, unable to look away.

"Ouch!" Chris jerked sideways, away from his girlfriend. "Yes, I see. You don't have to pinch my skin off."

Hazel ignored him, smiling at us. "Look at you two getting along." Despite her guileless tone, I spotted the evil glint in her eyes.

I retracted my hands from Brandon and stepped back. "Well, you know . . ." I cleared my throat. "Enemy of my enemy and all that."

"Agreed," Brandon said, a bit too cheerfully. "Right. I'll pick you up on Wednesday at seven."

What? "Why?"

"For the plan," he said, as if it were obvious.

"But that's a public holiday." The only plan I'd had was to stay home and avoid Brandon from the convenience of my own bedroom. I couldn't be around him too much. These feelings that seemed to be growing in me needed to be weeded out, and to do that I needed time and space. Brandon's plan sounded like the opposite of that.

"Seven!" he repeated, then sprinted off in the direction of the football field.

He had way too much energy, I thought, as he retreated. Something not unlike fondness bloomed in my chest. I visualized crushing it with the heel of my shoe.

When I turned around, my cousin and her boyfriend were locked in some silent conversation. Hazel lifted her chin, victorious, while he sighed deeply.

"What?" I asked, suspicious.

"Nothing," Chris said.

"Actually, one thing." Hazel held up her phone. "Found this on Jenni's page. I'm guessing you haven't seen it yet."

It was a photo from Saturday night. I didn't even remember when Jenni had taken the selfie on the couch. My face was blocked, but the hand that held Brandon's remained clearly visible.

"Something you want to tell me?" Hazel asked.

"Not really," I said.

# SIXTEEN

I ignored the first message notification, but the second woke me up. I reached out and fumbled along the edge of my packed dressing table, flipping a hairbrush and a tube of leave-in hair moisturizer onto the floor before locating my phone.

I squinted at the screen. The messages from Brandon lit up.

Are you ready???

I'm outside.

Somewhere in my sleep-addled mind, curiosity sparked. But not bright enough to push me out of bed. I dropped my phone onto the table, rolled back into the sheets, and fell asleep again.

Seconds or hours later, Hazel shook me. "Tess, come on. Get up. Brandon's downstairs."

"What?" I muttered, trying to slide away from her.

"Brandon is downstairs. Don't you remember? You made plans with him?"

"Yeah, for seven."

"It is seven."

It took me a second to realize the truth of what she was saying. I sat up. "In the morning?"

Hazel snorted. "You two really need to work on your communication."

"It's a public holiday. Why would I be up this early?"

"Why don't you ask him? He's right downstairs."

"Oh my God." I flopped back onto the pillow, staring at the ceiling.

"And if I were you, I wouldn't waste time. He's with Mummy now. Probably having another tea party."

I groaned and forced myself out of bed.

A few minutes later, I found them at the kitchen table, Aunty Gloria explaining our plans for this afternoon. Every Divali, her sister held a celebration party at her house. We were expected to attend. I'd completely forgotten about it. An excuse not to go out with him had been right there, and I'd fumbled it.

"So have her back by five," Aunty Gloria was saying, her back to me. "That should give her enough time to get ready."

"Of course, Aunty." Brandon noticed me over her shoulder. His soft smile sent my heart racing. "We'll be back by then."

"That's good to know," I said, walking in. "Since I have no clue about where we're going or why. But at least I know it will end."

"Looking on the positive side." Aunty Gloria nodded. "That's what I like to hear." She rose from her seat. "You two go on, I've got to start preparing my gulab jamun for tonight."

"Aunty." Brandon rested his elbows on the counter. "If you can find it in your heart to spare me a few of those, I'd be eternally grateful."

Aunty Gloria cocked an eyebrow. "Bring her back before five and we'll see."

"We must be back on time," Brandon said firmly, as we entered the living room.

"Back from where exactly?"

"Back from executing my plan."

I turned to face him, my sudden stop bringing us close in a near-collision. We stepped back from each other, the separation simultaneous. Oddly enough, *he* seemed to be more flustered than I did, running a hand through his hair.

"Brandon," I said, "I know that you love irritating me—"

"Who? Me? Never."

I swallowed the urge to laugh. Surely, I couldn't be so far gone that I'd find that funny. "But I cannot agree to go with you unless you tell me where we're going."

He tipped his head to the side, apparently considering this. "Okay. I see your point. It's just . . ." His smile slipped a little, along with the show of confidence he'd been putting on. "I don't want to get your hopes up."

What hope? I didn't do hope. Hope broke hearts and obscured the reality of a situation. What I needed was action. "Just tell me."

He sighed. "Have you heard of Dessa King?"

"*The* Dessa King? The soca music artist?"

The Dessa King who'd won International Soca Monarch at the age of sixteen? The singer who'd had a lull in the middle of her career, but recently made a massive comeback after collaborating with the superstars, DJ Bacchanal?

"Ah. So, you have heard of her. You a fan or something?"

"Obviously."

He frowned. "I told you, I didn't want to get your hopes up."

"Brandon, if anything, I'm more doubtful than ever. How would you even contact her? Do you know her management or something?"

"No. Though I did try reaching out to them. Unsurprisingly, they have not answered." He waved the thought away. "The real plan is to ask Dessa herself. And I've learned from a semi-reliable source that she's going to be shooting her new music video on Maracas beach today."

"Semi-reliable?"

"Like I said. Keep those hopes low."

"Trust me, they are," I assured him. "Wait? We're going to the beach?"

"Yes. Maracas."

Oh. "That explains the pants." I'd been wondering why he'd worn lime-green knee-length shorts. They were swim trunks.

"I figured you'd appreciate the bright color," he said.

I did, actually. Not that I planned to admit it.

"So?" he asked, shifting from one foot to the other. "Are you coming?"

"I don't know, Brandon." I loved the beach, and it had been far too long since I'd been to one. The longing to sink into the cool embrace of the sea almost pushed me into agreeing. "Do you really need me to go with you?"

"Of course," he said. "My plan requires at least two people. Someone will have to be the distraction."

"You—" I couldn't hold back my laughter anymore. This was ridiculous. I didn't even think it qualified as a plan; it was so flimsy. "This is not going to work."

"Probably not," he said. "But what if it does?"

If it did work—by some miracle—then that could maybe solve everything. Dessa's status as the moment's hottest soca music star stood unmatched. Her platform was big enough to draw loads of attention to anyone she worked with.

"So . . . ?" Brandon asked. "Are you in or out?"

"I don't know."

"What are you two doing here?" Uncle Russell entered the room, dressed for another day at the mas camp. "You're not trying to skip school again, are you?"

"No," I said bitterly. "It's a public holiday."

"Oh, right." He headed for the kitchen. Public holiday or not, it really didn't make a difference in his line of work. "What are you two up to then?"

Before Brandon could fully fill him in, I said, "He's trying to convince me to go to the beach with him." If Uncle Russell thought I'd been spending too much time on band-related activities, I doubted he'd approve of the reason behind Brandon's excursion.

"Sounds good," Uncle Russell said.

I felt a spike of resentment at his easy dismissal. "It's not like

I have anything else to do today." I didn't bother hiding the bitterness in my tone. Usually, I'd spend every school holiday at the mas camp. But not this time, apparently.

"All the more reason for you to go," Uncle Russell said, then left the room.

Fine. He wanted to shut me out of the mas camp, then I'd help with the promotions instead. By the time he found out what we'd been up to, we'd have saved the band with Dessa King's endorsement.

"Let's go," I told Brandon, then looked down at the loose T-shirt and jean shorts I'd been wearing. "Correction. Give me ten minutes, and then let's go."

"Only ten minutes?" He sounded skeptical.

"Yes." I narrowed my eyes, refusing to let the challenge slide. "Ten minutes. Time me."

He whipped out his phone. I ran for the stairs before he even started the clock.

Since most of my dressing time usually involved deciding what to wear, I started with a very clear outfit in mind. I picked my cutest black-and-yellow swimsuit and covered it with a yellow floral-print sundress. Within five minutes, I'd dressed, tied my hair back with a headband, grabbed my bag and my rubber slippers, and left my room.

Melissa met me at the bottom of the stairs.

"I need to talk to you for a second," she said, her voice low, her expression pinched. My mind immediately went to the band. "Is something wrong?" Maybe she had some insight into Uncle Russell's chilly behavior.

"It's about Brandon," she said.

Definitely not what I expected. I glanced around to make sure he wasn't close by. Lowering my voice, I asked, "What about him?"

"I don't even know if I should say anything. It might be nothing but . . ." Melissa bit her lower lip.

"Just say it," I pressed, unbearably curious. And also, my time on the clock was almost up.

"You know I've never cared too much about the Royalty feud, right? I play along for your uncle's sake. But as far as I'm concerned, it's a waste of time."

"Yes," I admitted. "It's been pointed out to me that some people feel it's silly. Even though it's a very real and ongoing threat. Why?"

"Well, I hope like hell I'm wrong about this, but I've been talking over our recent problems with my boyfriend—he's actually really smart and insightful—and he pointed something out." She smiled, a distant, dreamy expression falling over her face. "I haven't introduced you yet, have I? Tess, he's gorgeous. And a good listener. Plus, he kisses like—"

"Good for you," I cut in. "What's your point?"

"My point is—how did Royalty know to approach Jenni right after Brandon did?"

"I hate to break it to you, but your gorgeous, insightful boyfriend isn't the first one to ask this."

"Do you have an answer?" When she saw that I didn't, she leaned in. "What if it was Brandon who told them?"

"Yeah. That makes no sense."

"I know it's wild, but stay with me for a second. How do we know that Mr. Kingston really fired him? We only have his word for it. What if they've been paying Brandon to spy on us and give us bad advice. He could've pointed us in Jenni's direction, well aware that she'd end up with Royalty in the end."

"Oh my God," I said in wonder. "All this time . . . Please, *please* tell me I haven't been sounding this ridiculous about the rivalry. You're edging into a full-blown conspiracy."

No wonder Hazel made fun of me for it. Yes, I may have had a similar thought before we hired Brandon, but I doubted he could uphold that level of deception this long.

Right?

I shook my head. "Melissa, that's too out there. Even for me."

"Fine. Don't listen to me. Just be careful, okay?" She backed up. "As I said, I hope I'm wrong. But think about how convenient it is that he switched sides and offered us help, right when we needed it."

"Brandon isn't that good of an actor," I said.

Or was he?

As we'd spent more time together, I couldn't deny that I'd started to see a side of him that I hadn't before—depths that hadn't been visible in the shallow façade of his online persona. Wouldn't that imply some level of deception? Lord knows I'd been gullible in the past when it came to David. Could I be making the same mistake again? Seeing only what I wanted to see?

"Yeah, you're probably right," Melissa said, her skepticism still evident in the set of her jaw.

"Ha!" Brandon entered from the living room. "I was just going to wait in the car. Your ten minutes is up."

"I've been dressed for ages," I protested. "It was Melissa who held me back. Melissa, tell him."

"Nope." Brandon continued straight out the door. "Ten minutes is ten minutes. Still counts!"

I watched him go, warmed by a mix of amusement and irritation. Melissa met my bemused smile with a frown. She opened her mouth to say something, but I spoke faster.

"It'll be okay," I assured her.

# SEVENTEEN

The North Coast Road was known for two things: stunning scenic views and awful roads. Luckily, we set off early that morning, which meant less traffic. This would change as the day grew later.

"Are you sure you're okay?" Brandon asked.

"Yeah." I focused on the drizzle scattered across my window. It was preferable to watching the street as it snaked along hillsides. Passing clouds chased us all the way to the coast. Brandon slowly, carefully navigated the hairpin turns and narrow roads, but it didn't stop me from clenching at the sight of every oncoming car that passed a little too close to us.

Brandon glanced at me, his sunglasses flashing in the sunlight. "I shouldn't have brought you up here," he said, not for the first time.

"I'm fine," I insisted, also not for the first time. "Just distract me. Talk to me about something."

"About what?"

"I don't know." A pickup truck appeared ahead. I closed my eyes and waited until it passed us. "Anything."

"Would it help if I told you I do this drive at least once a week? So I've got experience."

"No. If anything, I'm more concerned about your judgment. Why would you be foolish enough to subject yourself to this so often?"

"Because I live in Maracas."

"No, you don't." If he did, he'd have to make the hour-long drive to school every weekday, and that was beyond ridiculous. "You live in St. Joseph. I've heard you mention it."

"No, my sister and her family live in St. Joseph. During the school week, I stay with them. I come home for the weekends."

"I did not know that." Just another item on the growing list of things I didn't know about him. "But family or not, this drive is too much."

"I know, but I miss them." He shrugged. "Plus, my parents have a restaurant up here. My father, let's say *strongly encourages* me to help out, when I can. According to him, it's important for me to have some experience at a *real job*."

"As opposed to a fake job?"

"As opposed to social media."

"Ah."

"Ah, indeed," he said. "Why do you think I respond so well to your cracks about my life choices, Boop? It's because I've heard it all before, and far worse." His light tone didn't match his words. "And the thing is—I don't mind working at the shop. The only

191

part I hate is the way he's constantly reminding me that I should be there, helping, even when I am."

Out of the corner of my eye, I tried to read his expression. But Brandon watched the road ahead, apparently unbothered—or at least, he did a very good impression of it.

"Hey, the lookout's coming up," he said. "Do you want to stop? We can get some snacks, and you can take a break from trying not to throw up."

"I'd appreciate it."

A minute later, he pulled into a little parking area. A cluster of tents housed a few stalls with items for sale, including handmade souvenirs, street food, snacks, and sweets. Beyond them stretched the cliffside and a gorgeous view of the coastline.

We got out of the car and Brandon grabbed a small camera bag from the backseat.

I watched him warily. "I better not end up on your Instagram. Not unless you want to feed the rumors."

Jenni's party post hadn't gone unnoticed for too long. The image of Brandon holding some girl's hand circulated online and in school, along with suspicions of her identity.

"People might think I'm your mystery girlfriend," I said.

"You *are* my mystery girlfriend." Brandon shut the door and slung the camera bag over his shoulder. "Technically speaking."

The laughter that bubbled out of my mouth sounded nervous to my own ears. "*Fake* mystery girlfriend," I corrected him, ignoring the way my stomach flipped. "So it's probably best we continue to keep it a secret."

"Why?" he asked, as we approached the tents. "You ashamed of your fake secret boyfriend or something?"

"Yes. On multiple levels."

"Wow." Brandon headed straight for one particular tent. "Well, now you've hurt my feelings."

I pouted, pretending to feel remorseful. "What if I buy you a bag of tamarind balls? Would that make you feel better?"

"Ah, bribery. You do know the way to a man's heart. No wonder we're in fake love." He paused at a table loaded with all manner of preserved fruits and sweets. He nodded in greeting to the saleswoman, who was busy helping other customers. "Make it a bag of coconut sugar cakes and you've got yourself a deal."

A minute later, Brandon had struck up a conversation with the woman who worked there, the customers who arrived before us, and a few who joined after.

"Here nah," he told his small but growing audience. "Miss Laurel has the best coconut sugar cakes on the island. If anyone tells you anything else, they lying. Her secret is that she uses just the right amount of ginger—"

Miss Laurel reached across the table to swat him, but he jumped out of the way. "Is not a secret if you telling everybody jus' so," she said.

"Who they going to tell?" He waved toward us. "Look at those honest faces."

I smothered laughter behind my hand.

Brandon caught my eye and smiled. "Except that one." He pointed at me. "She looks like trouble."

My jaw dropped with exaggerated outrage.

For the next few minutes, I watched him charm them, and by extension, charm me. My chest felt tight with a mix of awe and jealousy.

After the other customers departed, their hands and bags full of Brandon Richards–recommended snacks, Miss Laurel pulled Brandon aside. "I haven't heard back from your father," she told him. "He tell you anything about the guide I send by him? If they include the restaurant on the tour, it could mean more business."

"You know how he is." Brandon shoved his hands into his pockets. "Always busy. He must have forgotten."

She nodded; her face pinched in unhappy resignation. "I know what you mean. I'll call and ask him myself then." She sucked her teeth. "How someone so busy-busy like him make a lackadaisical son like you, I will never know." She gave him a wink to show she was teasing. "Thanks for the sales."

"Not a problem," Brandon said, his smile stiff.

I stood there, stunned that she could call him lackadaisical in one breath, then thank him for raking in a hundred dollars in sales for her in the next. Didn't she realize what he'd just done wasn't easy? Not everyone could do that.

After they said their goodbyes, we left the tent and approached the edge of the lookout. I walked right up to the barrier, taking in the verdant cliffside, and the curves of the coastline stretching and retreating from the luminous sapphire blue of the sea. Next to me, Brandon pushed his sunglasses up, pulled out a weathered Canon camera, and snapped a few photos.

As we stood there, the wind snatching at my hair, I thought back to what he'd said in the car—the comparison between my cracks about his life choices and his father's criticisms. It made me uncomfortable. For all the insults Brandon and I had traded over the years, it would be a lie to say that I hadn't meant any of them. But I'd never thought they carried much weight coming from me—someone he clearly despised.

Except he didn't hate me. He'd said so himself.

For so long, I thought he didn't care about anything, all insults sliding right off his back. But what if they hadn't? The idea that I might've hurt him troubled me.

"Smile," he said, his only warning before he took my picture.

"Brandon." I lifted a hand to block my face.

"What? It's not for posting. It's for you."

"I don't remember asking for one." My phone buzzed against my leg. I pulled it out of my pocket and checked the new message. It came from an unknown number.

Hey Tess. It's David. Still your number??

"Something wrong?" Brandon asked. He'd lowered the camera to look at me.

I checked the message again to make sure it said what it said.

"Hold on." Brandon retrieved his own phone when it started to ring. "I need to take this."

While he talked, I lifted my eyes to the sky, squinting against the glare of the sun. Wispy gray clouds sailed in the distance. The scent of wet foliage lingered in the air.

I checked the message again. It still said the same thing.

"We have to go." Brandon's voice cracked with urgency. "Now. Come on."

For a second, I hesitated, dazed and so confused. Then Brandon started for the lot, and I realized he meant it. I pocketed the phone and hurried to meet him at the car.

Whatever David wanted would have to wait.

We arrived at the beach a few minutes later. Brandon parked and we jumped out. He grabbed his camera bag and a large manila envelope and led me toward the pavement where a young girl waved to us. She had to be about ten or eleven years old, dressed in a black-and-white *bebe* printed T-shirt and a short jeans skirt. Her braided hair had been pulled into a high ponytail that swished as she walked toward us.

"Are you sure they're leaving?" Brandon asked her.

"Yes," she said. "I told you, I saw them packing up."

Brandon checked the time on his watch. "I heard they were supposed to be shooting until lunch."

"I don't know. Maybe they finished the music video early." She rolled her eyes, and in that moment, her resemblance to Brandon became so apparent I knew they must be related.

"Your sister?" I asked Brandon.

"My baby sister," Brandon said. "Lucy."

"Not a baby." She assessed me, a slight frown on her face. "You're Tess? Brandon told me about you." She tipped her head to the side—the same way I'd seen Brandon do so many times. "You don't look like a soul-sucking Jumbie."

"Ay! Watch it, Lucile." Brandon startled like he was the one who should be offended. To me, he said, "I said that ages ago."

"How would a soul-sucking Jumbie look?" I asked Lucy, ignoring him. If anything, I'd said way worse about him in private. And in public.

Her hands clasped behind her back. "I don't know. Sharper teeth?"

"Okay, enough." Brandon leaned down to meet her at eye level. "Now, focus. Where is Dessa?"

"Over there." She pointed behind us.

Brandon and I turned in time to see Dessa King standing a few feet away. She wore full makeup. Her hair was loose in long auburn waves, and a shiny black fabric was draped over her shoulder like a shawl. About a dozen people crowded around her, holding out their phones, filming or begging for selfies. Before we could move, speak, or plan anything, she slipped into the backseat of a large black van.

"Wait!" Brandon called out, though it was obviously pointless. Dessa King and her driver could not hear him, and even if they did, they would not care. The van drove off, a few people waving and shouting their goodbyes.

My heart sank. "Well, that's it." Even though I thought the plan would fail, I couldn't deny my disappointment. "So, what's next? Plan B? No, we're on C now."

"Honestly," Brandon said, his back toward me as we watched

the van leave. "Can you please not . . . speak."

"Excuse me?" I asked, offended.

"I can't handle your *I told you so* right now." Brandon ran a hand through his hair. He staggered off to the side and sat on a low concrete barrier. "I knew it was a long shot, okay? But I still tried." He handed me the manila envelope. "Do you have any idea how long it took me to make this?"

I opened the flap and pulled out the glossy booklet inside. "Oh my God," I whispered, flipping through the contents. "Brandon . . . is this . . . the information about Grandeur that I gave you?"

"Some of it. I cut out the boring parts, added some photos and graphics. I have a friend who works at a printer, and she hooked me up." His shoulders slumped. "Since Dessa's management ignored my emails, I figured we should have something substantial to show her, if we got the chance to talk to her."

"This proposal looks really professional. It must've taken ages."

"Yeah, well . . ." Brandon lifted a shoulder in an apathetic shrug. "Dessa's not going to see it. So it doesn't matter."

Except it did matter—to me.

Brandon had created a whole proposal for Dessa, presenting Grandeur at its best. Skimming through it, I felt an overwhelming sense of pride and awe. I laughed, my amusement bittersweet. We'd failed again; the future of Grandeur still uncertain. But if we hadn't missed Dessa that morning, I may not have discovered how much Brandon really cared.

"Ah-hem." Lucy pretended to clear her throat.

"Yes, Lucile?" Brandon said. "You know you can leave whenever you like."

Lucy huffed, folding her arms. "I was going to tell you that maybe you should talk to those guys over there." She pointed toward a pair of men—one in an unbuttoned silk shirt with many gold chains and rings, the other in a long-sleeved shirt and slacks, far too overdressed for the beach. "They were with Dessa earlier. One of them was directing the music video. *But* since I should leave . . ."

"Seriously?" Brandon straightened up. "Which one is the director? What am I saying? Obviously, it's the one with the jewelry."

"Here." I slipped the folder into the envelope and handed it to him. "You'll need this if you're going to talk to them."

"You're not coming with me?"

I shook my head. After watching Brandon charm the customers at the confectionary tent, and seeing his printed proposal, it became clear to me that he was good at what he did. He connected with people.

"Remember what happened with Jenni?" I asked. "I think my presence is more harmful than helpful."

"I really wish you wouldn't bad-talk yourself like that."

"Because that's your job?"

"Exactly." He took the envelope from me, our fingers brushing. The contact sent a pleasant thrill along my nerves. "I'll be back in a minute," he said.

I watched him go, a buzz of energy humming beneath my skin.

• • •

Brandon's chat with the director took more than a minute. In the meantime, the stretch of shimmering blue water called to me.

I shed my slippers and dress, and left my things tucked at the base of one of the many palm trees that sprang from the off-white sand. The big blue sky stretched overhead; the sun was warm against my shoulders. Music floated from one of the many beach limes congregating.

Though Maracas was almost never empty, the arc of the bay stretched out for over a mile, providing lots of space. When I'd walked into the blue-green sea, the cool water lapped against my legs, slightly choppy. Due to the strong currents here, I didn't go too far out, stopping about thigh-deep and lowering myself into the water.

That was where Brandon found me a few minutes later.

As he approached the shoreline, I waved to make sure he'd seen me, then nearly bit off my tongue when he reached back to pull off his shirt. He dropped it on a beach chair and tucked his shoes underneath. I tried not to look like I was staring as he revealed a torso of slim but defined muscle, the sun illuminating the golden undertones of his warm brown skin.

The waves at my back gently nudged me forward–nudging me toward him. I dug my heels into the sand to steady myself.

"Where did you leave your bag?" he asked, sinking lower into the water.

I exhaled slowly, forcing my focus toward his question, and away from the flurry of nerves that erupted in my stomach. "Your sister said she'd keep it for me."

Brandon grimaced slightly, shifting so we were side by side, facing the shore. "That means we'll have to stop by the restaurant to pick it up."

"Weren't we going to stop there anyway?"

His brows rose. "You want to?"

I did, actually. "Are you saying you dragged me all the way out here with no intention to provide lunch? Rude."

"Ah, so it's about the food. Nothing to do with wanting to see the place where I work."

"Yes, there's a tiny bit of that too."

"At least you're being honest." He rested his palms on the water, watching the surface ripple around them. "Aren't you going to ask me how it went with the director?"

I'd assumed from his somber disposition that it hadn't gone as well as he'd hoped. If it had been good news, he couldn't have contained it this long. "How was it?"

"Kale—that's the director—said he'd pass the proposal on to her."

"Do you think he will?"

"Considering he didn't so much as glance at it—and spent most of the time trying to convince me that *I* should get into music and hire him to make a music video—I'd say it's unlikely."

"He recognized you?"

"Yes, he follows me. For all the good that did."

"We don't know yet. Maybe he will help."

Brandon didn't answer, squinting toward the shoreline. I followed his gaze.

A man knelt at the edge of the water. He held out a ring to a woman who was losing her mind with excitement. She nodded frantically and the man slipped the ring onto her finger, rose to his feet, and drew her into his arms. Their friends and nearby strangers clapped and cheered. Even Brandon joined in.

"Ugh," I said. "Why would anyone propose on a busy beach in the middle of the day? Imagine if the ring fell into the water. Or if someone tried to steal it."

"No, I will not imagine that." Brandon scowled at me. "You don't know if the beach means something special to them. I think it's sweet."

"It's public. And cringey. I blame movies for making people think that big, grand gestures are aspirational."

"Wait a minute." Brandon faced me. "Now you're going after movies? I can't let this slide. Are you saying there isn't a single grand romantic gesture that affected you? None at all? Not even Heath Ledger singing 'Can't Take My Eyes Off You,' or Henry Golding's proposal on the plane?"

"No way. Public nuisances. Both of them. Especially Henry. I cannot watch that scene without feeling sorry for every other passenger, ready to go and having to wait because of this random couple."

Brandon laughed. "Wow."

"What? It's true," I insisted, but couldn't help laughing along with him. "Caring about someone makes you vulnerable enough.

Why would you want to lay it out in public like that? Worse yet, what if he'd gotten rejected in front of everyone?" I nodded to the couple on the beach. "That could've been a mess."

"Well, that's the point, isn't it? The fact that he's willing to risk rejection and embarrassment is what makes the gesture so powerful. That's how you know it means something."

"By sacrificing your dignity? No, thanks."

"I'm getting the impression you're not a romantic."

I shrugged. "Blame it on my role models, I guess."

"Uncle and Aunty? They seem—oh." His expression softened as his confusion cleared. "Your parents."

I nodded.

Back on shore, the newly engaged couple held hands as they waded into the water. They were smiling, their happiness radiant, like they were lit up from the inside.

"Everyone always said my parents made a great couple. A perfect match." Both supported the local arts. Both had many friends. Both were fully committed to their careers. "What people didn't see was that they were living completely separate lives."

We all were.

My parents were the ones who taught me the ways people let you down. After all the times I'd try to talk to Daddy, but he didn't hear me, too distracted by a phone call. All the times when Mummy would take an extra meeting and forget to pick me up from school. I loved them, but after a while, there'd been so many broken promises, forgotten trips, and missed events it became easier not to expect anything from them.

"Carnival was the exception. In our house, it was bigger than Christmas. Bigger than birthdays. My parents took time off from work just for it. Some of my best memories were of the three of us at mas camp. Mummy worked there, so Daddy would pick me up from school, and we'd join her."

Those evenings passed in a blur of creative focus and idle chatter, the light chemical scent of dyed fabric in the air. Daddy would inevitability glue something he shouldn't, Mummy singing along with the latest soca music playing in the background. It was the only time when our lives seemed to intersect. All three of us. Together.

"And now, Grandeur is failing," I said, overcome by a wave of resignation, and a yearning for a sense of perfect belonging I hadn't felt in years. Not since I'd lost my parents. Working at the mas camp was the closest I could get.

My throat tightened. I hoped he didn't notice as a tear slipped down my cheek, my face already wet from the sea. "I tried—*we* tried, Brandon. But I think it's time to admit it. The band's done."

Brandon stayed silent for a moment, then tentatively asked, "You're giving up?"

"No. I'm accepting it."

"Tess." His arm jerked in an aborted movement, like he'd been about to reach for me, then changed his mind. "You can't give up now. Not yet. If this Dessa thing doesn't work out, we'll try some one else. Someone bigger."

Someone bigger? "Brandon—"

"No, hear me out. I heard that Eliza Musgrove is visiting—"

"There's no time. We might already be too late. Most people have already bought their costumes by now."

"Then we'll try again next year."

"My uncle says there won't be a band next year, if things don't improve this year," I said, frustrated that he didn't seem to get it. "This year's sales are *bad*, Brandon. The worst it's been since the company started. Apparently, it hasn't been making a profit for years."

"For real?" Brandon asked, eyes wide.

"Oh, yeah. And it gets worse. Our business manager left suddenly a few months ago. Melissa has been trying to fill in, but she's barely holding it together. My uncle's arthritis is getting worse, which means he needs more help. Unfortunately, my uncle is, well, *my uncle*, who hates asking for anything. And to top it all off, he's been weird lately, shutting me out and I don't know why—" I ran out of air before words.

Inhaling sharply, I realized how much I'd said.

"Wow." He sank a bit lower in the water, like he'd literally taken on the weight of my words. "That's a lot."

"Yes, but, Brandon, you cannot tell anyone about this. Especially not the part about Uncle Russell's arthritis. He doesn't want anyone to know. I think it reminds him that he's getting older and that bothers him."

He frowns. "Will people really care, though? I think arthritis is common enough, and not just for older people. My big sister has it, and she's only twenty-eight."

"Yes, but my uncle is really sensitive."

"Russell Messina is sensitive? Are we talking about the same person?"

I knew he was only joking, but I was too upset to find any humor in it. "Yes. He is. And he's very proud of the band, so you absolutely cannot tell anyone any of this. If this does turn out to be our last year, he wouldn't want people remembering it as a failure."

"I don't know. If people knew that this might be Grandeur's last year, and we told them about all the difficulties you've been working with, that would get attention. It might even help the sales."

My blood chilled. I grabbed onto his arm and held it. "You can't. Uncle Russell would hate that. He wants his success to be based on his work, not because people feel sorry for him."

"Yeah, sorry." Brandon ducked his head. "I was thinking like a consultant. I hate that my mind went there so quickly."

"Just promise me you won't tell anyone. I'm serious, Brandon. Promise me."

He lifted his gaze to meet mine. "I am not going to tell anyone. Of course not. Contrary to what you may think, I'm not a complete asshole."

No, he was someone else entirely. Someone sweet and funny and caring. Someone truly wonderful. And now that I'd noticed, I couldn't see anything else.

"I know," I said. "You're only part asshole."

Brandon's laughter started softly at first, then it grew into this giant, uninhibited force, no trace of the too-cool-to-care persona he'd crafted for the internet. With sunlit droplets of water clinging to his skin and a broad smile on his face, he'd never seemed more real, more alive. The urge to stretch over and kiss him rose like a tide in my chest, nudging me forward on a wave of gratitude and something else I wasn't ready to name.

And then it came.

A snort.

He quickly covered his mouth, effectively silenced.

I watched him for a moment. "Did you just—?"

"No."

"But I could swear I heard—"

"No, you didn't."

I stared at the stubborn set of his profile, my amusement mounting with each passing second. My cheeks hurt from trying not to smile.

Finally, he rose from the water. "Are you hungry? I'm hungry. We should go."

"Now?" I asked, making a show of reluctance. "You sure?"

"Yes." Water sloshed around his feet as he walked out.

"You don't want to wait for a bit? And just sit in this moment . . ." My laughter bubbled up. "Brandon? Brandon!"

He ignored me, heading for shore.

# EIGHTEEN

Brandon led me to the food shops. After passing a couple of them—Catherine's Bake and Shark, Tony's Bake and Shark, and Sharkie's Bake and Shark—I began to notice a pattern. I mentioned this to Brandon, and he had the nerve to pretend to be confused. But when our eyes met, he broke into laughter.

Finally, we arrived at *Liv's* Bake and Shark, and Brandon led me inside. The small restaurant appeared even busier than the others we'd passed, a long line leading to the counter; the handful of plastic tables present mostly occupied.

I tapped my chin, pretending to read the menu board. "I wonder what I should order?"

"I know you joke," Brandon said. "But for real, the shrimp and fries is the best thing on the menu."

"If I visit Maracas and not eat bake and shark, was I ever really here at all?"

"Come on, you're really going with the obvious choice? What

happened to that contrarian spirit of yours?"

I jealously eyed the open container on the table nearest to us. "She's hungry, and that shark looks good."

"Fine. I'll take the shrimp so you can at least try it. Then you'll know you're wrong."

"Oh God. This is like the gyro thing all over again."

"Which I won. Don't forget."

"Would you let me?"

The couple in front of us stepped aside, and we approached the counter. The woman on the other side frowned. "Brandon, what you doing in the line?"

"I'm not in the line, Ma. Tess is. I just happened to be standing with her. And ordering for her. One shark and one shrimp and fries, please."

"*Tess?*" Brandon's mother's eyes landed on me. Despite her bland white hairnet and matching smock, she wore a full face of expertly applied makeup—cherry red lips, false lashes, and professional-level contouring that would make Kylie Jenner sit up. She beamed at me, far more welcoming than I'd expected.

"Here's your bag." Lucy popped up from somewhere behind us. She handed me my purse. "Your phone vibrated a few times. And I think you got a call."

"Thanks," I said, but as quickly as she'd arrived, she took off. My heart sank as I remembered David's message. Somehow, I'd forgotten. I checked the screen and confirmed he had called me.

Why? What could we possibly have to say to each other?

"You didn't tell me you were bringing anyone today," Brandon's mother said to him, absentmindedly touching her hairnet. "I would've kept the good table open. Or had your food ready so you don't have to wait."

"That's okay," I said quickly.

"Ma, please." Brandon sounded exasperated. "No worries. We'll eat on the beach."

"No, no." She lifted the flap of the counter and stepped out from behind it. "Come, you can sit here." She led us over to a table for four near the door, plucked a paper napkin from a dolphin-shaped holder, and used it to dust a bit of sand from one of the seats. "Here, all good. You two sit. I'll send your food over."

"Shouldn't I pay first . . . ?" I asked, confused, and looked to Brandon for clarification. He provided no help, one hand covering his face, his mortification bleeding through his fingers.

"No, no, you're good," she said, retreating to the counter. "And call me Liv."

"Ah, thank you. Liv." Who would turn down free food? When she left, I pulled out the recently dusted chair and sat. It rocked to one side, slightly unbalanced. "Why is she being so nice to me?" I asked.

"Because you're with her son," Brandon said too quickly. "Why wouldn't she be?"

I didn't buy that for a moment. Before I could ask more, Liv returned to the table with two sets of plastic-wrapped forks. She set them down in front of us.

"Brandon," she said. "Go and check in the back. I asked your sister to replace the tamarind sauce ten minutes ago. I don't know what she's been doing. And while you're there, you can crush up some ice. A new delivery just came in."

"But, Ma, I'm not working today."

"Would you like something to drink, dear?" Liv asked me, ignoring him.

"A bottle of water would be good." If this was free, I felt weird about ordering anything more expensive.

"No problem," Liv said, then turned to her son. "Ice. Now."

Brandon sighed. In a stage whisper, he said, "I knew this would happen. I knew if we came here, she'd find something for me to do."

Liv folded her arms. "And the longer you stay here complaining, the longer it will take to get done."

Brandon huffed and followed his mother behind the counter. She stayed out front to assist a new customer, while Brandon disappeared into the small doorway in the back.

For a moment, I sat there, hands on the table, unsure what to do. Was it weird to miss Brandon's presence already?

As if on cue, my phone chimed with a message. Resigned, I finally read what David sent.

I know you don't want to talk to me.

I exhaled through gritted teeth. He said he knew and proceeded to message me anyway. Unbelievable.

It was great seeing you last weekend

I don't know if you heard my parents got divorced

This year sucked but I'm happy to be back

Damn it. I did feel a twinge of sympathy at the mention of

his parents' divorce. It must've been hard for him. In one of our many midnight phone calls, I'd shared my own suspicion that if my parents were still around, they would have gone down that road eventually.

I tapped the screen, considering my reply, when the table rattled. I looked up to see a tray of condiments set before me, Lucy sitting in the chair directly across.

"You know my name's not Lucile?" she said. "It's just Lucy. I don't know why Brandon calls me that."

"Well, your brother calls me Boop." I set the phone down. "I've just sort of accepted that a lot of the things your brother does don't make sense."

She smiled. "I like you, and not just because you're helping us. Do you play chess?"

It took me a second to process the question, she'd switched tracks so quickly. "Not often. But I can." I was about to ask why she wanted to know, when something she'd said earlier sank in. "What do you mean I'm helping you?"

"Lucile." Brandon approached us, food boxes in hand. He stood beside his sister. "Stop bothering her."

"I'm not bothering her." Lucy glanced at me as if seeking confirmation.

"She's not bothering me," I said firmly. "So far our chat has been very interesting."

"I bet," Brandon said. "Lucile, don't you have a job to finish?" He pointed toward the side counter where a guy violently shook and squeezed a condiment bottle in an attempt to extract the last dregs. "Go help him before he breaks something."

Lucy sighed with the gravity of someone forty years her senior. "All right nah." She stood and retrieved the tray. "I found out everything I need to know anyway. She can play chess, which makes her way better than your last girlfriend. Don't mess it up."

"Okay!" Brandon said. "Thank you for your input, Lucile. Now, move along."

"I going, I going." She balanced the tray on her arm and shuffled off.

Brandon set down the boxes and dropped into the empty chair. He dragged his seat closer, our knees bumping under the table. "Sorry about that," he said.

"It's fine," I said, then didn't retract my legs. We settled against each other. It was a move, subtle but risky. Careful not to stare, I assessed his reaction. To my disappointment, he didn't seem to have one.

My phone buzzed, the screen lighting up with a message notification. I snatched it off the table, worried Brandon would see it and know who it came from. Without thinking, I read it.

I miss you

All the warmth seeped out of me. How dare he?

"Tess?" Brandon sounded concerned.

Choked on fury, I couldn't answer him right away. Instead, I stabbed the power button until the screen went dark, the message out of sight. The phone shut off.

"Sorry." I sat up, retracting my leg. "It's nothing."

Brandon pushed my box closer, before opening his own. "You sure?"

"Yeah." I opened the container to reveal a stack of steaming fried fish and fresh coleslaw stuffed into a lightly toasted bake. For a second there, I'd almost forgotten what heartbreak felt like. But three words from David and it all came back. Sitting here with Brandon suddenly felt like a huge mistake.

"Are you absolutely sure?"

"*Yes, Brandon,*" I said, exasperated, but refusing to meet his eyes to assure him. Silence stretched for a bit, but I could feel him gearing up to ask again, so I changed the topic. "Lucy said something strange."

"Lucy says a lot of strange things. Ma says it's a side effect of her genius—which, to be fair, she did skip two grades, so she might be."

Two grades? "That's impressive."

"She's also a big-time chess player. Nationally ranked in the top ten." Despite his exaggerated nonchalance, his pride for his sister leaked through. "She even got invited to play in a big tournament in Grenada next year."

"She did mention chess. But it wasn't that. She said something like *even though I'm helping her*? What does she mean? And does it have anything to do with why your mother nearly threw a parade when she learned who I was?"

"Ah. So, you didn't miss that."

Finally, I looked up. "Brandon, what's going on? What did you tell them?"

Brandon cursed, and my stomach dropped. Was it so bad that he didn't want to tell me?

Then, I traced his attention to the man standing in the doorway behind me.

"Why are you taking up a table out here?" The man entered the hut, his heavy footsteps thumping against the wooden slats on the floor. He took in our table, the food, and me. His unshaven jaw clenched. "I thought you were busy with a school assignment today."

"And I thought you were running errands," Brandon muttered beneath his breath.

"What's that?" the man asked.

"I said I thought you knew I'd changed my plans. This is Tess. She's helping me with the assignment. Tess, this is my father."

Mr. Richards' lips curled into a smile—and with that small change, he transformed. His gruff demeanor retreated into the shadows of someone distractingly handsome. He could've been a movie star, and from the way he entered the room, chest first, he knew it.

"Who's this now?" Mr. Richards asked in a joking-but-not-really tone. "Not another one of your internet friends? I can't take no more of them."

Brandon's posture tensed. "No."

"Good, because the last one you brought here ordered everything on the menu and didn't want to pay. Had to explain to him we can't pay the bills with exposure."

"I told you, Pa, Travel Wizz was a huge food blogger." Brandon pinched and ripped a napkin to shreds on the table. "Sometimes his segments show up on the Food Network website. If you'd let him film, we could've been featured."

"And I told you, we don't need any exposure. We've got all the customers we need and then some." He gave Brandon a pointed look. "At the moment, the only problem we have is we're short-staffed."

At the counter, Liv rang up another order. She glanced over at us every few seconds.

Mr. Richards stopped beside our table. "So, Tess—you're the new girlfriend?"

"No," I said.

"Actually, it depends on who's asking." Brandon tried to lighten the moment. It didn't work. "It's an inside joke between me and Tess," he explained to his father.

"Of course it is," Mr. Richards said, still smiling. "Because that's your whole life, isn't it? Jokes." His cheerful tone was so discordant with his words it made the underlining bite so much sharper. "Mind you, you better get real serious about football quick-quick. Those people in Florida not letting you in their school to play around."

"Never mind it *is* a game," Brandon said.

Mr. Richards didn't seem pleased about that response and appeared to be about to make these feelings known, when Brandon's mom interrupted.

"Sammy." Liv's smock was slightly skewed in her rush to get

to us. "The last set of fries came out looking a little burned up. I think the oil in the fryer need changing."

"That's not the oil," Mr. Richards said, already moving. "That's Roxanne leaving it in too long again."

Mr. Richards's shadow retreated from the table. The second he left, Brandon's shoulders eased.

"Everything good over here?" Liv asked us. "You need anything?"

The lingering awkwardness made me hesitate to answer. In my silence, Brandon spoke up, "Yeah, we need some ketchup. And garlic sauce. And a mindwipe so we can make Tess forget she saw all that."

I gave him a small smile, wanting more than anything to reach out and take his hand.

His mother squeezed his shoulders and kissed his forehead. "My little comedian," she said softly. "Never change."

Brandon grinned, the light that dimmed upon his father's entry returning to his eyes. "You hear that, Tess. My mom thinks I'm funny."

"That would make two of you," I said.

"You see what I'm dealing with, Ma? Every day at school. No respect at all."

His mother smiled at us. "Yes. I think I do."

The drive back from the beach took twice as long because of traffic, the streets into Port of Spain congested with far more cars than they were built to allow. Somehow the radio ended up on a station with more chatter than music, not that we cared, talking right over it. The way we spoke to each other always had a game-like quality. Back and forth, the topics knocked between us like a tennis ball—a feature that remained even when we weren't arguing. In fact, I think if anyone heard us now, they wouldn't detect much of a difference.

"Broadcast journalism?" I chewed on the end of a slice of red mango. "Like what Aunty Gloria does? Why? So, you can inflict yourself on an even bigger segment of the population?"

"Yes," he said. "It would be my honor to *gift* the nation with even more opportunities to see this face."

"How generous of you."

"I know. And Aunty was nice enough to give me some advice over tea the other day. I've already applied for a course that runs over the July-August break."

Ah, so that's what they'd been discussing over tea. "You sound like you've got it all sorted."

"I know some people can make the jump straight from social to traditional media, but UWI has a pretty good journalism degree program with courses in Television and Multi-Media. I'm actually really excited about it."

"That's why you turned down the school in Florida?" I asked. "Except, it seems like your father doesn't know about that?"

"No, I haven't told him yet. I know I should, but the timing's bad." He dragged a hand through his hair. "The only way my family could afford to send me to Florida was with the football scholarship, and the only reason I kept playing was to keep Pa happy. Don't get me wrong, I get why he's so invested. His family didn't have a cent to spare when he was growing up, so even though the shop's doing well enough, he wants to make sure we never have to experience that."

"Still," I said. "It's not like professional football is the most secure job ever."

"No, but he understands it. Social media, marketing and publicity, broadcasting—none of it sounds like a real job to him." His shoulders sagged. "It's whatever. I don't really mind."

From the look of him, I didn't believe that for a second.

"But I hate when he pushes his mind-set onto Lucy. He tolerates her playing chess a little more than my *hobby*, but he still thinks it's a total waste of time. It's hard to watch him degrade the thing she loves, especially since she's so good at it."

"You're good at what you do too," I said with far too much sincerity. The second the words were out of my mouth, I wanted to curl into a ball of shy embarrassment.

"Careful, that sounded like a compliment."

"I just meant your work on the band's social media hasn't completely sucked so far. And I like that you've been documenting the year, in a way. If this does turn out to be our last year, it's nice that we'll have it to look back on."

He nodded his head. "That's one of the things I love most about posting online. It's a record of your life. I can't tell you how many memories I might've lost otherwise."

"See, I get that," I said, utterly enamored with his smile despite myself. "It's the part about putting it out there that's my problem."

He shrugged. "I don't see it as any different from hanging framed photos. Good memories aren't meant to be kept in the dark. I like to have them in the open. Easy for me to look at and remember."

"Never thought of it that way." I considered the many photos, clothes, and other belongings collecting dust in the second floor of my old house. For so long I'd kept it locked up, sure the memories would only hurt. I supposed there would be a lot of good sealed in there as well.

"What are your plans for Carnival?" he asked suddenly.

"Why?" I asked, suspicious.

"Just curious. I'll be out on the road with the band in the morning." His fingers flexed on the steering wheel. Was he nervous? He seemed nervous. "I could use a hand, if you're up for it."

"I can't. Every year, I help with the band's costume repair service." Along the parade route, Grandeur had a tent where masqueraders could stop off, take some shade, drink water, and have their costumes fixed. "We're like a pit stop crew. We identify the problem, fix it as fast as possible, then send the masqueraders back out there. FYI the solution is almost always glue. *So* much glue."

He laughed aloud, and I felt absurdly pleased. His laughter was quickly becoming one of my favorite sounds in the world.

"Does that mean you're working through the whole festival? You don't get to join in at all?"

"No time. But I'm not bothered. You know I'm not into parties anyway. Never played mas or anything."

His nose wrinkled with confusion. "What are you saying?

How is it possible that you've never played? Carnival is like half your personality."

I glowered at him, not impressed with that assessment. "The festival is a *party*."

"I hear you, but it's not computing."

"Yes, I know, I'm a bad Trinidadian. I've heard it before. But even though I love watching the festival and dressing people up so they can enjoy it, it's not for me."

"What about J'ouvert?"

"What about it?" I asked. J'ouvert was the unofficial start to the festival. The name translated to *daybreak*, but it actually started even earlier, in the dark hours of Carnival Monday morning. Some saw it as just a warmup to the main festivities, others saw it as a special event all on its own. "I've never been."

"Well, there you go. It's earlier, so you can have a little fun, a little jump up, before you join the pit crew."

"Yeah, but it's still . . ." I sighed, frustrated that he didn't seem to get it.

"I know, I know. But J'ouvert is special. To me, it feels more . . . grounded in a way. The turnout isn't as big as it is later in the day. And it's the best time to see the more traditional costumes like the blue devils and midnight robbers."

"Oh, God, I used to be so scared of them when I was younger," I said.

"Everyone is. Hell, I still am. I'm not ashamed to admit it." Brandon smiled as I laughed. He stopped the car in front of our gate, then waited as I opened it. "I think that, as someone who loves the festival as much as you do, you should try to experience J'ouvert at least once."

I shook my head. "Brandon, I already know how I feel about these kinds of events, so why bother?"

He started the car up the drive. "Because you've never tried this particular event. And, even more than that, you haven't tried it with me."

"Are you . . ." I checked to see if he was serious. That sounded like he'd intended for us to go together just for fun. But that didn't make sense. It had nothing to do with his job or the band. How far was this truce supposed to extend?

Not that I liked the idea of regressing to the way we were. After everything I'd learned about him, I didn't think I could hate him again. Maybe he felt the same?

"Am I . . . what?" he asked.

"Nothing, it's just . . ." I laughed, more than a little nervous. "You don't want me to go with you." A statement. No question. "I'm not fun. I'm the opposite of fun. I'm this big black hole, sucking up all the fun." And he was like the sun, bright and beautiful and drawing everyone into his orbit. He could pick anyone else to take with him. He *should* pick anyone else.

"That's not true." He shifted in his seat, his fingers tapping on the steering wheel. I'd noticed he fidgeted when he was nervous. I had an unbidden urge to reach out, to still him. To place my hand over his, if he'd let me. But I suspected that if I did, it would have the opposite effect, and I'd be swept into the chaos with him.

"Like I said, you've never been with me," he said. "We have fun together, I think."

He stopped the car and I barely noticed, too caught up in reading the lines of his side profile, analyzing his words. Was he saying what I thought he was saying?

I wished he'd look at me.

"You think so too?" he asked.

My entire body buzzed like a live wire. "Are we still talking about J'ouvert?"

He finally turned to face me. "Tess, I . . ." He stopped, squinting through the window behind me.

"Brandon?" Unless I was mistaken, he'd been about to say something important. The abrupt loss of his attention was jarring. "What?" I followed his gaze to David.

My ex-boyfriend.

"What's he doing here?" Brandon asked.

"I . . . don't know." He was sitting on the steps, his posture slightly tensed, but otherwise showing no indication that this wasn't normal. "He's been messaging me, but I didn't think he'd show up."

"You've been messaging him?"

"No." My irritation sparked in the face of his annoyance. "He's been messaging *me*."

Wait. Why was I explaining this to him now? What I needed to do was get David away from my house. I grabbed my bag and undid my seat belt.

"Are you getting back together with him?" Brandon asked, confused.

Oh, for heaven's sake. "Not now, Brandon." I shoved open the door. When I stepped outside, David stood. He dusted off his pants and came toward me. "What are you doing here?" I asked him.

He lifted a hand to block the glare of the blazing sun. "You weren't answering my messages. I wanted to talk to you."

"That doesn't mean you can show up at my house."

"That's what your cousin said." He had the gall to laugh. "That's why she made me wait outside. I only got here a few minutes ago. She was trying to call you."

Damn it. She might've been trying to warn me, but I'd forgotten to turn my phone back on.

Whatever. "You need to go."

"I only need a minute."

"I don't. I have nothing to say to you."

He didn't answer back immediately, his attention straying to my right. The driver's side door slammed shut. I didn't need to look to know Brandon had gotten out.

"So what?" David said. "You two really are together? A part of me wondered if it was just something you said to piss me off, but I guess not." He tapped his cheek. "Never thought Brandon Richards would have a girlfriend and not feel the need to plaster it online." His gaze slipped to me. "You don't think that means he's ashamed of you or something?"

"Wow, I forgot what a raging jackass you can be." Brandon

walked around the front of the car to stand next to me. "Why were we friends again?"

"Good question," David said. "I've been wondering the same thing since you've apparently hooked up with my ex-girlfriend."

"I'm not some toy that got traded," I said. The tension in the air had me stepping between them, just in case. "We broke up over a year ago. I can hook up with whoever I want to. It's none of your business."

"But this isn't *anyone*, is it? It's someone who was my friend. Someone who was supposed to have my back." He waved a finger between Brandon and me. "And now I'm wondering how long this has been going on."

"You're embarrassing yourself," Brandon told him. "Just go."

"I will. But first, you've got to admit the truth. You've been planning this for a while, haven't you?"

"David, please." My temples throbbed with the beginnings of a headache. "Just go."

"He's been lying to us, Tess," David said. "Did you know he wanted me to dump you? That he'd bad talk you all the time, trying to manipulate me. Trying to convince me that you were too weird. Too mean. Too boring."

Beside me, Brandon had gone very still.

I watched him from the corner of my eye. "Did you?"

Brandon shook his head. "No. Yes. But it's not . . . he's taking it out of context."

"What context?" David's face contorted with disgust. "Like the times you tried to push me toward other girls. Like, *Have you met*

225

*Kerri? Don't you think she's prettier than Tess? Sweeter? You two have
so much more in common. And at least your friends won't hate this
one."*

This time I couldn't even look at Brandon for an explanation.
It felt like a shard of ice had been shoved into my chest and I was
finding it hard to breathe around it.

"Tess, I swear it wasn't as bad as that," Brandon said, his words
a flood of alarm. "David doesn't know what he's talking about.
Yes, I said those things, but I didn't mean them."

"Exactly!" David threw his hands up like he'd won something.
"You were trying to manipulate me into breaking up with her so
you could have her for yourself."

I snorted; his conclusion seemed so unlikely it wasn't worth
considering. The only explanation had to be that Brandon meant
those things at the time, and now he felt bad about it.

I rubbed my forehead. "Brandon, you should go too."

"Tess, please don't listen to him. David doesn't know what he's
talking about."

"Yeah, I do. And now she knows it too."

"Oh, shut up," Brandon said. "I wanted you to break up with
her because you kept cheating on her. I hated watching you string
her along."

Oh my God.

Brandon cursed. "No. Tess, I didn't mean—let me explain."

But I was walking away from him, heading for the house. I
passed David in a rush, my mortification complete and painful.
"Both of you can get the hell away from me."

When I hit the steps, the front door opened. Aunty Gloria stepped out, resplendent in a dark green sari embroidered with gold. She assessed the guys with calm kohl-lined eyes, her smile a mask of ethereal beauty that barely concealed an iron core. "Tess, it's time for you to get ready. We'll be leaving soon. Say goodbye, boys."

"Tess," David tried.

"Say goodbye." Aunty Gloria's words sliced through the air, cutting off any room for negotiation.

I heard their mumbled goodbyes as I fled into the house.

Hazel caught me before I'd gotten too far. She appeared to have been caught off-guard, in the middle of dressing. Only one eye was lined, and she wore an old T-shirt over her salwar. "I'm so sorry. Mummy let him in before I got to him. I didn't know what to do without explaining everything to her, which I know you'd hate. And you weren't answering your phone—"

"Hazel, it's fine," I stopped her. Inhaling deeply, I tried to calm down, but my breath hitched on the exhale. "Okay, no. It's not."

"What—" She snapped her mouth shut at the sound of the front door closing and Aunty Gloria approaching. She tugged my wrist, and we retreated upstairs. After she shut her bedroom door, she asked, "What happened?"

"Did you know David was cheating on me?"

"While you were together?" Her eyes widened. "No way. If I had, I would've had a little talk with him about it."

I couldn't help a little bubble of laughter. From what Brandon told me about her other *talk* with David, I could only imagine the verbal assassination she'd have executed.

"Actually . . ." She glanced toward the window. "Is he still here?"

"No, your mom scared him away." The amusement that sparked in the face of Hazel's protectiveness dimmed. A hollowness took its place. "You want to know what the worst part of it is? It turns out Brandon knew all along and he never said anything."

"That's the worst part?" Hazel said, frowning. She searched my face, and after seeing whatever she saw, her brows shot up, almost disappearing into her hairline. "*Oh.*"

"Yeah."

# NINETEEN

That night, we arrived late at Aunty Seema's house, the place already packed with the members of Aunty Gloria's family, neighbors, and friends. The weatherman predicted rain, but the starry night sky held clear. The food had been set out: roti with spicy potato, pumpkin, and channa. White rice and dhal. Saheena and pholourie. Mouthwatering sweets like kurma, barfi, and parsad.

Red clay deyas had been lit. Their lights lined the front of the house and adorned the cut bamboo stalks that had been bent into large arches. Every now at then a great *crack* would cut through the night, someone setting off fireworks or bursting bamboo in the near distance.

I sat off to the side of the party, under the brim of a leafy chenette tree. Geckos chirped and yard fowls rustled among the bushes. I ate gulab jamun off a plastic plate, watching as Hazel helped her young cousins light sparklers. Aunty Seema's voice floated through the open window to the kitchen, loud and vexed.

She declared the party was too much work, and she wasn't hosting it again—as she said every year.

A scraping noise drew my attention to Aunty Gloria, who was dragging one of the white plastic chairs over. Smiling, she placed it right beside me and sat. The sequins on her sari shimmered in the night. "How are you doing over here, sweetheart?"

An ominous feeling, heavy like a weight, settled around my shoulders. I knew the scene with Brandon and David outside the house hadn't looked great, but I'd still hoped she wouldn't make me talk about it.

"You know . . ." She crossed her legs, sitting back. "For someone who claims to have no social life, it certainly looks exciting from the outside."

And there it was. I set my plate on my lap, bracing for more.

"Oh, don't set up your face. I know it's hard for you to believe, but I was young once. I experienced all manner of boy drama and heartbreak. Including the problem of having two suitors fighting over you."

Since she'd literally won the title of the most beautiful woman in the universe once, I didn't have a hard time believing that part. But our situations were different. "They weren't fighting over me," I said, then mentally corrected myself—actually, they had been in a way. David seemed to want to reestablish something. And Brandon . . .

At the thought of him, pain sliced through me.

He'd called a few times, until I messaged him to stop. I asked him to give me space and he did.

Honestly, I didn't care that Brandon insulted me behind my back. We'd said worse to each other's faces. It bothered me that he hadn't told me about David's cheating. Not back then. Not now, when we were tentatively getting along. It shattered the fragile . . . whatever we were building.

"It was nothing," I told Aunty Gloria. "Just a misunderstanding."

"Okay," she said lightly. "You don't want to talk about it. No problem. I get it." She was silent for all of two seconds, before adding, "For what it's worth, I think Brandon is a very sweet boy—"

"Aunty Gloria, please," I begged.

"—and whatever you two do or don't become in the future, it was nice to see you going out and making a new friend. You seemed happy. There. I said it. I'm done."

I highly doubted that, but I said nothing.

To my relief, a distraction came in the small form of Hazel's five-year-old cousin, Anil. He ambled over to present Aunty Gloria with a lit sparkler.

"For me?" she asked, accepting it.

Anil nodded jerkily, then ran off to rejoin the others.

Aunty Gloria held out the sparkler, offering it to me. I shook my head. She retracted her hand, worrying her lower lip with her teeth. "We have a lot in common, me and you," she said after a while.

I couldn't think of a statement less likely to be true. Not counting when she'd told me she was done with this conversation.

"Did I ever tell you about my parents?" she asked. "They passed away when I was about your age. My father about a week after my mother."

I shook my head. I knew they'd passed, of course, but I didn't know the timing was so close.

"People used to say my father died because of a broken heart. At first, I thought it was a metaphor, but it's a real thing. Very rare, but very real. The idea shook me. Why would anyone want that? To love someone that much?" The light of the sparkler expired between her fingers. "I never made some sort of concrete decision to do it, but after he passed, I did pull back from everyone in my life. Moved abroad as soon as I could. Avoided coming back to Trinidad and seeing my family, knowing all the sad memories it would dredge up. Then, I met your uncle."

A smile played on her lips, soft and full of affection. "He was another Trinidadian living in London at the time. I already knew he'd planned to move back here when we started dating, and that was actually one of the things that drew me to him. Nothing keeps a relationship from becoming too serious like thousands of miles." She laughed. "Big mistake. When he moved back here, I missed him so much. I had to come and visit. I had to see him."

Anil returned with another sparkler. He handed it to Aunty Gloria and wordlessly ran off again.

"While I was here, of course, I had to see my family. And they insisted that we show Russell all my old haunts—my old schools, the liming spots, the small corner grocery that my father owned. And, of course, the family house.

"Once we started walking through the place—it was empty

then, all my sisters moved out—I was hit with memory after memory. Making hummingbird feeders with my mother and hanging them on the front porch. Hearing the living room TV all the way upstairs because my father listened to it way too loud. The afternoons with my sisters, climbing trees and playing hide-and-seek in the orchard. And the more I relayed these memories to your uncle, the more I started to remember. So many wonderful times I'd forgotten until then."

She waved the sparkler for a bit, the spark stretching into fleeting curls in the air. "I realized I didn't want to be on my own anymore. I wanted to be here. With my family. With Russell. And I'm glad that I did. The good memories—the ones from before and the ones I've made since—they burn so much brighter than the darker ones."

"Nothing lasts forever, though," I said, as the sparkler extinguished. Even the brightest moments ended.

"Life does move on," she said, reaching over to squeeze my hand. "That's why I keep the people I love close. And I make as many good memories as I can."

Anil brought over yet another sparkler.

Aunty Gloria leaned forward to speak to her nephew. "Love, can you bring one of these for Tess as well? I think she's feeling a little left out."

Anil blinked. Then, without a word, he grasped the sparkler out of Aunty Gloria's hand and gave it to me. Aunty Gloria and I laughed as he ran off.

"Smart boy," she said. "Saved himself some time."

I stared at the sparkler in my hand. The fire moved rapidly down the length of the stick. The sulfury smell tickled my nose. "I don't think I'm ready to visit the house just yet."

"That's fine. The house will be there," she said without a trace of frustration or disappointment. "But people, on the other hand—they're fickle. They have all these soft, squishy feelings and they tend to wander off. And I know you said that it's nothing, just a misunderstanding, but I've never seen anyone look as dejected as Brandon this afternoon."

"Aunty, please," I begged again.

"I'm just saying, if he is someone you care about—even if it's just as a friend—don't keep him at a distance for too long. Sometimes I scare myself thinking about how close I came to losing your uncle that way."

"Brandon isn't . . . He doesn't . . ." I didn't know what to say. "Honestly, I have no idea what's going on."

"Well." She tapped her chin. "He took you to the beach today. In my book, beach dates are a good sign. It means he wants to spend time with you."

"No, that's not why we went there. We were actually trying to meet Dessa King. The singer. Brandon had this idea that we could try to convince a celebrity to endorse Grandeur. But we were too late. We didn't even get a chance to talk to her."

"Wait—Dessa King?" Aunty Gloria tapped my knee. "Why didn't you ask me? Did you forget that I'm also somewhat of a local celebrity?"

Oh. "Well, Aunty . . . It's not that we don't think you'd be great at promoting the band, but you're . . ."

"Older? Not cool enough? You don't have to tap dance around it."

"I was going to say you might not appeal to our target audience."

"Sure," she said dryly. "What I meant was—why didn't you tell me you were trying to contact Dessa? I could've helped you."

I sat up, almost spilling my plate. "Do you know her?"

"Yes, I did a segment with her last year for the show. She talked about the work she's been doing with the Ministry of Community Development, Culture, and the Arts. *And* she's in my meditation group, which I know I've mentioned before. This has basically confirmed that none of you listen to me."

"Uh, yeah. Of course, we—"

"Don't hurt yourself coming up with an excuse. I'll message her in the morning. See what she says."

"Thank you," I said, gratefully accepting the out she offered.

Anil returned again, but this time empty-handed. "What is it, love?" Aunty Gloria asked, when he poked her knee. He pointed over to Hazel, who'd fallen onto the dirt ground, the cousins crowded around her.

Aunty Gloria and I jumped to our feet and rushed over. Aunty Gloria arrived first. "Hazel? What happened?"

Hazel blinked up at us, eyes glossy with tears. She had one hand clutched in the other. "I got distracted." She opened her palm to show us the burn, long and red, cutting across her skin like a new lifeline.

Aunty Gloria winced in sympathy, helping Hazel to her feet. I spotted my cousin's phone face down on the ground beside her. I bent to pick it up and flipped it over. A spiderweb crack had bloomed over the glass. The lock screen still lit up when I tapped it.

We brought Hazel to the chair I'd just vacated. While Aunty Gloria went inside to see what disinfectants Aunty Seema had stocked, I returned the phone.

"Screen cracked." I held it out to her. "But it's still working."

For some reason, this made her tear up. "I don't know what happened."

"It was an accident," I said.

"Not that." She took the phone from me, grasping it in her uninjured hand. "Chris messaged me. That's why I got distracted." Her voice hitched on a sob. "I don't know what happened. But he just dumped me."

The next day, during last period, I stood in front of my classmates, a pair of wings heavy on my back, a dress two sizes too small cutting off the circulation in my arms. I'd made the deadline for my English project by the skin of my teeth.

Standing at the front of the room, I discussed the different costumes used across *Romeo and Juliet* adaptations, and how the choices reflected the sensibilities of the time and culture of those who made the films.

My original plan had been to narrate only, off to the side somewhere, operating the laptop and projector, while Hazel modeled. Now, I'd had to do both. To say I'd felt awkward was an understatement. I'd made the costume with Hazel and Juliet in mind—the layers of gauzy fabric soft and delicate, like the hearts of the naive romantics they were. But after several hours of venting and crying the night before, Hazel had woken up a mess.

"I'm so sorry," she'd choked out. "I can't go to school. If he saw me looking like this, I'd die."

So my dear, sweet cousin—the holder of a near-perfect school attendance record—stayed home. And I, in the stillest hours of the early morning, altered the fit of the costume as best, and as quickly, as I could. It hadn't been easy. Taking in a dress is no problem, making it bigger is a different matter.

Still, I'd done what I could with the time I had, rehemming through my free period and most of lunch. Amid the stress, I actually found myself having fun. It reminded me of those last days leading up to Carnival, while the mas camp buzzed with customers seeking last-minute alterations and fixes.

By sixth period, I'd gotten dressed. I'd applied face and body gems at the corner of my eyes and along my collarbones and arms. I dusted silver glitter across my cheeks. A tiara crowned my head. The feathered backpack that I wore was attached to my dress, secured and disguised under a flap of textured material. The expanse of the wings curved into a gentle arch. The result was a blend of the iconic movie costume with Trinidadian Carnival aesthetics. An adaptation of an adaptation.

To my eye, it looked better than I'd expected, though every breath was a struggle in the not-made-for-me bodice. I was not meant to be Juliet, the role of the innocent lover not mine. And yet there I was, dressed as the winged messenger of heaven, reciting memorized quotes and trying very hard not to look at the boy who brought the abstract lines of Elizabethan English new meaning.

Finally, I got to the end of my presentation. Sister Thompson turned off the projector and flipped the lights back on. I lowered my cue cards, weak with relief that it was over.

"Questions?" Sister Thompson asked the class.

Kate raised her hand. When Sister Thompson called on her, she asked, "Did you really make that costume?"

"Yes," I said.

"And your uncle didn't help you?"

"No."

Sister Thompson sighed. "That wasn't quite what I meant. But thank you, Kate. Anyone else?"

"So, when we were working on the presentation as a group," Kate said, "you didn't feel the need to mention you could do this, instead of acting like a deadweight the whole time?"

"Okay, that's enough." Sister Thompson pinched the bridge of her nose. "Any questions about the content of the presentation and how it relates to the adaptation process?"

Kate continued to glare at me but said nothing more. Silence reigned in the classroom, for which I was grateful. I started to pack up, retrieving my USB from the laptop.

"Anyone?" Sister Thompson asked again.

The school bell rang, announcing the end of the day.

"Yeah, fine. You're dismissed." Sister Thompson reached for the laptop and disconnected the projector. Behind us, the light on the whiteboard disappeared. "Good work, Tess. You really impressed me today."

"Thanks," I said, not really listening.

"I was a little concerned when I removed you from the group, but you've shown an excellent grasp of the purpose of the project."

"Yeah, that's . . ."

At the back of the room, Chris slipped out the door. The coward. He'd been dodging me all day, and it looked like I was about to lose him again. He had to be out of his mind if he thought I'd give up. No one broke up with my cousin out of nowhere—without any reason—and got away with it.

"Excuse me, Sister," I said, then charged after him, my wings whacking a few classmates on my way out the door, the anger that had simmered in my gut for the last eighteen hours ready to boil over.

"Hey!" I called out, catching up to him. "Chris! Don't run away from me."

Chris turned around, Kate and Brandon beside him. "I'm not running away."

"You sure about that?" I marched right up to him, my wings fluttering a little with the momentum. "Because only a coward would break up with someone over a text message and give no explanation."

"What?" Brandon sidestepped away from them.

I pointed in Chris's face. "The very least you could do is have the decency to talk to her. Tell her what happened. And I don't mean over the phone. I mean in person."

As classrooms emptied, more students gathered to watch the show.

"Leave it, Tess." Chris's nostrils flared. "Hazel and I both know what she did." He glanced over to Brandon. "Help me nah, man?"

"Why?" Brandon answered. "She seems to be handling it pretty well on her own."

Chris shook his head, a wry smile on his lips. "So, Hazel was right. Something is going on between you two. After all the grief you gave me about getting too serious too quickly, you turn on me for a girl you just got with? You're a total hypocrite."

"You *do* fall in love too quickly," Brandon said. "And I'm not sure what you expect me to say here. It sounds like you're wrong."

"So, you're just going to stand there and listen?"

Brandon shrugged. "Yeah. Why not? I've got some time."

"Brandon, stop it," I said. This was my time to have a say. They could chitchat later. "Do you know where my cousin is right now?" I asked Chris. "She's at home, crying. Heartbroken. I don't think you understand how devastated she was when she got your message. It shocked her so bad, she got distracted and burned herself."

"Is she—" Chris's mask fell for a second, before he threw it back up. "That's not my fault. Whatever is wrong with your cousin, she's not heartbroken. I can promise you that."

"And I can promise you that whatever you think Hazel did, you're wrong. She's one of the only genuinely good people in this world full of assholes. And when you realize that and come to your senses, you're going to regret treating her like this."

"I highly doubt it," he said, and then had the gall to storm off before I could.

I stood there, breathing hard, fists clenched, trying to suppress the urge to go after him. Brandon stayed, even as the rest of the gathered students dispersed. I made the mistake of glancing over at him. Our eyes met.

"Is—"

He didn't get any further than that before I spun around and stormed off, making sure to whack him with my wing as I did.

Unfortunately, he followed me back to the classroom. I ignored him, stuffing the rest of my belongings into my backpack.

"Tess," he said softly. Carefully.

I braced myself, expecting some plea to talk. An appeal to please listen to him.

"Is Hazel okay?" he said.

I stopped to look at him. Unbelievable. I hated him for lying to me and adored him for asking after my cousin. How could one person inspire so much feeling?

"You said she got burned." His brow furrowed. "Is it bad?"

"No, she's fine." I leaned against the front of my desk. "It was just a small sparkler-related accident."

"Good. That's good." He shoved his hands into his pockets, shuffling his feet. "Sorry, I know you don't want to talk right now."

"I really don't. Not unless you're here to tell me why your friend dumped my cousin via text? Because that's the only thing I'm willing to hear from you right now."

"The only thing?"

"Yes."

"Not even if I wanted to tell you that I'm an idiot? That I should've told you about David's cheating?"

"Yes," I said.

"That, even though I did try to warn you away from him, and you told me to stay out of your business, I could have—*should have*—tried harder?"

"Especially that." I folded my arms, refusing to let go of my anger so easily. It didn't matter that he had a point. That if he had told me anything bad about David back then, I probably wouldn't have believed him. If anything, I would've clung to David harder.

"Okay." He leaned against the teacher's desk. His posture mirrored mine. "What if I wanted to tell you that you're amazing? That watching you tear into Chris—tear into someone who is not me, for once—was surreal? You looked like an avenging angel, brutal and gorgeous, and I don't think I've ever seen anything hotter in my life."

"That too," I said, though my voice was softer. Not unaffected. But Brandon was a good talker, charming even under pressure. I had to remember that.

Brandon bit his lip and nodded. "Believe me, Tess, I don't know what's going on with Chris, and I doubt he'll tell me now. He thinks I've been . . . compromised by our association."

"Are you?"

He shrugged. "The fact that I'm here means something."

It probably did. And as confusing as it was to skirt around any outright admissions, I appreciated his restraint. I couldn't deal with anything more right then. Not when my cousin sat at home, crying. Not when I still couldn't handle all these feelings.

"How do I know you're telling the truth?" I asked. "You could be covering for a friend again. And I swear to God, if you are—" I unfolded my arms, the move reminding me of my costume. Standing there, dressed like this—it suddenly struck me as unbearably ridiculous. "Honestly, I can't be serious with this thing on."

I reached back to undo the flap that released the backpack, but I snagged my hair on my armband instead. I hissed in pain.

"Wait, let me look." Brandon came over and stood behind me, a warm, solid presence. "Hold on." With careful, light touches, he undid whatever went wrong back there, releasing my arm.

I dropped my hand. "Looks like I found a flaw in the design."

"No, I don't think so," he said, releasing the flap. The backpack dropped a little as he freed it. "It just means that you need a little help taking it off."

I watched him over my shoulder. His hands were gentle as he helped me slip the straps off. My breath quickened, my skin prickling with awareness of every move he made. When he lifted the backpack, his hands brushed against my bare arms, the touch setting off sparks that lingered.

"There." He set it on the desk next to us. "Better?"

A little lightheaded, I didn't answer.

He misread my silence, his expression melting into something guilty and contrite. "I swear, Tess, I really don't know what's going on with Chris. And I'm not saying that out of loyalty or whatever. He hasn't told me."

"But you can find out."

"And then you'll be willing to talk to me?"

"I don't know. Maybe." Or maybe we could just stay like this; my will to hold on to my anger was already slipping. I wanted nothing more than to fall into him. His voice, his smell, his warmth pulled at me like a current, drawing me closer.

The same moment I leaned in, he stepped back, his face set with resolution. He nodded. "If that's what it takes, then I'll find out."

He started to leave, and I realized he meant right now.

"Brandon, wait."

He returned to my side, his expression hopeful.

I swallowed, clearing my throat. "Did Melissa call you today?"

"No. About what?"

She must've been waiting until school was over. "We got in contact with Dessa. She's going to be visiting the mas camp on Saturday morning."

His eyes widened. "For real? The director actually came through?"

"No. It was actually Aunty Gloria. She knows Dessa, apparently. I don't know why I didn't think to ask her earlier. I suppose that's what I get for underestimating Gloria Messina."

"Wow. I'm glad it worked out."

So was I. Even though Aunty Gloria had admitted that Dessa

sounded skeptical about the collaboration over the phone.

"You'll be there on Saturday, right?" Despite my complicated feelings about him at the moment, one thing I knew with absolute certainty was that Grandeur needed him. He might be the only one who could talk Dessa into endorsing us.

"Of course," he said, then waited. When a few beats of silence passed, he asked, "Was that it?"

I nodded.

He didn't hide his disappointment well. Then again, I doubted my attempt to do the same was any better.

# TWENTY

I checked the time on my phone again. Despite my attempts to freeze the numbers with my mind, the minutes kept ticking away. Dessa was late, Brandon wasn't here yet, and Aunty Gloria kept fiddling with the refreshment spread she'd prepared and set out on the receptionist's desk.

"I hope she comes soon." Aunty Gloria removed the kettle to reheat the water yet again. "I don't like that the breadfruit fritters are sitting out here like this, getting cold in the air-conditioning. Unlike the guava tarts, they do not hold up to reheating."

We'd all gathered in the lobby to wait. Our tiny welcome team was composed of my aunt and uncle, Melissa, Morris, and I. Hazel had also tagged along, her parents readily granting her request to accompany us. The chance to meet her favorite soca singer had been the first thing to lure her out of the house in days.

The rest of the staff and volunteers were given the morning off to avoid commotion and distractions while Dessa visited.

"Stop fussing, Gloria," Uncle Russell said, as she returned with the reheated water. He'd been scowling, stiffly sitting on the plum-colored couch since we'd arrived. He seemed determined to be as sullen and unhelpful as possible. "I do not see why you're going through so much trouble for someone who doesn't respect us enough to show up on time."

Morris—who sat behind the receptionist's desk, altering a costume with a needle and thread—grunted his agreement.

Aunty Gloria set the hot water down, alongside the rest of the tea set. "I told you Dessa said she'd try to come around nine. I'm sure she's very busy."

"And we're not?" His perpetually dry tone took on an edge. "Do you have any idea how much work we still have to do? And here we are, pausing operations for a full morning, just for her."

I winced, hating it when they fought. It rarely happened, the both of them usually so in sync. But in these rare times they fell out, it reminded me of my parents. And while I knew, rationally, Aunty and Uncle were not them, I still got hit with the same suffocating, panicked feeling that everything was unraveling.

I glanced at Melissa, hoping that she might intervene. Melissa didn't notice, smiling at whatever she was reading on her phone. Since the new boyfriend had appeared on the scene, she'd been relentlessly cheerful, even in the face of the band's continued problems.

I switched my attention to Hazel, seeking assistance from my cousin instead. She wasn't listening, earbuds in, her gaze glassy and distant. I was beginning to feel very alone.

I shot off another text to Brandon. The message sat in our chat, the last dozen or so all sent from me. None of them had been answered.

"Dessa is coming here as a favor to me." Aunty Gloria enunciated the words with needle-point sharpness. "She didn't have to, but she agreed. It wouldn't hurt you to show at least a little appreciation that she's showing up at all."

"Appreciation?" Uncle Russell asked. "Why? For this waste of time? We know she's not going to agree. And, frankly, I do not care if she does. We do not need some flash in the pan singer to promote my band."

"Do you have any idea how popular she is? Dessa is not a flash in the pan. She's been around for years. Just because you have no concept of the world beyond Grandeur doesn't mean it doesn't exist."

"This is ridiculous. People beg to wear my costumes. I do not beg them."

I couldn't listen to them anymore. Their acerbic tones made my skin crawl. I left the room, not even sure they noticed. The second I stepped outside, I started to breathe easier. The sun's glare refracted off the cars in the lot, prompting me to turn away.

Before I could pull up Brandon's number again, my screen lit up with an incoming call. In my rush to answer, I almost fumbled the phone right out of my hands.

"Brandon?" I answered in a rush of breath. "Where are you? Are you close?"

"Tess, I'm so sorry. I'm not going to make it this morning."

My stomach dropped. "What?" He couldn't do this to me. Not now.

"I'm so, so sorry," he said, his voice muffled by the rushing in my ears. "A family thing came up last night. I'd hoped I could still get to the mas camp if I left early this morning, but there's been a landslide."

I glanced toward the street that led to the mas camp, as if I could possibly see the evidence of this from here. "How far away are you? Dessa is late too. Maybe you could still—"

"It's blocking the whole road. I'm not going anywhere for a while."

"Oh."

"Yeah."

I leaned against the wall. My back warmed from the heat baked into the concrete.

He exhaled loudly. "I really am sorry."

What were we supposed to do now?

We'd been counting on him to guide us through this meeting. I didn't know Dessa personally, and while Aunty Gloria did, she didn't know anything about Grandeur. Brandon was supposed to bridge that gap, but without him here, it would be left open.

"What was the family thing?" I asked. "I hope everyone's okay."

"Yeah, it's just . . . you remember that chess competition in Grenada?"

"The one Lucy got invited to? Yes."

"Yesterday, my father found out that her club isn't sponsoring the trip. He forbade her from going. Lucy was upset and it was a

249

huge mess. I couldn't leave her and Mom to deal with it on their own. And then I . . . and then I told him I turned down the scholarship."

"Oh my God."

"Yeah." He barked out a sharp, dry laugh. "Pa didn't take it well. He's still not totally on board, but we did talk about it. For a while. It went on through the night, until it got too late to drive back. I really thought I could make it to Port of Spain this morning."

"I understand." It sounded like he'd really needed to be there.

"You were right. I love what I do and I'm good at it. But . . . I think the reason I held back on telling him wasn't because he'd be angry. It was because I thought he'd think less of me. I feel better now that I've been honest with him. Obviously, I couldn't keep hiding it forever."

"That's great," I said, happy for him.

A dark black car turned onto the property and paused at the security booth. The guard leaned out of the window to talk to them, pointing toward our end of the building.

"Sorry, I have to go," I said. "I really am glad that you and your father talked, but I think Dessa is here. Let's hope I don't completely mess this up. Or, at the very least, not insult her in the first five minutes."

"Relax. You've got this."

I laughed. "I really don't think I do."

"Yes, you do. You'll be fine. If you could convince me to see what's so special about the band, I have no doubt that you can do the same with her."

"That's nice to hear. Except I'm not exactly sure how I did that."

"Well, your binder helped a little. But what sealed it was the way you talked about Grandeur. You love making costumes, Tess, and that comes through. Just show her that passion. Talk to her honestly and you'll get her endorsement. You'll get her the same way you got me."

I smiled despite myself. "That was the nicest thing you've ever said to me." Probably the nicest thing *anyone* has ever said to me. I clutched the phone to my ear, wishing more than ever he were here.

The black car reversed into an open parking spot.

"Brandon, I don't think—"

"Then don't think," he said. "Drop the sarcasm and the indifference and be yourself. It'll work out."

"How dare you." I laughed despite my nerves. It felt like pterodactyls were performing aerial gymnastics in my stomach. "Sarcasm and indifference *are* my whole personality."

"Good point," he said. "Shoot, sorry, I've got to go. You'll be fine, Tess."

He hung up before I could ask more. Time was up anyway. The doors of the black car opened.


"Absolutely stunning," Dessa said. She'd been circling the mannequin wearing the frontline version of the blue heron costume for a full minute. "Look at it."

"I'm looking," Ken said. The tall, muscle-bound man had been introduced with no last name or title. For all we knew, he could've been her partner or a bodyguard. Or an overly invested accountant. "It's very pretty."

"Not just pretty," she said, precariously balancing the teacup in one hand while excitedly gesticulating with the other. "Stunning."

"It's our most popular costume this year." Uncle Russell stood beside the door, his arms folded. "Very in demand."

"I can see why." Dessa paused to sip her cocoa tea. She'd changed her hair from the auburn waves she'd worn on Maracas to long pink braids.

Apart from the fact that she was slightly shorter than I expected, Dessa seemed the same in real life as she appeared in the media. Not that I'd gotten over the strangeness of seeing her in person— of watching someone I'd only known through a screen moving through a familiar space. Every now and then, I'd be taken aback because she'd spoken directly to me—and with me—rather than to some interviewer off-screen.

"I mean, look at the detail," she said. "The different shades of silver and blue."

"If that's the costume you're interested in," Uncle Russell said, "I advise you to put in the order now, before we're out of stock. If they sell out, that's it."

Aunty Gloria laughed nervously. "I'm sure we can afford to set aside a costume for Dessa," she told him. "Give her a chance to make up her mind."

Uncle Russell said nothing.

An awkward silence fell. Dessa continued to browse the various costumes set out, and I wished for the hundredth time that Brandon was there. He would know exactly what to say to fill the dead air that permeated the room.

I shot Aunty Gloria a desperate, pleading look. She and I had done our best to soften Uncle Russell's antagonism, but he seemed determined to remain uncooperative the whole time.

"Dessa, could you use a freshening up?" Aunty Gloria asked, lifting her own teacup. "I know I could."

"Thanks," she told Gloria. "I'd love one."

"Russell." Aunty Gloria took the cup from her. "Come help me in the kitchen."

"Why do you—"

"Now, please," she said, a thread of steel laced through her words.

"Of course." He relented and stood up to follow her. "Please excuse us."

When they were gone, Dessa continued to peruse the displayed costumes. At some point, Melissa left to take a phone call. Ken and Morris sat at one of the cleared workstations, lightly chatting and devouring the breadfruit fritters. Hazel slumped in a chair in the corner, drowning in her oversized hoodie. After the initial excitement of meeting Dessa, she seemed to have drifted again.

Perhaps asking the staff to stay away had been a mistake. The mas camp felt lifeless, a hollow shell of itself. If Dessa had seen it in action, alive with all its moving parts and people, and felt that energy of everyone working together to produce something they loved, she wouldn't need convincing.

As I'd feared, it seemed to come down to me.

Lord, help us.

"So," I said, approaching her. "What do you think?"

"I think the costumes are stunning." She returned to the blue heron again. "This one in particular. I would absolutely love to wear this on the road come Carnival morning."

My heart lifted. "Really?"

"Yes. Unfortunately, I don't think I can endorse the band."

As quickly as my spirits rose, they plummeted again. "Can I ask why?"

She glanced over her shoulder, then dropped her voice. "It's not that I don't like the costumes—like I said, they're fabulous. Very much living up to Grandeur's reputation for quality."

"But?" I prompted.

"It's your uncle. Clearly, he doesn't want me here."

Damn it. So she had noticed. Not that I didn't think she would, but for a second there, I'd hoped the allure of the costumes might've enticed her to overlook it.

"I've been a fan of his for years," Dessa said. "My grandmother had his coffee table book. Every time I stayed with her, I'd spend hours looking through it, admiring the pictures, reading about his life. He's very talented. However, that doesn't excuse rudeness. In my business, I've met so many arrogant men who acted like they knew everything. Like they're above everyone. And I'm disappointed to learn that Russell Messina is one of them."

"My uncle's not . . ." I started, then stopped.

Not what? Arrogant? Could I really get away with such a bald-faced lie?

*Talk to her honestly*, Brandon had said.

So much easier said than done.

"I'm not going to tell you my uncle's not arrogant. You're right—he's been awful today. And I'm not going to make any apologies on his behalf. But I can offer you an explanation, if you're interested."

"Go on," she said. "I'm listening."

"My uncle's been under a lot of pressure. The band's . . ." I exhaled slowly. "We're going through a rough patch. There's a chance this might be our last year."

"Really?" she said, surprised. "What happened?"

With a wave of my hand, I led her to the nearest workstation. After we sat, I told her what had been happening. I started with the rivalry with Royalty, moved on to the messy launch events, and how we'd failed to recruit Jenni.

I couldn't believe I was saying any of this. After spending the previous hour talking up Grandeur, trying to impress her, here I was, airing out a large chunk of our dirty laundry, hoping for the best.

"So, you see," I said, "we really need your endorsement. Otherwise, this might be it."

Dessa frowned. "I'm sorry to hear that. Grandeur has been around for ages."

"Yeah. Uh . . . could you not tell anyone what I've just said? My uncle wouldn't want it getting out."

"Of course. I think I understand some of what he's feeling now. My career started when I was a child, and nearly ended by the time I was a teenager. I'd peaked at sixteen, all the plans I had for my future disappearing. The only thing I'd ever wanted to do was sing. Without that, who was I? That loss was a hard, very lonely feeling to deal with."

My heart clenched with sympathy. "I'd feel the same way if Grandeur closes. All I've ever wanted to do is work for the company like my uncle—like my mom. Just thinking about it scares me. I can't imagine what it was like for you living through it."

"But that's the thing, babes—I wasn't done, was I?" She tapped the table. "I'm still singing and loving it more than anything. And in the gap years, I discovered a love for marine biology. I'm in the middle of studying for a degree right now."

"Really?" I asked, surprised. "Like fish?"

She laughed. "I'm just saying, it wasn't time wasted. Maybe that'll work out for you. Maybe the band will stick around and you'll be a designer, and it'll be everything you've ever wanted. Or maybe you'll discover other passions you want to explore. I mean, even your uncle hasn't been making Carnival costumes his whole life, right? For a few years, wasn't he working in the theater instead?"

"Yeah, he was," I said, surprised she'd brought it up.

She winked. "Learned that from the coffee table book."

I laughed. "I'm impressed. Not a lot of people know that."

"I'm surprised they can't tell. His designs have a certain

256

theatricality to them. I love that he uses stories to guide the concepts each year. Actually, I don't think y'all told me about the story for the theme this year."

"You . . . want to hear it?"

"Yes, of course," Dessa said.

"Okay . . ." I hesitated at first, thinking about Jenni's disinterest when I'd tried to tell her. "Well, this year's theme is based on a bedtime story my grandmother passed on to my uncle. It's about a Trinidadian fisherman who loses his lover. After learning that Tobagonian mermaids will trade his human heart for immortality, he tries to sail there. But a hurricane hit and he's blown way off course. On his trip back, he embarks on an odyssey-type adventure, encountering various animals and mythical monsters. By the time he finally reaches Tobago, his heart is healed, and he changes his mind. Living forever without love no longer appeals to him."

"Lovely," Dessa said.

"Yes, but unfortunately, the realization comes too late. The mermaid he's been seeking steals his heart anyway."

Dessa frowned. "That's a bit depressing."

"It depends on how you look at it," Hazel said. She was sitting up, watching us. Apparently, even now, she couldn't resist a story. "They say that the mermaid stole his heart. I've always chosen to interpret it metaphorically. He just fell in love again."

Of course, she'd see it that way. "Hazel's a romance writer," I explained. "She loves love."

"So do I." Dessa smiled at Hazel. "That's a clever way of looking at it. It's hopeful. I like that."

"My apologies for making you wait," Uncle Russell said, reentering the room.

Aunty Gloria hurried in behind him, throwing me an apologetic look. It wasn't necessary. Frankly, I had no idea how she'd kept him away as long as she had.

"That's fine." Dessa rose from her seat. "We're done here."

Uncle Russell lifted a brow. "I see. I'm sorry we couldn't be more helpful."

Dessa smiled. "On the contrary, I found both of your girls very helpful and very convincing."

My hand flew to my throat. "You'll do it?"

"Yes."

I jumped to my feet. "That's . . . I can't even express how . . . We'll organize a photo shoot as soon as possible. Let us know when you're available, and we'll schedule a fitting for your costume."

"All that's fine." Dessa laughed. "But there is one thing, though. A suggestion I'd like to make."

"Go on," Uncle Russell said in a wary tone. He folded his arms, apparently ready to refuse.

"I was thinking, in addition to a photo shoot, we'd do something a little extra. I don't know if you heard, but I've been filming a new music video . . ."

# TWENTY-ONE

A week later, the new Grandeur website had gone live. Dessa King had posted teasers for her new music video, her blue heron costume prominently featured in every promotional clip. To celebrate, we hosted a premiere party at the house and invited all the staff, volunteers, and friends. The living room had been decorated with fairy lights and tables laden with food and drinks. It almost felt like a redo of the launch party.

On my way downstairs, I stopped off in my cousin's room. Hazel sat on the edge of her bed, lacing up a pair of white Converse. When I nudged the door open more, she sat up to reveal a plain green hoodie, the sleeves bunched up on her arms. Her curly hair had been brushed into a tight ponytail.

"Go on." She held out her hands. "Get your worst out. I know I'm underdressed and boring."

"No, you look great." And she did. A few days ago, she'd been doing a scarily accurate impression of a pile of dirty laundry. Today, she was clean and combed. And she looked like herself.

Getting to this point hadn't been easy. Last Monday, she'd returned to school. For the first few days, Chris wouldn't talk to her at all, and if he did it was only in the most caustic tone. Despite this, Hazel reached out to him multiple times, but after repeated brush-offs, she'd taken to avoiding him as well.

My interactions with Brandon had also been limited. He seemed to be taking my request to delay any deeper conversations very seriously, determined to discover Chris's reasons for dumping my cousin. This meant when we spoke, we only spoke about the band, and every time the tension between us would thicken, leaving me breathless and frustrated.

Then yesterday, everything flipped.

After school, Brandon caught me on my way out the gate. He led me around the back of the maintenance shed, to a spot known to provide enough privacy for hookups—or at least the illusion of privacy, seeing as everyone knew about it. I'd been curious to see if it proved to be a more secure spot than under the flamboyant tree.

When we stopped and faced each other, I took him in, and my mind slid right into the gutter. I didn't even try to stop it. Obviously, I couldn't roll back my own ultimatum. But if he kissed me, I'd let him.

"I've got what you want," he said.

My mind, from the gutter, chimed in, *Yeah, he does.*

Unfortunately, Brandon's thoughts lay elsewhere. "Chris still refuses to give me a straight answer, so I decided to try another tactic. Lord knows he can't resist talking about his feelings to *someone*. For months, I'd been hearing nothing but how smart and pretty and perfect Hazel is."

"Uh-huh," I said, only half-listening, the other half of my brain preoccupied with trying to work out what made his face so appealing.

"I decided to ask around," he said. "Like what I did at Royalty, except this time I was a little more careful."

"Sounds good." Was it the angle of his jaw? The lush curve of his lower lip?

"Are you listening to me?" he asked.

"Yes."

"My eyes are up here."

I lifted my focus off his lips. "Yes."

"Normally, I wouldn't have a problem with wherever your mind just went, but I need you to listen to me. This is important." He held my shoulders. "Chris dumped Hazel because she cheated on him."

He might as well have doused me with ice water.

"What?" I asked, my voice so loud that it echoed.

Actually, no. Not an echo. Someone had said it with me.

Hazel gaped at us from a few feet away. Her hand with the bandage pressed against the water-stained wood of the shed.

"He thinks I did what?" she said.

I stepped away from Brandon. "Hazel? Were you looking for me?"

"Yeah. And it wasn't hard to find you. Literally, everyone in the parking lot is talking about how you two snuck over here to make out."

I wrinkled my nose. "Ugh."

"Hey." Brandon sounded offended. "You should be so lucky."

I really should be. Would love to be. "Not that. I don't like that people are talking about us."

Our schoolmates had worked out that I was the secret girlfriend from the photo. During my confrontation with Chris, he'd given it away, something I hadn't noticed at the time, but became apparent later.

For some reason, after publicly professing a profound hatred for each other over the course of several years, the idea that Brandon and I were now dating raised some eyebrows.

"Tess, you do know if we . . ." He fumbled for words, but I got exactly what he meant. "If we—you know—some people are going to pay attention."

Honestly, I hadn't really thought about it. Now that I was, I couldn't say I liked the idea.

"Excuse me." Hazel reminded us of the main problem at hand. "Why does Chris think I cheated on him?"

Brandon glanced at me, seeking assistance.

"Go on. After you told me, I planned to tell her anyway."

He sighed. "Kate said that she saw you kissing some guy in your car. It was in the MovieTowne parking lot last week. She even took a photo of your car and sent it to Chris to confirm."

"That can't be true," Hazel said. "I didn't cheat. And I haven't even been to MovieTowne in ages."

Brandon winced. "Kate sounded convinced. And it was your car, Hazel. I've seen the photo. I can show it to you." He pulled up the picture on his phone and handed it to us.

It was Hazel's car. Same license plate number and everything.

For a second, my world flipped. Could it be true? Hazel, the only person I trusted totally, seemed to have been caught in a huge lie. Outed as a cheater.

Hazel's brow pinched. "I don't understand."

I didn't either. My stomach plummeted in a sick, swooping feeling. I'd defended her in front of everyone. Believed her so completely, I never questioned it. But here was proof. I didn't know how to handle it.

Suddenly, Hazel's posture straightened. She snatched her hand from the wall, a look of profound calm falling over her face like a veil. "Melissa."

Without another word, she left us.

In her absence, the truth swept in like a cool breeze. "Wait," I said, reaching out to grab Brandon's arm. "Melissa borrowed Hazel's car a few times while hers got fixed. What Kate saw was probably Melissa and her boyfriend."

"You sure?" Brandon asked. "She and Melissa do not look alike."

"Melissa and Hazel have similar skin tones and long black hair. If someone saw Melissa through tinted car windows, a mistake could happen."

We stared at each other, silent, shocked.

Brandon pointed his thumb in the direction Hazel disappeared.

"Right now, you don't think she's . . ."

Oh. "Yes. Definitely."

We took off, hurrying around the side of the building. I ignored the sneaky and not-so-sneaky looks from the other students, and searched for Hazel or Chris, sure if I found one, I'd find the other. Brandon spotted them first. Hazel had been crossing the parking lot, heading right toward Chris and his friends. The group crowded around a single phone. With their attention otherwise occupied, they did not see her coming.

Honestly, I expected the worst. Not that I would've minded watching Hazel eviscerate him, but I was worried about what he might say to her in turn. She'd been a dark cloud the past few days, floating through rooms, gloomy, and constantly on the edge of waterworks. I missed my cousin, and I was nervous that another slight from him would push her even further away.

But as we approached, Hazel and Chris had stepped aside to speak. The scene was much less public and way less dramatic than I'd expected. Later, when I'd asked Hazel about it, she'd admitted that she didn't want to make a spectacle. "Don't get me wrong, I still live for angst in books," she'd said. "But in real life, it's not as hot as I thought it would be."

By the time we got to Hazel and Chris, they were already arguing, voices low, words dripping with muddled hurt and accusation.

"How do I know Melissa wouldn't lie for you?" Chris said. "She does work for your father." His body half-turned away from her, as if on the edge of leaving. "I'd been suspicious long before Kate said anything. From the second we got together I had the feeling you were hiding something."

Hazel blinked rapidly. "What do you mean? I'm not—"

"Yes, you have. Sometimes, when you're on your phone, you hide your screen from me. I got a glimpse of it once, and it looked like a love note to someone named Heathcliff. At the time, I brushed it off, thinking I must've read it wrong."

"Heathcliff?" Brandon whispered to me, his shoulder brushing mine. "Who's that?"

"Hazel's star-crossed lover," I said, and sighed.

What a mess.

"I've been through this before," Chris said. "I ignored all the signs with Nora. But not this time. I know everyone thinks I'm dense. They think that they can play me for a fool, and I'm tired of it."

"I have never thought you were a fool," Hazel said. "Not once. That's why I'm so mad right now. You should know better. You should know *me* better." Her eyes widened, a look of horror slipping in. "But, of course, you couldn't."

"What?" Chris said.

Hazel ignored him for the moment, shrugging off her backpack. She unzipped it and pulled out her pink, battered, spiral-bound notebook.

"You were wrong. But you couldn't know that. I have been hiding things from you." She handed the notebook to him. "The entire time we've been together, I've been so worried about you comparing me to your ex-girlfriend. In a way, I guess, you kind of did."

He gingerly held the notebook, as if afraid it would explode on him. "What's this?"

"Proof," she said. "It's Heathcliff's and Julie's story." Her lips twisted into a self-deprecating smile. "Tess isn't the romance writer in the family. I am. After you made it clear you thought the books were silly, I was embarrassed to tell you."

Chris stared down at the notebook cover. "If you'd told me—"

"You still would've thought it was silly. Which really isn't fair, since you've never even tried reading one." She broke off, exhaling through her mounting irritation. "What you saw was me writing notes for a scene on my phone."

Chris's frown slackened, speechless.

Hazel zipped up her bag and slung it over her shoulder. "And I do think you should go ahead and ask Melissa to confirm. Not for me, or the sake of us, but for you. You should know not everyone thinks you're a fool. I did truly care about you." To me, she said, "I'm at the car when you're ready."

When Hazel walked off, Chris slumped backward. He stared after her for a moment before flipping the notebook open to the first page.

"I should go with her," I told Brandon.

"I thought . . . we could talk?"

"I know. But Hazel . . ." Once again, bad timing.

He nodded. "Later, then?"

"At the party. You'll be there, right?"

"I won't miss it."

"Last time you said that you missed Dessa's visit to the camp."

I'd only been teasing, but he shrank back a little. Worried that I'd come off too combative when—for once—that wasn't my intention, I tugged on the end of his shirt.

"Thank you." I looked him right in the eye, showing him I meant it. I had the impulse to kiss him. On his lips. No—on his cheek. No, that was too much. Or was it? While second-guessing myself, the moment came and passed, and once again I was left frustrated.

Now the music video premiere party had started. More than half the guests had already arrived by the time Hazel and I joined them downstairs. I greeted the familiar faces, searching for one in particular, anticipation pooling like warm honey in my stomach.

The air buzzed with conversation and laughter and music. Since Dessa's first Instagram post about the band, sales had risen beyond our wildest expectations. Because of the increased demand, my uncle had allowed me to come back to the mas camp for the upcoming three weeks of the Christmas holiday. Buoyed by relief, I'd been walking on air for days. Even the staff and volunteers seemed to have been bitten by a bug of excitement, even more invested in making this year our best ever.

For the first time in a long time, everything felt right.

A little distracted, I got roped into a conversation with Aunty Gloria and an elderly man that I'd never met before. He had a square head and freckles across his nose. His bony fingers wrapped around a cane that he thumped against the floor to emphasize his points—and he seemed to think he was making a lot of them.

"This must be Beatrice," the elderly man said.

The use of my legal name derailed my search, pulling my attention.

"She prefers Tess, Bobby," Aunty Gloria corrected him, bless her. "She doesn't like Beatrice. I think the young people these days find it old-fashioned."

Bobby huffed. "Nothing wrong with Beatrice. It's a strong, sophisticated name. My great-aunt's name was Beatrice."

"And your great-aunt was old." Uncle Russell slid into the spot beside his wife. He sipped from a glass of whiskey. "Not your best argument."

Bobby shook his head, smiling. "Russell, I was just telling Gloria how your niece looks exactly like her mother."

I blinked, surprised by the mention of either of my parents, who hardly came up in casual conversation with strangers anymore.

"It's your smile," he said. "When you light up, it's her in print."

Oh. I didn't even realize I'd been smiling just then. "Thank you."

"She was a gorgeous woman," Bobby went on. "Turned every head from Toco to Cedros. Smart too. Is a shame she passed before she got Trix up and running. I think she really had something there."

"What's Trix?" I asked, the name tickling some long-forgotten memory.

"The name of her company. The one she'd started." He tugged on his lapels; his chest puffed. "I was her first investor." His eyes lit up and he leaned forward, his cane sliding on the floor. "I don't suppose she left any unused designs lying around? We might be interested in buying them off you."

"I didn't know," I said, still processing this information. If she had designs, there was only one place they could be. The one place I hadn't been to in years.

Uncle Russell sniffed. "I'm going to get another drink," he said, though his glass was still full.

"Is the company named after me?" I asked Aunty Gloria.

"I assume so."

Warmth bloomed in my chest. "I didn't know."

While Bobby drifted aside to talk to someone else, I wondered about Trix, and what else I didn't know or might've forgotten. Over the past few days, I'd been thinking and hesitating, but this new information finally pushed me into making a decision.

"Aunty Gloria, do you think . . . I don't want to sell the house. But I think I'm ready to see it. To clear it out."

"Are you sure?" she asked, her smile soft. "We can do it in your timing."

"I think the time is now." Before I changed my mind again. No more putting things off or blocking them out. I was ready.

"Good." She nodded, squeezing my shoulder. "Let's give the Nelsons a chance to move out first. They said they'll need a few weeks?"

"Yes. Okay."

"Great." Her eyes ticked over my shoulder. "We'll talk later. For now, I think someone is looking for you."

I turned and saw what she meant.

Brandon had arrived, maneuvering through the sea of people, unaware of the attention he commanded. He looked good in a white shirt, the material light and the fit flattering. He already had a drink, somehow, his head held high as he searched the room. When he found me, I felt both unlocked and ensnared by the look on his face. I approached him.

"Come with me," I said.

He knocked back the rest of his drink and dropped the cup onto the side table. I led him into the alcove under the stairs.

"Hi." I faced him, suddenly nervous. All day, I'd been waiting for this moment, and now that I had him, I didn't know what to say.

"Hi," he said, a curl of amusement to his tone. "It's—" He broke off as Melissa stumbled right into us.

"Oh, sorry," she said as Brandon reached out to steady her. The second he let go, she swayed precariously to the side. Her glazed eyes focused on us. "It's you! And you!"

"Are you drunk?" Brandon said. "Isn't it a bit early? The party just started."

"I'm not." She blew at the strands of hair that fell against her mouth and stuck to her lip gloss. "I'm perfect . . . perfectly on time, all the time. Every time. Unlike you. We're lucky if you even show up at all." She poked his chest. "You never did tell us why you did . . . didn't show up to the meeting with Dessa. What was that about?"

"Melissa, cool it." I noted Brandon's clenched jaw, and added, "It was a family issue. He doesn't have to tell you his business."

"Hey, I'm just saying I find it all conveniently inconvenient. Once again, Brandon fumbles an opportunity to help the band."

I rolled my eyes. "Not this again."

Melissa raised her voice over mine. "You're so lucky that, somehow, Dessa agreed to work with us anyway. But I've been watching you, Brandon Richards. And you're either a snake in the grass or you're actually incompetent." She held out her hands. "Which is it?"

"Melissa!" I dropped my voice to a sharp whisper. "You're drunk and acting totally unprofessional. For you, this is basically a work event." I took Brandon's hand in mine. "My suggestion is that you leave now. Or sober up real quick, before my uncle sees you."

I tugged Brandon out of the alcove, prompting him to follow me. We passed around Melissa and ascended the stairs. Only when we got to my room and I shut the door, I said, "I'm so sorry. Melissa isn't usually like that."

Brandon wasn't looking at me, his hands stuffed into his pockets. "She had a point, though. I did mess up. In the end, it was you and Aunty Gloria's connections that saved the band. Don't get me wrong—I'm so happy for you. But I hate that I didn't do more to help."

"Are you kidding me?" I stepped closer to him. "You've given the band an online presence, oversaw the new website, and took us from hundreds of followers on Instagram to almost ten thousand in a matter of weeks. That's not nothing."

"I don't know. I can't help thinking that maybe my father was right. Maybe I should've focused on football. Or something I'm better at."

"Okay." I sighed. "You know how much I hate feeding your ego, so listen up, 'cause I'm only saying this once—Brandon, you're funny. And entertaining. And charming. People like you. Like watching you. Like listening to you. Not to mention, that proposal you made for Dessa—my God. It was so good. When you showed it to me, I could've kissed you right then."

He squinted at me. "So it was the proposal that hooked you, huh? Interesting. Not what I expected."

My heartbeat picked up. "Yeah. Among other things."

"Still, it was Dessa's endorsement that led to the big bump in sales. Not anything I did."

"And whose idea was it for us to approach Dessa in the first place?" I raised my brows, relieved to see the beginnings of a smile. "It was because of you I knew how to talk to her. It was your voice I heard in my head, advising me on what to say."

"My voice?"

"Yes. It was very annoying."

Brandon laughed. He reached out, lacing our fingers together and gently tugging me closer. We stood so close I could feel the warmth of his body, smell the subtle scent of soap on his skin.

"Why isn't this weirder?" I asked him. "Shouldn't it be weirder?"

"Do you want it to be?"

"No. But two months ago, we hated each other."

Brandon frowned. "I told you, I've never hated you. I—"

My phone chimed. I pulled it out of my pocket. "Hold that

thought. I'm very interested in hearing it. But this might be Hazel letting us know the video is up." I checked the screen and burst out laughing. "Unbelievable."

"What?" he asked, curious.

"It's David again. I don't know what kind of extrasensory perception he developed in Martinique. Somehow, he always knows the worst possible time to contact me." I shoved my phone back into my pocket. "Whatever. You were saying?"

Brandon pulled back. "He's still messaging you? Why?"

I shrugged. "Knowing him? Because he can, probably."

"And you haven't blocked him because . . . ?"

"I know it's petty, but I'm curious to see how long I can leave him on read before he gets the message."

Instead of laughing along with me, Brandon seemed upset. "You're not going to answer him?"

"No, of course not." Did he want me to?

"You know how David is. He's not going to stop if he thinks he still has a chance."

"He doesn't have a chance."

"Then block him and he'll get the message. It's not that complicated."

I backed away from him. "Thanks for the advice that no one asked for. But since it's my phone, I think I'm going to do whatever I want with it."

"Are you saying you really don't see anything wrong with the fact that you're still talking to your ex-boyfriend?"

"I told you, I'm not talking to him. He's—actually, you know what? I don't have to explain myself. Feel free to get out of my room."

"You—" Brandon started then stopped. He held up his hands in surrender. "Fine," he said, then yanked the door open and walked out.

I stared at the empty doorway. As seconds passed, I grew angrier and more confused. What just happened? Everything had been going so well and then we'd—

Brandon walked back in. "I'm sorry. I didn't mean to tell you what to do. Of course you can talk to whoever you want."

"Then why say it?" I meant to snap back, but the words were too pained, too fragile. I didn't want to fight with him. Not like this. Our previous bickering matches didn't hurt because they meant nothing. But now, when we were teetering on the precipice of something important, every word mattered.

"Because, apparently, I'm a jealous asshole who *still* can't say the right things to you."

Jealous? What—

"I've always thought you could do better than David." He stared at me with such intensity, I couldn't look away. "I thought so from the beginning. From the first day you showed up at school in that weird yellow-and-red frilly outfit."

"You remember that?"

"It's literally imprinted on my brain," he said. "Since then, I thought you should be with someone who loves your weird outfits. And is fascinated by the fact that you sew pockets into everything. Someone who won't cheat or betray or publicly embarrass you."

He rested his hands on my waist, luring me in with his sweet words and gentle touch. "You should be with someone who adores you. Someone who's an idiot for not understanding why he's always been so fascinated by you and craved your attention—until you started dating one of his friends, and he hated every second of it."

I stared into his face, his expression so honest and open it made me ache.

"Someone like me," he clarified. "I'm talking about me."

"I got that," I said.

Brandon's eyes dropped to my lips, and I felt a sharp tug of want in my stomach.

"It's funny you say that," I said. "Because I'd come to a similar conclusion myself."

"You have?" His smile was a mix of joy and shock with a heavy emphasis on the latter. Even though I'd felt like I'd been embarrassingly obvious about my feelings for days, he seemed genuinely surprised by this.

"I have," I said.

His kiss was gentle at first. Tentative, like a question. Even now, after everything we'd said, he was so careful with his affection. I tilted my head in answer, changing the angle, parting my lips to let him in. He inhaled sharply, his grip on my waist tightening. His fingers pressed into my flesh as he pulled me closer, the kiss deepening into something bolder, hotter, sweeter.

"Tess, are—oh!"

I opened my eyes in time to see Hazel come to a sudden halt in the doorway, so abrupt it looked like she'd slammed into a wall. She did an immediate about-face.

"Sorry!" Hazel called, over her shoulder. "Wanted to let you know the video's up. Didn't mean to interrupt, though. I'll save my *I told you so* for later. Okay, bye!" Then she was gone as quickly as she appeared.

I covered my face. "She's going to be insufferable about this."

"What does she mean she told you so?" he asked, hands sliding down my arms.

I suppressed a shiver. "Nothing."

Brandon squeezed my free hand, then brought it to his lips. "Did she tell you that I've been dying to do this?" He kissed my knuckles, then my inner wrist. "And this?" When I uncovered my face, he kissed the corner of my mouth. "Or that?"

"Basically."

God, he was going to kill me. When I leaned forward, chasing his lips, unsatisfied with his teasing, he pulled back. His smile—the little knowing smirk—irritated me as much as it had a million times before. But now, all I wanted to do was crush it under my lips and pull him closer.

My phone chimed again. And again.

Damn it, David.

Brandon's smirk slipped, but he made no comment.

"Come on." He stepped back, tugging me toward the door. "Let's go see the video with everyone. Then we can finish this later."

"That's rather presumptuous." Not that he was wrong.

From the look he threw over his shoulder, I could tell that he knew.

In the living room, everyone gathered around the TV. Hazel had the video loaded and waiting. As we approached, she saw us and started it. People clapped even before the song started. Goose bumps bloomed along my skin; excitement and pride swelled in my chest. The music played and Dessa's bright, clear voice sang along with the hypnotic rhythm.

*When the vibe is right*
*Then you know it's real*
*You can fight your fight*
*But it don't change how you feel*

Hazel came to stand next to me, on the opposite side of Brandon. She knocked my shoulder and whispered, "Next time close the door, nah."

I laughed, knocking her back.

My phone chimed with a message. Then another. And another.

Oh, for heaven's sake. I pulled my phone out. Brandon was right. The time to cut this off had passed.

I meant to block him. Unfortunately, I made the mistake of reading his messages first.

Hey

I saw the article about uncle

Sorry to hear about his problems with arthritis

And the band

I know it means a lot to you
I'm here if you need to talk.

My heart dropped. Despite knowing better, I replied to him.
What article?

So this is the right number. I was wondering

Irritated, and refusing to engage any further, I closed the chat and searched recent articles featuring Uncle Russell's name. It only took me a couple of seconds to find it on *The Write Vibez* website.

I let go of Brandon's hand and backed out of the crowd, away from the noise. The article had been up since that morning. No one had mentioned it at the party. Either they were being polite, or they hadn't seen it. It figured David, of all people, would be the one to bring it to my attention.

"Something wrong?" Brandon stopped beside me. "You're missing it."

I ignored him. Eyes on the screen, I marched right out the front door and down the steps. Behind me, I heard a roar of applause as something exciting appeared in the music video. Maybe it was the appearance of the costumes. I didn't know and I didn't care.

A few minutes earlier, I'd been dying to see it. But now, it all felt distant and irrelevant.

"What is going on?" Brandon asked, Hazel a few steps behind him.

"*The Write Vibez* did an article about Uncle Russell and the band. They wrote about everything. *Everything*. About how sales were tanking. That we hired you to manage our social media. How Jenni turned us down. They even—" I hissed through my teeth, trying to steady the hitch in my voice. "They even know about Uncle Russell's arthritis."

My stomach clenched at the thought of Uncle Russell's reaction to it.

The way they'd chosen to write about his condition was everything I'd feared, the tone condescending and barely masked with a thin veneer of sympathy. Exactly the type of article Brandon mentioned would be a good story to boost interest in the band.

I looked him in the eyes, begging, "Please tell me this wasn't you."

Brandon blinked. "What?"

"Tell me you aren't their source." All I wanted was an outright denial and I needed it immediately. "You're the only person I talked to about Uncle Russell's arthritis. Everyone else who's known has known for ages. So, the fact that this is coming out now—"

"You think I had something to do with it?" He looked so shocked, so hurt, every cell in my body wanted to reach out and comfort him.

But I couldn't. I had to know. "Did you tell anyone?"

"Tess," Hazel said in an annoyingly calm tone. "Let's take a step back for a moment. Give Brandon a chance to explain."

I held up a hand to cut her off. "Did you?"

"I . . ." His lips tugged to one corner, as if he'd been about to say something, and caught it at the last minute. The longer he didn't answer, the colder I felt.

"Okay, yes," he said. "I did tell Lucy. But—"

I couldn't believe this. How did I keep making the same mistakes? Hadn't I learned anything from David? Hadn't I told myself not to trust Brandon, not to fall for him?

I'd known better and still did it anyway.

"Tess, I swear to you, Lucy had nothing to do with this. She's eleven, for crying out loud!"

"You can't know that. She could've told someone."

"You think my little sister has the editor of *The Write Vibez* on speed dial?"

"I asked you not to tell *anyone*."

"It was an accident." An edge of fear infiltrated his voice. Whereas before, he'd been angry, now he sounded worried. He'd probably realized how badly he'd messed up. "We were talking about you and I mentioned how committed you were to the band, and all that you do for your uncle . . ." He lifted a hand, then dropped it listlessly. "It came out. I doubt Lucy even knew what I was talking about or cared."

I folded my arms. My skin felt too tightly drawn, my insides swelling with more emotion than I'd been built to contain. "Do you know what you've done?"

"Tess," Hazel said. "We don't know anything for sure."

"It was not Lucy," Brandon said enunciating each word like my problem had been understanding rather than believing him. "That I know for sure."

"Call her then. Ask her."

"No way."

"Why not?"

"Because that's ridiculous!"

I couldn't listen to him anymore, the feeling of betrayal and hurt left me numb. I turned and started for the steps.

"Of course you're running away again," he called out. "No matter what I do, you still assume the worst of me. Every time. Even after everything."

His words stung, but I did not stop. If anything, I'd been right to assume the worst. He'd just proved it.

I entered the house, avoided the guests, and ran straight for my room. Downstairs, another cheer rang out as the party continued. My uncle carried on, somewhere in the midst of all that, totally unaware. I'd have to tell him soon.

In the meantime, I blocked David's number from my phone, just like Brandon wanted.

Then I blocked him too.

# TWENTY-TWO

December was the only time of year that Morris allowed music other than calypso or soca in the mas camp. Throughout the month, the building filled with the cheerful sounds of parang music, some of it sung in Spanish, but most in English; all of it about food and celebration.

"Do you know, for ages, I thought the lyric was *she gone, father*," I told Morris, as Scrunter's *Leroy* played. I added arches to a stack of dyed blue feathers by running each one through my pinched fingers. "That's depressing, I thought. The mother left her family on Christmas morning. When, all along, she'd just *gone parang* with her friends."

He grunted, tapping the glue gun to make sure it was hot enough. "Used to think Mommy kissing Santa Claus was about infidelity."

"It's not?" I asked, screwing up my face in confusion.

He grunted again, this time with a flash of teeth. I swore that one day, I'd get him to break into a smile. One day.

"Good news, everyone!" Melissa came rushing in, waving her hands over her head like she was directing a plane to park. Uncle Russell followed a few steps behind.

"It's official," Melissa said. "I'm pleased to announce—we've sold out!"

Cheers erupted from every corner of the workshop. I shared a look of surprise with Morris.

We hadn't sold out of costumes in all the years that I'd been living with the Messinas. The extra stock was usually sent over to Barbados to be sold at a huge discount for their Crop Over festival later in the year. Dessa's impact on our numbers was truly staggering. While the others gathered around Uncle Russell to offer congratulations, I could not move from my seat, weak-kneed with relief.

We'd done it. We'd truly done it.

I retrieved my phone from my bag, about to call Brandon when I remembered I couldn't. The fall from the high was instant and dreadful.

In the days leading up to Christmas break, we hadn't spoken, and apart from one accidental shared look during the final school assembly of the term, we'd had nothing to do with each other. I tried not to think about it.

"Thank you, everyone." Uncle Russell raised his voice above the commotion, then he waited for us to settle down. "I want to take this moment to extend my sincerest appreciation to all of you. Grandeur would not be what it is without your contributions—both the first-timers and those of you who've been with us for years. To Morris—"

Another cheer rose up, and I clapped along.

"—thank you, old friend. You've kept the camp going. I could not do this without you."

"Agreed," Morris said, inciting laughter from us.

Uncle Russell gave the impression of rolling his eyes without actually rolling them. "And, even though they aren't here today, I would like to mention Brandon Richards and Dessa King. I don't pretend to understand the first thing about internet culture, but their success cannot be denied."

I clapped along with the others, feeling like a fraud.

Uncle Russell didn't know what Brandon had done, and I didn't plan to tell him. My uncle had been as crushed by the article as I'd expected. Though he did not show it outwardly, anyone who knew him could see he'd become quieter and even more disengaged than usual.

Thankfully, the post hadn't gotten much attention, the hype from Dessa's music video blotting it out. But while the company had been unaffected by the invasion of privacy, damage had still been done.

At least now I could help at the mas camp again, a consolation that I hadn't taken for granted. I'd been here every day since school closed for the holidays. It had felt good to get back to doing what I was meant to do. Something I was great at. Something I couldn't mess up.

"And finally, I want to thank my niece, Tess." He nodded at

me, which might as well have been a bear hug on his scale of affection. "She's been an asset to the band in more ways than I can express."

I smiled in reply. Everyone turned to me and applauded. I dropped my eyes to the table, the mix of joy and mortification overwhelming.

*This*, I thought, *this is all that matters.* I could devote myself to the band and my craft, and it would be worth it.

"And it is because of this huge win today that I feel comfortable enough to make my own announcement." Uncle Russell looked away from me to address the whole room. "My parents started Grandeur. I've been a part of the company in one way or another since birth. I always thought that if it were to come to an end, my parents would want it to be on a high note. And I believe this moment is it."

No cheers followed. No applause. Nothing but the sound of the glue gun clattering on the desk after it slipped from Morris's fingers.

"This will be Grandeur's last year, I've decided," Uncle Russell said. "Thank you all for making it a wonderful, memorable experience." Then, he left the room, wearing a polite smile. Like he hadn't just dropped a bomb on all of us.

"And now comes the chaos," Morris muttered, before everyone swarmed him, demanding answers.

I slipped out of the melee, the sound of blood pounding in my ears.

Uncle Russell sat in his office, behind his desk, apparently working on his laptop. He briefly glanced up from the screen when I walked in, before dropping his eyes again.

"You cannot shut down the band," I said without preamble.

"Tess, I realize it is a big change for you—"

"Not just for me. What about all those people out there? What are they supposed to do now? Some of them have been working here for years."

"Almost everyone out there works part-time, and the others are skilled enough to get jobs for other bands. They will be fine."

"And what about Morris? And Melissa?" *And me?* "Did you even give a thought to what they may want? This isn't all about you."

"Last I checked, it is about me. I told you—this is my band, and I can do whatever I want with it." He sighed, the sharpness in his tone easing. "Listen to me, child, I don't want to fight—"

"I am not a child," I said, frustrated.

"You say as you're stomping your feet and throwing a tantrum because you're not getting your way. I know it's hard, Tess, but it's time for me to accept that my era has passed. We no longer fit into this industry—"

"You literally just announced that Grandeur had its most successful year in over a decade," I said. "How does that mean your time has passed?"

As I spoke, he was shaking his head. "The sales had nothing to do with the costumes, or the band itself, and everything to do with your publicity stunt—"

"So?" I threw my hands up. "Why is that a bad thing? We tried something new, and it worked. This is how publicity works these days."

"It's not how I do it. It's not the way it's supposed to be done."

And then it hit me. "This is about the article, isn't it?"

"Hardly. As insulting as it was, I do not care about it, and clearly, neither did anyone else."

"Exactly." That was the problem. "No one cared about it." No one had cared about him. "You're closing Grandeur, not because the band is irrelevant, but because you think you are. This is all about your ego."

"Excuse me?" Uncle Russell said, clearly offended.

"Do you know how many times I've defended you?" To Dessa. To Brandon. To myself. "I told them you were a bit arrogant, yes. It's just a quirk of your character. But, no, you really are that selfish."

"That's enough." He rose to his feet and pointed to the door. "I suggest you take a moment to cool down, and then we can discuss this calmly."

"No. I see it now. You let Brandon and me work on the online promotions because you didn't believe it would succeed. And now that it has, you're upset because someone else was responsible for the band's success. Not you."

"Enough, Tess—"

"People still love your designs." Why couldn't he see that? "All we did was bring attention to them. We reached people the way that everyone does now. But God forbid we try new things. No, we should keep operating exactly as we always have been, then wonder why nothing gets better. If anything's holding back the band, it's you!"

I ran out of air, drew a deep breath, and meant to go on, when I noticed a small smile on his face. Not a happy one, but something somber and distant. It caught me off guard, and my words dried up.

His voice, when he spoke, was infuriatingly cool. "I think you've just proven my point."

"What?"

He returned to his seat. "It will be fine, Tess. I promise. This is for the best."

It was like talking to a rock.

All the anger drained out of me, in its absence all that was left was the dull ache of loss. I left the office then, not sure where I was going. I just knew that I had to get out of there.

My old house wasn't haunted. But a part of me liked to think my parents were still in there. My mother sitting cross-legged on the living room floor, the contents of her latest project scattered across the carpet, music blasting through the speakers of her old-timey radio. My father locked in his study, steadily typing on his desktop, the door firmly shut to keep the sound out.

But there were no ghosts, only memories. They left impressions in the walls. In every corner. In every room.

I really did not want to go in there.

"Are you okay?" Aunty Gloria asked, as we stood on the threshold. "You don't have to do this, you know?"

"I know." But I needed to.

My first step into the house was the hardest. I instantly looked toward the living room, expecting to see Mummy curled up on the couch, her legs thrown over the armrest as she flicked through some fashion magazine. To see my father, always on the phone, loafers quiet against the blue carpeting as he crossed the hall. He'd stop in front of the pictures that hung on the wall next to the stairs and adjust the framed family portrait that never stayed straight.

But there was no couch. No carpeting. No pictures. No parents.

Hazel slipped into the hall beside me. She looked around, curious. "It's smaller than I remember," she said.

She was right. It did seem smaller. And it smelled wrong—like chemical cleaners and aged wood. The walls, the floors, and the ceilings had been cleared, the house's bones bare and worn. Speechless, I headed up the staircase. At the top, a door had been built and kept locked. This prevented the tenants from going up there. Aunty Gloria joined me and used the key to open it.

The second floor smelled both better and worse, the air stale and musty, but underlined with something familiar—an indescribable scent that I associated with home. A smell I didn't realize I'd forgotten until that moment.

In my old room, Aunty Gloria went straight to the bookshelf.

"Did you read all these?" she asked, her fingers skimming along the spines of my little library.

"Several times," I said, joining her.

I'd collected mostly horror and mysteries. *Nancy Drew*, *A Series of Unfortunate Events*, and *Scooby-Doo*. *Bailey School Kids*, *Goosebumps*, and *Fear Street*.

"We can give them away," I said, pulling out my well-worn copy of *The Thrill Club*—a favorite of mine. An inscription had been scrawled on the inside of the front cover.

*Happy birthday, Trix! Try not to read the whole thing in one day. Love always, Daddy.*

"Except this one." I checked to see if that would be okay with Aunty Gloria, but she wasn't paying attention, examining the many fashion magazine collages I'd stuck to my wall.

"Tess!" Hazel called out from across the hall. Her tone sounded a bit panicked, so we wasted no time joining her in the guest bedroom. When we got there, she pointed at the open closet. "What is that?"

I peeked inside, saw what she meant, and laughed. "Oh. That's Zelda." I dragged out the old mannequin and set it in the center of the room. The years had done Zelda no favors, and her appearance had leaned toward the uncanny from the start.

"She was Mummy's," I explained.

"Lord, have mercy." Aunty Gloria recoiled. "I remember this thing. Used to haunt my nightmares. I swear, your mother kept it around purely because she knew it terrified us. She found that amusing."

"Sounds like Mummy," I said. She had the best sense of humor.

Zelda didn't scare me, though. There were days when it was just her, my mom, and I. Mummy would use this room as a workshop, and I'd sit on the floor, imitating her process with the fabric scraps and leftover accessories.

"Did she give Zelda a name that sounds witchy on purpose?" Hazel asked, inspecting Zelda's rimless, white eyes.

Aunty Gloria snorted. "If you told me it was cursed, I'd believe you."

I was about to go on defending my old friend, when a stack of boxes in the closet caught my eye. A single flap had been bent back, revealing the cover of a familiar sketchbook. I hauled the boxes out, one by one.

Inside, I found all my mother's sewing equipment and fabrics. A couple of unfinished projects, sketches, and pattern guides. At the very back were mood boards, some vague and others with concrete concepts ready to go.

"I want to keep these," I said, then turned to face Aunty Gloria. "Please? I know you just cleared out the house—"

"Anything you want," Aunty Gloria said easily. "It's your home too, sweetheart. If it makes you happy, you can keep everything."

Something in my chest loosened.

"Including Zelda?" I asked.

She wrinkled her nose and with obvious reluctance, relented. "If that's what you want."

"Thank you," I said. And though she didn't realize it, I wasn't just thanking her for the mannequin, but for everything she'd done from the day she'd moved me into her house and made it my home too.

"But first . . ." Aunty Gloria nudged Zelda with her shoe. "Let's run this little demon through some garden sage smoke before we take it anywhere. Just to be safe."

# TWENTY-THREE

That night, after retiring to my room, I pulled out Mummy's concept boards and sketchbooks and laid them out on the floor. She'd dated a lot of her work, which made it easier to set them in chronological order and observe the changes to her style over time. A lot of her later costumes seemed to veer away from traditional feathers and beads to fitted bodywear and swimsuits.

I stared at the collection for a long time, wishing I could ask her to explain. I could make a guess about her intentions, but it wouldn't be the same as hearing her tell me herself.

At some point, I must've fallen asleep, because I woke up precariously balanced on the edge of the bed, my left arm numb because I'd rested on it. I stumbled to my feet, careful to step around my mother's things as I headed to the bathroom. After washing up, I headed down to the kitchen.

My uncle sat at the dining table. In front of him lay a handful of my mother's designs—the same ones I'd had in my room. I hadn't noticed some missing. "When did you get that?"

"You fell asleep last night with the light on. When Gloria went in to turn it off, she saw all this on the floor, and showed me."

I drew a little closer. "They're Mummy's. We found them at the house yesterday."

"Yes, I know. I remember some of them. Do you know what they are?"

"They look like Monday wear," I said. "Was that even a thing back then?"

My uncle snorted. "Yes, Tess. It was a thing seven long years ago. It was even more controversial then."

Monday wear was exactly that—an outfit meant to be worn on Carnival Monday so the costume could be saved for Carnival Tuesday. A few bands were incorporating it into their lineups, even though many saw it as watering down and further commercializing the festival.

"But Mummy wanted to design them?" I guessed.

"She did. She wanted us to get in on the trend early." He scratched his chin. "I rejected the idea immediately. And when I did, she called me old-fashioned and stubborn. Told me that I never tried anything new. That I was holding back the band. Sound familiar?"

"A little."

His lips pressed into a tight smile. "Eventually, your mother said she couldn't take it anymore. She felt limited creatively. And she quit the band."

What? "No, she didn't. She loved Grandeur."

"She did. But she'd had enough of doing things my way, and she decided to start her own company. One that focused exclusively on designing Monday wear."

"Trix." I realized, slipping into the chair next to him. "Why haven't I heard about this before?"

My uncle sniffed. "I'm not particularly proud of the fact that we were fighting in her last days. Some of the things I said to her . . ." He tipped one of the sketches up to look at it. "As mad as I'd been at the time, a part of me actually admired her for quitting. She was branching out on her own. I thought . . ." He bit his lip and inhaled sharply. "*I knew* she would have accomplished something great."

A glimmer in his eyes hinted at unshed tears. It was far more emotion than I'd ever seen from him, and my own eyes welled in response.

"You are so like her. So talented. So determined. And hardheaded. I know I've been pushing you away from the band recently. But I'm worried. You're investing too much of yourself into the company. I would hate it if you woke up one day, realized you've got nothing of your own, and resented me too."

"That wouldn't happen." I leaned forward, needing him to hear me and understand. "I love Grandeur. I wanted to help. *Want* to help."

"I know. And this last year especially I really needed that help. But it's too much to ask from you. You should be out with friends on a Friday night. Focused on exams and applying to university."

"It's not too much."

"It is. You're still a child."

"I'll be eighteen soon. Old enough to know that I want to be a part of this."

Then again, as the memory of my conversation with Dessa flowed back to me, it occurred to me—if the past few weeks had taught me anything, it was that I didn't know everything. That people I thought I understood could still surprise me. That I could even surprise myself. And maybe it wouldn't hurt to leave the door open to a few possibilities I hadn't considered before.

"Maybe I'll want to branch out to something else one day," I said. "Maybe movie costuming or more traditional fashion. Or Monday wear like Mummy. But right now, you're not holding me back. You've been giving me the chance to do exactly what I want to do. What I love to do."

"I know that now. But, Tess." He shook his head. "It *is* too much."

My heart sank. I shifted, about to shove my chair back so I could stand and leave.

"Which is why we need to hire more staff."

I froze. *What?*

"We could expand a bit," he said. "Increase the number of sections next year. Bring in some new designers with fresh perspectives. Get Melissa an assistant."

"Why would we do all that if we're closing?" I asked cautiously.

My uncle gave me an unimpressed look. "Tess, please keep up. Clearly, I'm saying I've rethought my decision. We'll use the profits from this year to expand the company and make some changes."

"Really?"

"Really. You were not wrong. Once I looked past my own ego, as you so eloquently put it, I realized Grandeur isn't just me. It's all of us. It's the decorators, the seamstresses, the masqueraders—everyone in the company. And when I looked at it like that, I saw no reason why we shouldn't keep going."

I jumped to my feet and let out a shriek, so very unlike myself. It startled us both.

"I'm so sorry," I said. "I don't know where that came from. It will never happen again."

He nodded, still looking a bit shaken. "I'm going to take that to mean you approve of this decision."

"I do, yes. Thank you."

He patted my shoulder. I was relieved to see his usual stoic expression returned, with only the slightest tilt to the corner of his lips betraying his amusement.

Hazel rushed into the room. Upon spotting us, she came to a stumbling halt. "Did you already hear?"

"Good morning to you, Hazel," Uncle Russell said. "Slept well?"

"No, actually, I woke up with this crick in my neck—" She waved her hand. "It doesn't matter. There's something I need to tell you. But first, you need to know that he's okay. He *is* in the hospital. But he's going to be fine. So don't panic."

"What are you talking about?" I asked. If her intention had been to prevent panic, she'd done a terrible job so far.

"Brandon was in a car accident. He's fine, but he's hurt."

For a while, all I could hear was a thunderous rushing noise in my head, everything after *car accident* drowned under the sound.

"He's okay?" I asked after a minute. Maybe longer.

Hazel snapped her mouth shut, apparently in the middle of saying more. Something I'd clearly missed. "He's okay," she said firmly. "The problem was, his leg got pinned for a bit. When they pulled him out it was broken, and he has to have some surgery to fix it."

"I think I'm going to be sick," I said.

Uncle Russell yanked out the chair and had me sit. "Was anyone else hurt?" he asked—an obvious question. But even the obvious eluded me at the moment.

"It was just him injured. But it sounds like it was the other car's fault for speeding around a blind corner." Hazel rested a hand on my shoulder. "I'm sorry. I knew this was going to upset you, but I thought you'd want to know. Even after all that drama with *The Write Vibez* article, of course you'd still care about him."

"Hold on," Uncle Russell said. "What about that article? What does it have to do with Brandon? Was he the one who gave them the story?"

Hazel, bowled over by his correct leaps in logic, didn't even have a chance at denial. She looked to me for help, which was as good as confirmation.

"I see." My uncle's lips thinned.

Shoot. I'd never planned for Uncle Russell to find out. How did the morning devolve so quickly? Just a minute earlier, Uncle Russell had told me that Grandeur would continue, and now I had to admit I'd broken his trust.

"It's my fault," I said softly. Reluctantly. "I'm sorry. I'm the one who gave him all the information. Then he went and told his sister, and it got out. I hadn't meant to tell him. It was an accident."

"You didn't mean to tell him?" Hazel asked.

"Of course not," I said. "Why would I do that?"

"I told Chris." In response to our stunned silence, she added, "What? He's my boyfriend. I trust him."

I noted her present tense but was too appalled to point it out to her.

"This explains a few things," Uncle Russell mused. "I had been wondering why Brandon wasn't around as much." He patted my arm. "Don't worry, child. There will be others."

Was he comforting me? Why? "Aren't you mad?"

"Of course I am. Clearly, the boy broke your heart. But you are young. You will bounce back."

"Uh . . . that's not . . ." Had he missed the part where I'd betrayed his trust? "I meant—aren't you mad at me? I'm partly responsible for the article?"

"Well, I'm certainly not happy about it. But as you pointed out—no one cared. I'm much more upset that he hurt you. I'll let Melissa know he's fired." He glanced around. "Where is she, by the way? She was around earlier."

There was a thud and the pantry door creaked open. We turned to see Melissa staggering out. "I can't listen to this anymore."

Hazel rushed over to help. "Oh, jeez. Are you okay? Do you need something? A glass of water?"

Melissa refused her hand. "No. Leave me. I'm a terrible person. I don't deserve your water."

"Melissa," Uncle Russell said calmly. "Just so you are aware, this is highly unprofessional."

"I'm sorry, sir." She inhaled, straightened her spine, and ran her hands over her outfit to smooth it out. "I got some bad news last night. I went into the pantry to do my breathing exercises."

And have a little cry, I guessed from the state of her eyeliner.

"Good God," Uncle Russell said. "Is your job really that bad? We are definitely getting you an assistant."

"No, it—actually, yes, I would like that very much. But the reason I'm upset is because I heard everything you said and I just—" She teared up, her shoulders sagging with defeat. "Please don't fire Brandon. Don't blame him or Tess or anyone else. The article is my fault. Last night, I found out that the guy I've been seeing is good friends with Prince Kingston. Prince was the one who arranged the article."

"Oh, Melissa." Hazel covered her mouth. "I'm so sorry. I know you liked him."

"I did! And when I confronted him about it, he actually confessed that Prince was the one who encouraged him to ask me out in the first place. He wanted to see if he could get any inside info on Grandeur out of me—which he did. My boyfriend told me he's still into me regardless. I think that was supposed to make me feel better."

"Let me get this straight," Uncle Russell said. "Did *all* of you tell your boyfriends my personal business?"

"Brandon wasn't my boyfriend," I said. But he might've been. Oh God.

"Tess, here's the part that I'm still stuck on," Hazel said. "You were mad at Brandon for accidentally telling his sister, when *you* accidentally told him. And you didn't think that was a little hypocritical?"

Could she not? I already felt bad enough as it was. "Hey, I wasn't the only one who thought something was going on with him." I laid out my only defense. "Melissa thought he was still working for Royalty. And he made no secret of the fact that he was only in this for the money."

"Who doesn't take a job for the money?" Hazel said. "That's what a job is for. Not to mention—do you even know why he needed the money? Didn't he tell you?"

"No. What?" I asked, with a sinking feeling that her answer would only make me feel a million times worse.

"His sister's chess tournament. For her to go, their family had to pay her way. Since he knew his father would refuse to contribute, Brandon had to save up and pay for it himself."

"Brandon . . . did mention something like that." On the day of Dessa's visit, he'd said his father found out the chess club wasn't paying, which meant his father must've found out that Brandon was. Mr. Richards must have not appreciated his family hiding it from him.

I rested my head on the table. Done.

"Tess, what were you thinking?"

"I don't know." But now all the awful things I'd said were

replaying in my head. I'd treated him so badly—accusing, rejecting, then avoiding him. He'd been right. Even though he wasn't David, I'd expected the worst of him.

"What's going on here?" Aunty Gloria's voice came from the doorway to the living room.

"I'm not so sure anymore," Uncle Russell said. "Just grateful I'm not seventeen."

"Me too." Aunty Gloria said. "I've seen the photos of your hairstyle back then. No one wants that."

He huffed out a laugh, his chair dragging on the floor as he rose to his feet. "Would you like me to make eggs this morning?"

"I'd love that," she said. "I'll start the coffee."

"Scrambled for me, please." Melissa dropped into the seat Uncle Russell had vacated. To us, she said, "I should probably dump him, shouldn't I?"

"Yes!" Hazel and I said in unison.

My cousin pinched my side. "You know you're going to have to apologize to him, right?" She didn't need to clarify who she meant.

I raised my head, shifting away from her. "Yes. I am aware."

But what could I possibly say to make this right?

# TWENTY-FOUR

"Stop fretting. It will be fine." Hazel led me into an elevator and hit the button for the floor where Brandon was staying.

I didn't answer, clinging to my silent treatment, though it seemed like I had very little say in the matter regardless.

Earlier that afternoon, on our first day back at school, our teacher had organized a get-well-soon card for Brandon and asked everyone to sign it. Since there were about one hundred and twenty students in the whole form, the card was actually a folded sheet of glitter-dusted cardboard paper the length of my arm. We'd had to line up at the teacher's desk and sign before we left the classroom for the day.

When my turn came, I'd held a gel pen to the paper and hesitated. My mind blanked. Nothing I could write felt like enough. But crowded in by my classmates, I felt a bit of pressure to put *something*, so I wrote a simple platitude, matching the many others already scrawled and signed, aware of Hazel at my back, watching over my shoulder.

After I left the classroom, she stormed out after me. "*Hope you're better soon?*" she asked. "Are you serious? That's it? That's all you have to say to him?"

I continued walking toward the car. "It's a class card, what should I have said?"

"I don't know. I'm sorry? I'm a fool? Please take me back?" The soles of her sneakers slapped against the asphalt behind me.

"How could I possibly put that on the card?"

Had she lost her mind?

"You do realize this will be your first communication with him in weeks. He *is* going to look for your message among the rest—you know he will. Do you really want *hope you're better soon* to be the first words he gets from you?"

I yanked open the car door but did not get inside. "What do you want me to do? If Brandon was here, I'd apologize to him. But at the moment, he's at the hospital recovering from surgery."

"I want you to do what you should've done days ago."

"What's that supposed to mean?"

She said nothing.

It was only when we were already on route to the hospital, that I'd realized what she'd had planned.

"I can't." I turned back to the elevator.

"Remember what I said." Hazel tugged my arm, yanking me down the sterile, disinfectant-scented hallway. My sneakers squeaked against the overly polished floor. "Either you go in there and talk to him, or I'll go in there and tell him you tried to talk to him and chickened out."

"Why are you pushing this?"

"Because two people who feel the way you two feel about each other shouldn't give up so easily."

"Like in your books?" I asked, incredulous. "Hazel, we're not characters in a novel. We're not Heathcliff and Julie. Life just doesn't work that way. Are you listening to me?"

Hazel suddenly stopped, nearly jerking my arm out of its socket. "Chris?"

Chris looked up. He was in the near-empty waiting room, sitting slanted across two chairs. He seemed just as surprised to see us as we were to see him, the notebook in his grasp falling into his lap. He twisted to face us, his feet hitting the floor. "Hazel—hi."

"Hi." She swallowed so hard I could hear it. "You weren't at school today."

He stood, then started to take a step forward before changing his mind. "I skipped. I wanted to keep Brandon company." He laughed, rubbing the back of his neck. "Well, I say *company*, he says, uh, *smothering*."

Hazel let out a small laugh.

"He kicked me out for a bit," Chris said. "He's free now if you want to see him. His mom went to pick up Lucy. They're supposed to be here later, but—"

"You weren't supposed to read that." Hazel's attention strayed to the notebook in his hands. Her notebook. The one she'd given him as proof. "Not the whole thing. That's not why I gave it to you."

"Yeah, I . . ." Chris glanced down at it. He had a finger slipped between the pages to hold his spot, about halfway through. "I've never actually read a romance book before. Someone told me I should give it a try."

Hazel closed her eyes, laughing. "Not that one. It's not even a full novel. It's barely a draft."

"I like it though." He flipped the notebook over, looking at it. "It's sweet, and the humor—it sounds like you. It's taking me a while to get through because your handwriting is truly awful."

"Oh, God." Hazel covered her face.

I used this opportunity to back away. With my cousin distracted, maybe I could go and she'd forget the reason we were here. It was a long shot but I had to try.

"Tess, are you leaving?" Chris asked.

I stopped. "Sorry, I thought you two would want to talk alone."

"Didn't you come to see Brandon?" he asked. "His room's that way." He pointed.

Hazel said nothing, lifting her hand and pointing too.

Resigned, I walked toward the hall, as directed. My languid pace contrasted the rapid beating of my heart.

I passed two young doctors in white coats, sharing a clipboard and whispered conversation; a nurse wearing a bright-pink smock who seemed to be muttering to herself; and Prince Kingston, who was so distracted on his phone he nearly bumped into me.

"Tess," he said, a smile on his face.

He seemed absolutely delighted to see me. I couldn't say the same.

"Are you here visiting your boyfriend?" he asked. "I just spoke to him. When I heard our former employee was in an accident I wanted to check in."

"Out of the kindness of your heart?"

"Because we've recently reviewed the circumstances of his termination and determined that we may have been too hasty. I offered him another chance to collaborate with us again." When I said nothing, he asked, "Aren't you curious about his answer?"

"I already know his answer." Brandon had proved himself time and time again. At this point, how could I not trust him?

Prince laughed. "Well, we've extended the offer, and it's a pretty lucrative one. He can think about it. I'll see you around, Tess."

"No, I don't think so," I said, stopping him in his tracks.

Brandon once told me that all we needed to annoy an enemy was to thrive. But in the last few days, while Grandeur had been thriving, I hadn't thought of Royalty once. And I realized, I didn't want to ever again.

"I'm done with this rivalry," I said. "Competing with you hasn't done anything but cause trouble. It's been distracting us from what matters, and that's making the band the best it can be. So, you do you, Prince. I honestly wish Royalty all the best, and hopefully, we'll have no reason to talk to each other ever again."

I didn't wait for his answer before walking away.

Leaving him like that, I felt a surge of confidence. But by the time I reached the room where they kept Brandon, it all drained away.

There were four beds, two on each side of the room. Brandon was alone, though the bed across from him was clearly in use, unoccupied at the moment. I thought he was asleep at first, his head turned toward the frosted louvered windows. Slants of light fell across his white bedsheets. He wore a hospital gown that looked thin and scratchy, his injured leg slightly elevated.

I was about to leave, but he turned to look right at me. His face remained stoic, but I noticed his fingers grasping at the covers beside him. I breathed through a sharp stab of pain lodged under my rib cage. I didn't realize how worried I'd been until that moment.

When I reached his bedside, my attention snagged on the curved scar on his chin. It reminded me that he'd lived through my worst nightmare. I knew all too well how bad the outcome could've been.

If anything had happened to him . . .

"Well, it's worse than I thought," I said.

"Because I look the same?" he finished without missing a beat.

"Because you look exactly the same. Unfortunately." I pointed at his chin. "Except for that. That's brilliant. Your followers will love it."

"If they do, then they're going to lose their minds when they see my leg."

My chest tightened. "Is it really that bad?"

"It's not pretty, but the doctor said the surgery went well. I'll be walking in a few weeks. But my hypothetical football career is over." His lips twisted in a tight smile. "On the bright side, my father has come around to broadcast journalism, now that his preference is off the table. Too bad it took a car accident for him to finally accept it."

I flinched, sure I'd detected a pointedness beneath his words. His father wasn't the only one who'd taken too long to come around.

"Aren't you going to mention it?" he asked.

"What?"

"I know you would've seen him on his way out. So, go on. Ask what Prince was doing here."

"It doesn't matter."

"Of course it matters. Don't you want to know what we're planning? How I'm conspiring to take you and Grandeur down now?"

I fisted my hands to stop them from shaking. "I know you wouldn't do that."

"Yeah, now that Melissa admitted to everything. God knows my word counts for nothing."

*Of course it does*, I should've said. Instead, like a fool, I blurted out, "You know about Melissa?"

His eyes shuttered, closed off to everything, even anger. He had nothing for me. I felt it like a physical blow.

"Yes," he said. "Hazel told me when she apologized *days* ago."

Damn it, Hazel. I shouldn't even be mad at her for doing the right thing—the thing I should've done ages ago—but I was. Why couldn't she wait?

"I'm sorry," I said, but I could see the apology did not reach him. The words fell like rocks onto the floor. He remained unmoved.

Was I really too late?

"Brandon, I—"

"There you are." Jo entered the room, both hands laden with plastic bags. Rondell and Jenni came in behind him. "We took a wrong turn and ended up outside the morgue. Never backtracked so fast in my life. Hey, Tess."

The others' greetings followed his, the three of them crowding around Brandon's bed. Jenni hopped up and sat on the edge, her long legs swinging off the side. "If your aim was to get out of school for a few days, I think you went a little overboard," she said.

"Yes, you've figured me out," Brandon said. "I messed up my leg and totaled my car just to skip a few days of school."

Jo's jaw dropped. "Oh, man! The car's gone?"

"Yes, and don't think I didn't notice that your reaction to what happened to my car is twice as dramatic as any concern you've shown for me."

"I really liked that car."

I backed out of the room, the four of them too preoccupied with the many snacks Jo had brought Brandon to notice. It was like we were back at Jenni's party, and I was disappearing into the couch again. The last thing I heard before I left the room was Jenni saying, "Nice scar," and Brandon laughing.

Chris and Hazel were still in the waiting room, sitting closer, far cozier than two people who'd recently broken up would sit. I could only assume there'd be an update on the status of their relationship.

They rose from their seats upon seeing me. Something in my expression had Hazel drawing closer, reaching out in concern. "Was it his friends? Did they interrupt? We gave them wrong directions to buy you some time."

I shook my head. "We were done anyway."

They shared a loaded look, and I turned away, unable to stomach their coupley silent communications. For now, I needed to lick my wounds. I'd try to be happy for my cousin tomorrow.

# TWENTY-FIVE

Hazel kept checking on me throughout the drive home. Not lingering looks, but quick assessing ones. I didn't know what she was seeing or waiting for. But I gave her nothing, staring straight ahead, as still as stone even as I shattered inside.

Eventually, her patience snapped. "I don't understand. Did you apologize?"

"Yes."

"It doesn't make sense. You must've done it wrong."

"Hazel," I said, frustrated. "You and Chris got back together. Can't you take that as a win? Whatever romantic notions you feel the need to project on Brandon and me—"

"It's not about romance!" she said. "It's the fact that you made a connection with someone. I've been worried—*so worried* about what happens when I leave this year. I'm scared you're going to be alone."

What the hell? "So this was all pity? You're—what? Looking for a replacement?"

"You know that's not what I mean."

"No? Because it sounds like that's exactly what you mean. You feel so sorry for me, guilty that you're leaving, so now you're pushing me into this relationship—"

"It's because you close yourself off! To feelings, to people. I can so easily see you retreating into yourself next year, hiding in your dorm room, pretending that you don't need anyone."

"I don't need anyone."

"Yes, you do, Tess. You really do. If only to pull you out of your own head and remind you that there are people who love you and care about you." Her breath hitched. "I swear, this is not about romance. And it doesn't have to be Brandon. I just thought he might be someone you'd let stick around."

So had I.

I lifted my eyes to the roof, blinking back tears. Guilt tore at my insides. Hazel shouldn't have to worry about me. Not for this.

But was she right?

In that hospital room, my first impulse had been to retreat, terrified of rejection and intimidated by Brandon's friends. I'd made jokes, afraid to be vulnerable. My very late, very stilted apology hadn't been enough, and I'd known it at the time, but instead of trying harder, I'd withdrawn to my comfort zone—the safety of being alone.

"This fool must be joking." Hazel slowed as we approached

the gate to the house. David waited, his car parked on the side of the road. "Of course he's still hanging around. At least Mummy didn't let him in this time." She parked the car. "Stay here. I'll tell him to go."

"No," I said. "Wait. I'll talk to him."

Hazel paused, her hand on the door. "Are you sure? You don't have to."

"I think I do."

Because, even if Hazel didn't realize it, this was what she'd meant. This was part of my problem. Talking to David would reopen old wounds, which was why I'd been avoiding it. But she was right. I couldn't close myself off forever.

I opened the car door and stepped outside.

Almost an hour later, David left. This time, I doubted he'd be returning. As I walked into the house, I thought about what he'd said, and how much hurt could've been spared if we'd been honest with each other.

"I didn't cheat on you."

"But Brandon said—"

"Brandon told you what I told him." He'd scratched his chin. "I lied. But not to you."

We were leaning against the front of his car, the metal of it warm to the touch. A sunset of pink and orange streaks lit up the sky. The faint tinkling of steelpan music floated in from a distance.

"I shouldn't have told people about your father either," he said. "It was part of an image I wanted to keep up. Brandon was the funny, popular one and I was the cool one who didn't care about anything. I don't know why it seemed so important at the time. But then I lost you. And Brandon. And after that, it didn't seem so important anymore."

My heart softened with sympathy, but nothing more. "Thanks for telling me."

"I should have told you sooner." He kicked at a loose pebble, the soles of his sneakers dragging against the ground. "So, you and Brandon . . . ? That's really a thing?"

"It's a thing," I admitted—and really that may have been the best way to describe it at that moment, our circumstances as they were.

He leaned off the car and straightened up. "I did suspect something, you know? Back then, I had a feeling there was something behind all that animosity."

"I didn't see it."

He squinted at me. "Really?"

"Back then, I only had eyes for you," I told him.

"And now?"

Now I wanted Brandon to forgive me.

After he left, I entered the house. I found Hazel sitting in the living room, a Beverly Jenkins novel open on her lap. The television was on even as she pretended to read. Like I'd ever believe she hadn't been watching us from the window the entire time.

"How was it?" she asked, turning the page.

"Fine." Hard to listen to. Painful at some points. "I'm glad I talked to him."

She flipped another page too quickly to have actually read anything. "Good. I'm proud of you."

On TV, *Crazy Rich Asians* played. The movie was already halfway through, but I'd seen it more than enough times to follow along. Aunty Gloria joined us later, around the scene of the wedding. By the time we got to the part on the plane, a plan was already forming.

I waited a few days to make sure he'd been discharged from the hospital. It gave me enough time to work out what needed to be said, and to practice how to say it. No one knew what I'd planned. In fact, I hadn't been sure I'd actually do it, right up to the moment I hit "Record."

"This is so ridiculous," I blurted out, three seconds into filming.

I'd propped my phone against the side of my sewing machine, pushed my desk chair back to the wall with the Carnival poster.

"I'm sorry if I seem awkward here, but I don't do this. I don't talk to cameras. Or post myself online. Except, apparently, I do—if it can reach the right person. If by risking rejection and embarrassment, I can show him how I feel. Let him know that I am sorry. So, here I am, speaking to everyone. But especially to you, Brandon."

I broke into nervous laughter, overwhelmed. "God, I'll have to figure out how to edit this later. Hopefully, you still think public declarations are romantic or this is going to be——"

I stopped, breathed, and focused on the camera. Stick to the script, I reminded myself.

"This is me saying, if you're interested in extending our truce indefinitely, then this time, I promise, I'm all in."

I stopped the recording, played it back, then nearly cringed out of my skin because of my voice. Was that what I really sounded like?

After pacing for a few minutes, I posted it, unblocked and tagged Brandon, then made my account public. It didn't need to be perfect. Who was going to watch it? No one would care but me and—hopefully—him.

Then, I waited.

After the first hour of nothing, I worried. After the second, my head started to throb, and I couldn't stare at the phone screen any longer. When I crawled into bed that night, I took with me a headache and the sickening certainty that my plan was a bust.

There was always a chance he hadn't seen it yet, and I hoped that was the case. I had no backup plan if this didn't work.

The next morning, I woke up to over two thousand likes and hundreds of messages—gloating from Hazel, teasing from classmates, congratulations from Chris. Even Sherlyn chimed in, though it was only to criticize my lighting. After a quick look through notifications, I discovered that Dessa King had added my post to her stories, which accounted for most of the random clicks.

But no message from Brandon. No likes. No phone calls. Nothing.

As alarming as the whole situation was, his silence resonated more than anything. The mortification at having the video viewed so many times by so many people did not surpass the disappointment I felt at knowing it must've been ignored by the one person it had been made for.

I got dressed and headed downstairs. It was Saturday, which meant mas camp. With only a few weeks left to the festival, we were officially in the Carnival season. While the rest of the country attended endless events and fetes in the leadup to the big days, we were finishing up the last of the costumes and tending to any final alterations that needed to be made.

I forced myself to think about the work that needed to be done, and only that, rather than my failed grand gesture—so wrapped up in my thoughts, I almost walked right past Brandon and Aunty Gloria on the couch.

I backed up.

"Oh good, you're up," Aunty Gloria said, sparking the most visceral déjà vu of my life. The only huge difference between this scene and the other was Brandon's leg in a cast, which was propped on the coffee table. He was even finishing up tea from the same cup, as nonchalant as ever.

"I'll give you two a moment." Aunty Gloria gathered their cups and left. I assumed she'd gone into the kitchen, but in my shock, my focus on Brandon so unwavering, she could've jumped through the ceiling for all I'd noticed.

"You saw my post?" I asked him, approaching the couch. My gaze slid over his face. He seemed to be okay. When I'd visited him at the hospital, I didn't notice he'd been missing a certain warmth. Now, it burned brightly.

"I did," he said. "Otherwise, this would be a very big coincidence."

I stopped beside the couch, the tips of my fingers brushing the armrest, the need to reach for him almost impossible to resist. "You didn't like it."

"Of course I— Oh. You mean I didn't literally *like* the post. No, I figured I should do this part in person." His lips twitched with amusement. "Didn't you once tell me you didn't require likes for validation?"

"What part?" I prompted him.

"The part I need to do in person?" he asked, then tipped his head to the side. "Come, sit next to me. I'm too used to talking to you face-to-face. Have you ever noticed we're almost the same height? I am *slightly* taller, though."

I sat beside him. "Sure."

"What? You don't believe me? The second this cast is off, we can check."

As he spoke, he kept moving—touching his shoulder and his cheek, tugging at the collar of his T-shirt. As usual, he couldn't seem to stay still. This time I didn't hesitate to move closer, drawn into the chaos, ready to embrace it.

"Brandon," I said. "What part?"

He cupped my chin, his thumb brushing my cheek. The touch was as gentle as the affection in his gaze. For a moment, we stared at each other, and I was struck by the ridiculous notion that I never wanted to look away from him.

He ducked his head and pressed his lips to the corner of my jaw. "The part where I tell you I'm all in too," he said, the warmth of his breath against my skin.

"Oh." I somehow found the words even as I melted against him. "Good."

"Yes, I think so," he said, laughing quietly. "Thought I should tell you in person, as soon as possible." He pulled back, smiling. "I know you like your privacy. And after that very public declaration, I want to spare you any more embarrassment."

"If we're together, I doubt that's a promise you can keep."

"Oh? So we're together now? That's presumptuous."

"Brandon," I said, grasping his T-shirt. "For someone who usually knows the right things to say, you need to learn when to stop talking."

"Well, lucky for me, I have you to—"

I kissed him. Partly to shut him up. Mostly because he was here, and I couldn't resist any longer.

# EPILOGUE

## SIX WEEKS LATER

I tore across the house in search of my phone. "Where is it?" I muttered, shifting around the contents of the coffee table, lifting pillows, and overturning cushions. "It was in my hand a second ago."

"Here it is." Aunty Gloria shuffled out of the kitchen, holding up my phone.

Still dressed in her royal blue pantsuit from work, she looked ready to fall asleep on her feet, yawning every other minute. Despite her obvious exhaustion, she seemed happy to be back at the station. According to her, she'd needed a vacation from her vacation, whatever that meant.

"You left it next to the fridge." She handed it to me.

"Thanks." I did vaguely remember taking it into the kitchen. But this was a lot of action for three-thirty in the morning. I still wasn't fully awake yet.

Uncle Russell came in from the hall. "Your ride is here. I just let them in."

"Thank you!" I rushed past him. Then backed up. "I swear, I'll be at the tent no later than ten. Are you sure that's okay?"

"Yes, of course," Uncle Russell said. "You know things don't pick up till after midday anyway. Plus, we have lots of help. Go enjoy yourself."

"I'm sure she will." Aunty Gloria wistfully glanced off into the distance. "I remember my J'ouvert days. Up at three, we'd mash up the streets. Then, we'd power right through the rest of the day, snatch a few hours of sleep at a friend's house, and go right back out next morning."

"Yeah, we're not doing all of that."

She shook her head "Young people today. You don't have the stamina."

"I can't speak for all young people, but I know I don't."

I grabbed the rest of my things. Then before leaving, I glanced back at them. Perhaps I was feeling a bit sentimental—I always was coming down to the end of another Carnival season. And this one, in particular, felt a bit more meaningful than most.

That being said, I wasn't entirely sad my time had opened up. I could shift focus to exams and work on the costumes for the drama club. For Sherlyn's last production, she'd decided to put on one of Shakespeare's comedies. Not usually my favorite of his works, but I'd been enjoying the challenge.

Hazel met me at the front door. She finished lacing up her sneakers and straightened up. "Did you find your phone?"

"Yeah." I patted my side and the hidden pocket I'd sewed into my black shorts. Most of the outfit I'd made myself, inspired by one of Mummy's sketches. The final look was cute but disposable. I'd been warned today could get messy and prepared accordingly.

Outside, the night was dark and windy. The breeze carried a citrus scent from the orchard, the oranges and portugals ripening. All was silent, too early for even the overeager roosters who tended to crow long before dawn.

Chris jumped out of the waiting silver minivan and pulled the doors open for us. It was completely unnecessary, but Hazel rewarded him with a kiss anyway. The two of them had been extra loved-up lately since Chris's football scholarship and early acceptance to university came through. With Hazel all but guaranteed to get into Columbia with her phenomenal SAT score and grades, they'd be going to New York next year together.

"You two look great," Chris said, though his eyes never left Hazel. His thumb skimmed along her glitter-dusted cheek.

"You too." She tapped the brim of his mint-green cap.

Hazel hopped into the passenger seat. I climbed into the back, delighted to find it already occupied.

"Well don't you look comfortable," I said. Brandon had his eyes closed, resting his back against the window, his legs outstretched on the seat. "I hate to come in and ruin it."

"Impossible," he said, opening his eyes. He shifted, lowering his feet to the floor, wincing a little and trying to hide it. "Having you next to me can only be an improvement."

He looked gorgeous, if a little tired in the early hour of the morning, dressed in a pair of jeans and a black vest. I sat and curled into his side, my head resting on his shoulder.

"You'll take it easy today, right?" I said seriously. He'd only removed the cast a few days earlier and shouldn't be overexerting himself.

"Don't worry about me, Boop." He kissed my forehead. "I promised we'd go to J'ouvert and I meant it. I'll think of something."

"Sure." I arched an eyebrow, pretending to be skeptical to make him laugh. But I believed him.

Two hours later, we were riding on a music truck, Machel's latest song—the frontrunner for Road March—blasting through the speakers behind me. Brandon had recognized one of the DJs and talked him into letting us sit on the back.

I swear, he really did know *everyone*.

With my mud-splattered feet swinging off the side, I sang along to the lyrics. In the commotion, I spotted Chris and Hazel wining and jumping up, part of the crowd, moving with the music. Everyone here was covered in paint and mud. It was joy and celebration at its least self-conscious. At its most free.

Distracted by a band of blue devils, I didn't notice the yellow paint until it dripped down my arm.

"Brandon!"

His shoulders shook with laughter. One hand covered his mouth. The other held the incriminating near-empty cup of paint. "Whoops. I didn't think it would be that much. But I thought you could use a little more color."

"You're such an asshole."

"I know. You may have mentioned it once or twice."

I shook my head, fighting back laughter. "You really didn't think this through, did you?" Before he could ask what I meant, I crashed my lips against his, enveloping him in a paint-soaked embrace.

He really should've seen it coming.

Later, thousands of people would parade through these very streets, hundreds of them wearing the costumes I'd helped make. For so long I'd felt like I wasn't enough, alone and untethered. But in this country, in this festival, in the paint-spattered arms of the boy I loved, nothing had ever felt more right.

# ACKNOWLEDGMENTS

Second books are hard! Who knew?

I admit that there were days when this one felt impossible. Now that *When the Vibe Is Right* is finished and everything I hoped it would be, I have so many people to thank.

To my agent, Wendi Gu, for her counsel and endless encouragement. And to my editor, Donna Bray, for her clever insights, guidance, and patience while I found this story.

To the fantastic team at Balzer + Bray/HarperCollins: publicist Aubrey Churchward and marketing director Audrey Diestelkamp. Shona McCarthy and Jill Amack for copyediting, Sarah Madden for the fantastic cover art, Jessie S. Gang for the jacket design, and Alison Donalty for art direction.

To my 21ders group, who got me through my debut year and beyond. To Timna, Clarice, and Laura for their time and feedback. And to Miss Boochoon for introducing me to *Much Ado About Nothing*.

To Debbie for answering my many questions about mas bands. And to the incredible Carnival costume makers in Trinidad and Tobago, whose talent and commitment have inspired this story.

To all the awesome readers, booksellers, and librarians who read, reviewed, bought, and recommended my first book.

And thank you to Mummy, Rebecca, Stella, and my wonderful family. Love you.